Catherine tried to u
the incomprehensible.

This man, this stranger, was calmly standing there telling her that they had shared the ultimate intimacy.

When he spoke again, his voice was cold. "Is the thought of sharing my bed so distasteful to you?"

Catherine whirled on him, hands clenched into fists. "Yes! Should I be happy knowing that a lifetime ago I did sordid things with a complete stranger?"

His jaw twitched, and he spoke through clenched teeth. "We weren't strangers, and nothing we did together was sordid."

"How do I know that? How do I know anything?" Her breath came in ragged gasps. "It's not real to me. I don't remember."

He grabbed her arms and pulled her against him. "*I'm* real. Feel me, feel my heart beating against you." He was strong, and her struggle was futile. She pushed at his shoulders, but he cupped her hips, pressing her against him. His voice was raw. "You can deny me, Cat, but you can't deny yourself, what you're feeling now, what you felt then. You can't deny *this*."

Dear Reader,

Welcome to the Silhouette **Special Edition** experience! With your search for consistently satisfying reading in mind, every month the authors and editors of Silhouette **Special Edition** aim to offer you a stimulating blend of deep emotions and high romance.

The name Silhouette **Special Edition** and the distinctive arch on the cover represent a commitment—a commitment to bring you six sensitive, substantial novels each month. In the pages of a Silhouette **Special Edition**, compelling true-to-life characters face riveting emotional issues—and come out winners. All the authors in the series strive for depth, vividness and warmth in writing these stories of living and loving in today's world.

The result, we hope, is romance you can believe in. Deeply emotional, richly romantic, infinitely rewarding—that's the Silhouette **Special Edition** experience. Come share it with us—six times a month!

From all the authors and editors of Silhouette **Special Edition**,

Best wishes.

DIANA WHITNEY

One Lost Winter

Silhouette Special Edition

Published by Silhouette Books New York

America's Publisher of Contemporary Romance

For Suzanne Forster,
a wonderful writer and a wonderful friend,
with many thanks for your help and support.

SILHOUETTE BOOKS
300 East 42nd St., New York, N.Y. 10017

ONE LOST WINTER

ISBN: 0-373-09644-5

First Silhouette Books printing January 1991

Printed in the U.S.A.

Books by Diana Whitney

Silhouette Special Edition

Cast a Tall Shadow #508
Yesterday's Child #559
One Lost Winter #644

Silhouette Romance

O'Brian's Daughter #673
A Liberated Man #703
Scout's Honor #745

DIANA WHITNEY

says she loves "fat babies and warm puppies, mountain streams and Southern California sunshine, camping, hiking and gold prospecting. Not to mention strong, romantic heroes!" She married her own real-life hero fifteen years ago. With his encouragement, she left her longtime career as a municipal finance director and pursued the dream that had haunted her since childhood—writing. To Diana, writing is a joy, the ultimate satisfaction. Reading, too, is her passion, from spine-chilling thrillers to sweeping sagas, but nothing can compare to the magic and wonder of romance.

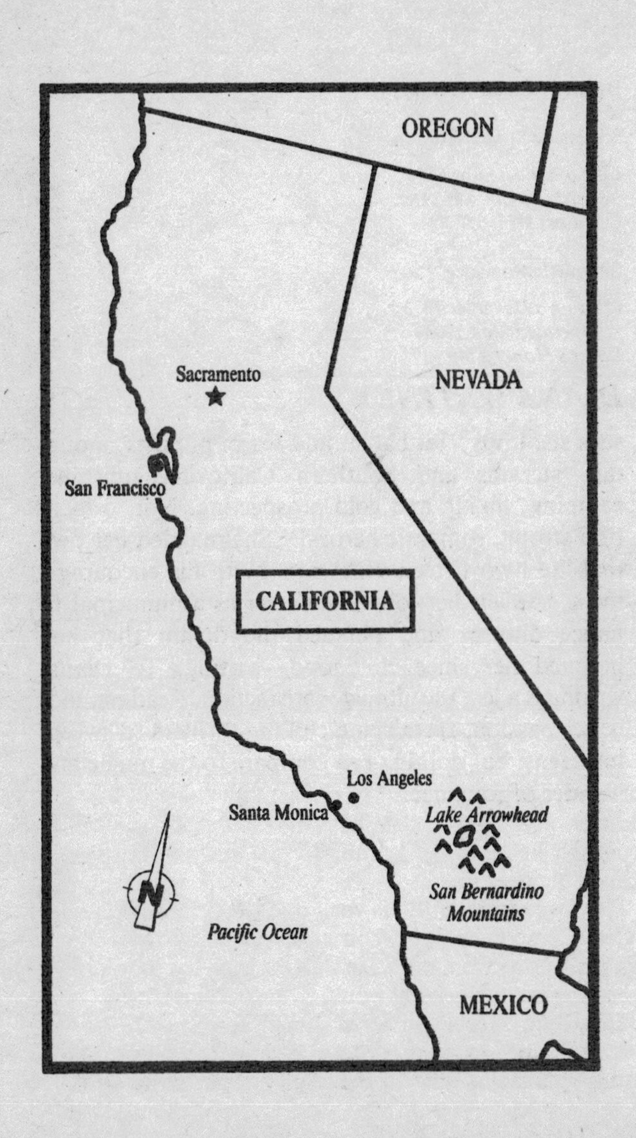

OREGON
NEVADA
Sacramento
San Francisco
CALIFORNIA
Los Angeles
Santa Monica
Lake Arrowhead
San Bernardino
Mountains
N
Pacific Ocean
MEXICO

Prologue

A bitter wind whipped over the mountain.

Cathy Greer careened across the icy ground with the desperation of a woman whose world would soon be shattered. She slipped then lurched forward, ignoring the numbing cold. Twenty feet behind her was the warm cabin and even warmer arms of the man she loved. She wanted to go back, to be with him. But she couldn't. Not yet.

Frantically, Cathy pushed on, every breathless step taking her farther from his comforting embrace and closer to the arms of disaster. Her heart pounded like a mournful drum. Snow crunched beneath her stumbling feet and the howling wind echoed her despair.

Her lover called out, his voice stern yet edged with tension. "Cat! Come back here. You can't run away from this. You can't run away from me." He was ordering her to return, commanding her as a general would command his troops.

How dare he speak to her with such arrogance?

Cathy wiped away angry tears and pushed onward, leaning into the punishing wind. If she could just get to the woods, into the protection of the tall pines, she could sort things out and get control of the hysteria building deep inside.

They'd never argued before, not like this. The angry words reverberated through her mind, tormenting her. No matter what Cathy had said, she hadn't convinced him that one wrong move would destroy their dreams and ruin their future together.

Didn't he know what he was asking of her?

He called her name again. This time there was fear in his voice, and Cathy longed to turn around. She ached to run back to him, seeking the solace of his warm strength. But heartache drove her stubbornly onward.

The forest loomed closer. Just a few more steps and Cathy would be at her special quiet place. There she could think. Questions pelted her dazed brain like the stinging, wind-driven snow. Somewhere buried deep in her soul were the answers. She just needed time to find them. She needed peace.

But exhaustion had taken its toll. Panting and sobbing, she stopped and steadied herself on a nearby tree, each rapid breath a cloudy white puff in the frigid air. She turned and looked back across the clearing toward the cabin. She saw him standing in the open doorway, backlit by the golden glow of the warmth within. Her heart melted.

Cathy thought back, remembering the first time she'd seen him. She had been lost then, engulfed in the frigid grasp of a raging blizzard. Suddenly, *he* had appeared, a warm safe haven in a sea of swirling white. She'd never forget the snow whipping his dark hair and the soothing comfort of his voice.

Cathy had fallen in love that day and she loved him still.

Suddenly, she was desperate to feel his arms around her shivering body, to feel his soft breath against her face. He would comfort her and make her believe that everything would be all right. Reflexively, she reached out and took a single step toward the man she loved.

A hard, cruel hand covered her mouth.

Cathy went stiff with fear, then began to fight like a cornered animal. She struggled fiercely, kicking and trying to scream a warning. Strong arms surrounded her, crushing her so tightly that she could barely breathe.

A familiar voice whispered harshly, "Hold still. Don't fight me."

Cathy stiffened as she recognized the voice of the one man she truly feared. He had found them, tracked them down. A metallic taste flooded her mouth, and she was overcome by absolute terror. He would force her away from the mountain—and tear her from her lover's arms.

She couldn't bear that. Even the mere thought of leaving the man she loved made her stomach churn and her legs go weak. Panic gave Cathy a sudden strength and she fought desperately against the intrusive grip.

Her captor's voice was gruff. "Stop this, Catherine. Stop, or someone will be hurt."

Panting and clawing, Cathy continued her valiant struggle, driven by desperation and sheer terror. Vaguely, she became aware of other voices reverberating through the forest. She went rigid and listened. There were several male voices, urgent and demanding and in the distance a dog was barking. Then the animal's frantic yelps turned into snarls of warning.

Cathy's eyes widened in horror. Armed men appeared from behind nearby trees—a dozen or more—and she realized that they had been hiding in the forest. They had weapons and were pointing those weapons at the cabin. At her lover.

Oh dear God, they wanted to kill him.

Suddenly one of the armed men screamed, "He's got a gun!"

"Drop it!" yelled another.

"Don't let him get away."

Cathy tried to cry out but the cruel hands still crushed her mouth. She clawed at the leather-clad fingers, whipping her head back and forth against the powerful male chest against which she was helplessly pinned. The stiff fibers of a hunting jacket rubbed her skin raw, and tears streamed down her face.

Please Lord, don't let them hurt him, she prayed.

Then a gunshot split the air like lethal thunder.

Cathy went rigid. The punishing fingers loosened, then fell from her face. Instantly she leaped forward, screaming wildly as she dashed toward the cabin. There were more gunshots and a frenzy of frantic shouts.

Then a bullet pierced the propane tank. Cathy saw the tiny hole appear an instant before the explosion rocked the land and knocked her backwards. Dazed, she pulled herself up and watched a spiraling plume of smoke and flame. Everything happened in slow motion and she stared in numb confusion as bits of wood and shingles looped through the air.

Cathy heard her captor's voice. The sound was distant and oddly garbled, like a record playing too slowly.

This must be a dream, she thought hazily. It was all just a horrible nightmare. At any moment, she would awaken and be safely tucked in her lover's warm arms. None of this could be real.

Please, God. Make me wake up.

Stumbling to her feet, Cathy staggered forward. Ignoring the din behind and flames in front, she wanted only to reach him. She *had* to be with him. She *had* to—

The second explosion hit like a giant fist, hurling Cathy into the air. She slammed into the icy earth and cried out his name.

Then the mountain sank into a dark black sea.

Chapter One

Beyond the lighted stage, darkness swelled with hushed anticipation. Tension mounted in a spiraling crescendo, then plummeted to the shattering climax. The final note floated sweetly, then faded into the collective, satisfied sigh of the audience.

Catherine LeClerc stood beside the gleaming piano, accepting the enthusiastic applause with relief and appreciation. It was over and it had gone well. Offering silent thanks, she gracefully exited the stage.

When safely obscured by the worn tapestry curtain, she exhaled slowly. Opening night was always the worst. The remaining concerts would be easier. Looking up, Catherine smiled at the grinning man rushing toward her.

"You were marvelous, *chère*," he gushed excitedly, his soft French accent adding emphasis to the praise. "*Bel et bien*, your best performance yet."

"Maurice, you always say that," Catherine replied, returning his excited hug.

"It is always true, my sweet." Maurice Bouchard's proud face gleamed in the soft backstage light. "Your dancing fingers hold a very special magic."

Catherine felt a surge of love and gratitude toward her dear friend. "These weeks have been your triumph as much as mine. Without you, these magic fingers would not be dancing on anything more interesting than a dreary typewriter." Fondly, she brushed the shiny lapels of his tuxedo and murmured, "You are the dearest man in the world. I could have done none of this without you."

And Catherine meant every word. As her manager, confidant and friend, Maurice had expertly guided Catherine's career. Long ago he had discovered Catherine's raw and reluctant talent and set about molding her into a sophisticated professional pianist. Now Catherine was completing her first United States tour, and those years of grueling effort had finally paid off.

In spite of Maurice's obvious contribution to her success, the handsome Parisian was embarrassed by her compliment. He coughed awkwardly, flushed to the roots of his sleekly styled hair and hurriedly changed the subject. "There is a gathering in your honor this evening."

Catherine's smile died. She hated the banal chatter of such highbrow events. Although some social obligations couldn't be avoided, Maurice circumvented most invitations with gracious aplomb. Apparently this occasion had special significance.

She regarded Maurice cautiously. "What kind of gathering?"

"Mrs. Waldenhoff is hosting an impromptu cocktail party at the Regency Hotel." Maurice looked extremely apologetic. "It could not be avoided."

Catherine rubbed her brow. Her manager was right; it couldn't be avoided. Mrs. Waldenhoff was a powerful influence in the Los Angeles performing arts community; the woman even owned this very theater.

But she was grateful that the party was being held at their hotel. After a brief appearance, it would be a simple matter to saunter casually toward the elevators for a covert exit.

Glancing up, Catherine noted Maurice's anxious expression and managed what she hoped was a reassuring smile. "How much time do I have?" she asked.

"You are expected within the hour." Maurice gently took Catherine's arm and escorted her through a maze of dank hallways toward the tiny cubicle that was her dressing room. Gallantly, he pushed open the door and flipped on the light, then stood aside and allowed her to enter.

A brilliant bouquet of pink roses lay on the vanity. With a gasp of delight, Catherine delicately touched one of the blooms. They were gorgeous, a soft pastel hue that reminded her of cotton candy. She had always loved flowers.

Fumbling with the tiny envelope, Catherine read the card. "'May the city of your birth honor your return. I miss you with all my heart. Love, Uncle Brad.'"

Maurice smiled broadly. "Ten cities, ten dozen roses. Ah, your uncle has developed the poetic soul of a true Frenchman."

Wiping her damp eyes, Catherine laughed. "Eleven years in Paris would put a little romance in the most cynical heart, but Uncle Brad has always been thoughtful. I wish he could have come..." Her voice trailed away as she leaned down to inhale the soft floral perfume.

Her uncle had begged off this trip saying that he couldn't leave his position as music director of the Versailles Philharmonic. Catherine hadn't believed that for a minute. In France, Bradford Madison was a respected maestro. He'd have had little trouble arranging a leave of absence, and Catherine knew he would have done just that—if the tour hadn't included Los Angeles, a city her uncle hated with an inexplicable vengeance.

Bradford had spent most of his life here, but eventually that life had soured. Los Angeles became a demon in her uncle's mind, a city that had destroyed his career, his marriage, even his life. Bradford had gone to France as a broken man. He'd sobered up, dried out and embarked on a new life. It had been a turning point in Catherine's life, too. Her uncle had been her legal guardian at the time, and she'd had no choice but to accompany him.

Those early days were still somewhat blurred in her mind. Catherine recalled brief images, but could never really focus on specific events. She remembered being lonely, though, and feeling oddly bereft. Those emotions were probably homesickness, the loss of old familiar surroundings. Or so she had repeatedly consoled herself.

Intuitively she knew the feelings had a deeper source. Sometimes, she'd seen a shadowed face in her dreams, heard an illusive voice in her mind. Then her heart would ache until she thought she would die of it—and she never understood the sudden eerie pain.

A sharp rap on the dressing room door broke into Catherine's reverie. A stagehand peeked in and whispered something to Maurice, who listened intently, then nodded a curt dismissal.

"What was that about?" Catherine asked.

"There are some people waiting outside," he said, then went to the small closet and retrieved the peach satin evening cape that matched Catherine's flowing recital gown.

"People?" Catherine took a deep breath. "Reporters?"

"A few perhaps, but most are your fans. You must greet them." Maurice held up the cape and slid the garment over her bare shoulders.

Catherine frowned, absently fondling the rich fabric. This was not her favorite part of the tour, but it came with the territory. Meeting patrons after a performance was gracious and expected. Theaters like this one were old and faded, rich in history but sadly lacking in funds. The financial prospects of goodwill gestures and free publicity certainly couldn't be ignored.

Maurice recognized her reluctance. "You will quickly drive the masses wild with your beauty, *ma charmeuse*," he teased. "Then I shall whisk you to festivities and be the envy of every young man in the room."

Smiling, Catherine scooped up the bouquet of roses and took her small handbag from the dresser. "It's more likely to be the ladies who will be green with jealousy when they see me with my handsome escort. I'll probably have to risk life and limb by throwing myself between you and a pack of love-crazed women."

On cue, Maurice blushed furiously. "You are a wicked woman to torment me with such foolishness."

Catherine laughed, enjoying the affectionate teasing that was such an integral part of their relationship. "It's not the least bit foolish. After all, those poor ladies can't know that your heart belongs to Genevieve. They would be inconsolable to know that after thirty years of marriage, you still have eyes only for your wife."

With an expression of pure chagrin, Maurice muttered a request for divine deliverance. Smiling in victory, Catherine followed her manager through the narrow corridors. Maurice's modest, unassuming nature was part of his charm, and she couldn't resist a final dig as they reached the stage door.

"Do you hear that soft buzzing noise?" she asked innocently.

He frowned. "I hear nothing but the sound of traffic from the street."

"That's not traffic at all." Her eyes gleamed. "It's the hopeful hum of vibrating female hormones on the other side of the door. Be gentle with them."

Shaking his head, Maurice feigned shock. "What am I to do with you?" he muttered, but his eyes twinkled.

Catherine's witty response was cut off as Maurice opened the stage door. She stepped outside and was stunned by a disconcerting throng of well-dressed people pressing toward her. Her happy mood melted into tense anxiety. She hadn't expected such a crowd and was unnerved by the swelling group. Moistening her lips, Catherine slipped into a practiced air of regal composure. She was uncomfortable, but Maurice had trained her well. If she performed properly, all these people would see was a confident, serene woman.

A flashbulb popped in her face. She shielded her eyes briefly and heard Maurice speaking softly to the photographer.

"Miss LeClerc, how does it feel to be back in L.A.?" shouted a reporter.

"It feels wonderful," Catherine answered smoothly, handing the bouquet to Maurice so she could accommodate the requests for autographs. A stylish woman held out a copy of Catherine's latest album for signature. Catherine obliged, pasting on a stiff-but-sincere smile as she tried to suppress a growing uneasiness.

This homecoming had been long past due, and she *should* feel wonderful. Instead, she felt oddly anxious. Los Angeles hadn't changed, but Catherine had, and her transformation had been profound. Eleven years ago a shy, confused girl had left California. A successful, confident woman had returned.

Her attack of nerves went beyond dismay at the surging crowd. Ever since Catherine had returned to California, she'd been plagued by an eerie mixture of sadness and anticipation. She'd had a bizarre premonition that something momentous was about to happen, something joyous or frightening—or both.

Now a chill skittered down her spine, and she had the unpleasant sensation that she was being watched. She shivered, feeling suddenly exposed and vulnerable.

But this was ridiculous. Of course she was being watched. Dozens of people were staring at her this very moment, and Catherine scolded herself for having such a vivid imagination.

A persistent reporter muscled forward. "When are you going back to France?"

"I'll be returning next week, after the tour."

From behind the crowd came another question that Catherine couldn't quite hear. Looking up, she scanned the crowd and saw someone wave an arm, but Catherine's gaze fell on a man standing alone.

This was no ordinary man. This was a man who turned heads and quickened feminine hearts. And this man was staring at Catherine with a seductive intensity that was mesmerizing and frighteningly intimate.

For a moment, Catherine was aware of nothing but the man's eyes and heard nothing but a rush of white noise in her brain.

He exuded a raw power that took her breath away. Her gaze was riveted on him, as though his mere look had turned her to a pillar of stone.

"Miss LeClerc?" When Catherine didn't reply, the woman spoke again. This time she sounded exasperated. "Miss Le-Clerc, if you please."

Catherine dragged her attention to a fur-wrapped matron extending a concert program.

The woman smiled invitingly. "May I have your autograph? I did so enjoy your performance tonight."

"You're very kind," Catherine murmured, sliding a covert glance at the dark-haired man.

Standing away from the main group, he was leaning against a light pole, his ankles crossed and his thumbs hooked in the pockets of his dress slacks. The casual stance reflected a man more comfortable in blue jeans than the black-tie evening apparel he now wore.

Casual posture aside, Catherine instinctively knew that this was *not* a casual man. This was a powerful man, with arrogant eyes and an aura of hidden danger that chilled her to the bone.

Again, she shivered and this time was unable to tear her gaze away. Maurice slid his arm around her shoulders and whispered a concerned inquiry. Catherine wasn't listening. She was watching the man, watching his eyes narrow and his mouth tilt in a mocking half-smile that offered a challenge and a warning.

Vaguely, Catherine was aware that Maurice was speaking to the group of fans, then he propelled her toward a waiting limousine. Safely inside, Catherine closed her eyes and took a deep, shuddering breath.

"Are you ill, *chère*?" he asked solicitously. "I am certain Mrs. Waldenhoff would accept your apologies—"

"No." Catherine dismissed his concern with a weak wave of her hand. "I'm fine."

Unconvinced, Maurice frowned. "You are as pale as a lily bloom," he mumbled, laying a warm palm against her chilled cheek.

Catherine was beginning to feel a bit foolish. "I'm perfectly all right. It's probably no more than a delayed reaction to the excitement of the tour."

But as the limo pulled away from the curb, Catherine couldn't keep herself from looking out the window. The man was still watching.

And Catherine was still shivering.

The crystal chandeliers of the Regency Ballroom were sparkling with warmth and gaiety. Tuxedo-clad gentlemen chatted in amiable groups while elegant women in sequined attire strolled in a determined effort to see and be seen. Champagne flowed freely and laughter punctuated the hum of the guests. So far the postconcert gala seemed a rousing success.

More comfortable now, Catherine willed her taut shoulders to relax and concentrated on Mrs. Waldenhoff's throaty voice.

"Miss LeClerc, may I present Dr. and Mrs. Walter Conlin," the hostess purred.

Catherine smiled and accepted the doctor's firm handshake. Maurice, who hadn't left Catherine's side all evening, kissed Mrs. Conlin's hand with such European panache that the flustered woman barely managed to totter away without swooning.

The introductions droned on, but Catherine didn't mind. She enjoyed meeting people, particularly those who shared her love of music.

It hadn't always been that way. As a girl, Catherine had hated the piano, reviling the drudgery of practice as some kind of horrible punishment for having been born to a family with musical genes. Before his untimely death, Catherine's father had been a classical violinist. Uncle Brad had composed scores and conducted orchestras for as long as Catherine could remember. Still she had loathed it all, wanting nothing more than to be a devoted wife and mother to dozens and dozens of fat babies.

But all that had changed suddenly around the time she and her uncle had moved to Europe. Catherine still couldn't remember why she'd decided to pursue a musical career; that period of her life was fuzzy, just out of memory's reach.

Long-forgotten events had preceded the life she now led and with which she was basically happy. Occasional loneliness and the lack of meaningful relationships were simply the cost of a successful career. Weren't they?

Suddenly, the hairs on her nape stood at attention.

Catherine looked up, knowing instinctively who she would find. She wasn't disappointed. It was the dark-haired man.

He was on the other side of the room speaking to Mrs. Waldenhoff, but his eyes, his dangerous eyes, were on Catherine, still watching her in that same penetrating manner.

In the bright light of the ballroom, she saw him more clearly now. The man wasn't particularly tall but he exuded an aura of power one would expect from a much larger person. Even dressed in a tuxedo there was a rough quality about him, a steely glint to his sharp features. His face was a mass of right angles and chiseled planes, with elongated eyes that were the color and clarity of a mountain stream. Straight low-set brows intensified the mystique of his unnerving esoteric gaze.

Catherine's eyes were drawn to his surprisingly soft, sensual mouth, which seemed strangely out of place in such a hard, determined face. As she stared in stunned silence, Mrs. Waldenhoff smiled brightly and led the man directly over.

The closer he got, the more unnerved Catherine became. Then he was there, so close that his scent enveloped her. The fragrance was sharp, tantalizing and as dangerous as the man himself.

Mrs. Waldenhoff gushed. "Catherine, this is Jonathan Stone, of Stone Securities Corporation. Jonathan is one of our most valued patrons and he has always been quite generous to the cultural needs of our fine community." The woman finished, blinking up at the charismatic man with an expression bordering on overt adoration. But he never took his gaze from Catherine, much to the older woman's obvious disappointment.

Jonathan Stone smiled, but his eyes were hard as flint. They were mysterious eyes, Scorpio eyes, eyes that seemed to be searching her very soul. Catherine steeled herself for the sound of his voice. Somehow, she knew it would affect her.

"It's an honor to meet you, Miss *LeClerc.*" The unpleasant emphasis on her name was startling, but before Catherine could respond, he took her hand, raising it to his mouth. Brushing her palm with his full lips, he murmured against her skin, "Your performance this evening was... quite interesting."

Catherine retrieved her hand from his grasp with as much grace as possible. She found her voice and managed a weak acknowledgment.

As compliments went, Mr. Stone's comment was less than stellar. There was hidden meaning to his words and the quiet inflection he gave them, but Catherine was totally bewildered. Everything about the man set her nerves on edge, but she didn't know why, nor could she fathom the reason behind his steely demeanor.

The tension between them was palpable. He was waiting. She was breathless, yet unable to look away.

Suddenly, he turned toward Mrs. Waldenhoff, tilting his head slightly as though giving some kind of signal. On cue, the woman swirled around and took Maurice's arm. "You must allow me to introduce you to the countess," she crooned silkily, then immediately propelled the startled Frenchman into the colorful crowd.

Satisfied, Jonathan Stone turned to Catherine. "And so we are alone."

Catherine looked up in astonishment, then gestured toward the surrounding throng. "We are hardly alone, Mr. Stone."

His eyes were veiled. "These people don't concern us, Catherine."

"I... don't understand." Reflexively, her hand touched her throat, and she stepped backward. Everything about him was disturbing, yet oddly compelling. Catherine felt like she was being torn, pulled in two directions by equal, yet invisible forces. She was suddenly frightened.

Jonathan appeared startled, as though he'd recognized her fear and was confused by it. The Scorpio eyes grew wary as his lips pursed in contemplation. There was something familiar about his expression, something hazy and slightly out of focus.

Then a strange thing happened. An image formed in Catherine's mind. She saw gray clouds pulsing and rolling as distant thunder rocked the frozen earth. A bitter wind whistled through barren branches, and the metallic taste of terror flooded her throat.

Suddenly, everything turned white, and Catherine was cold, cold to the bone. In that very instant, she knew that death was imminent.

Jonathan watched in stunned amazement as Catherine's eyes glazed and her skin paled to the color of bleached porcelain. Weakly, she touched her forehead and swayed. He instantly steadied her. At his touch, Catherine's eyes flew open and she stared at him. In her clear gaze, he saw bewilderment and fear, but not a trace of recognition.

Color returned to her cheeks in an embarrassed flush. "I—I'm sorry," she stammered, trying to step away from his supporting embrace.

Jonathan wouldn't allow it. The softness of her skin was too enticing, her sweet fragrance too arousing. "You need some rest," he said quietly, sliding his arm around her waist. "I'll take you to your room."

Maurice emerged from the crowd. He was obviously distressed and pried Catherine away from Jonathan's insistent grasp. "I shall see that Miss LeClerc receives the required attention," he said tightly, then quickly bundled Catherine away.

Jonathan watched, feeling as though a part of him had gone with her. An aching sadness swelled deep inside him, mingling with the smoldering rage that had been burning for eleven long years.

So that cool, sophisticated woman was the famous Catherine LeClerc, he thought bitterly. She was not what he'd expected. Yes, he'd anticipated her beauty, and she was still incredibly lovely. Her exquisite face was framed by a cloud of rich brown hair that had once blown free in the wind, but was now coiled into an elegant coiffure designed to compliment her sleek evening gown. Even her exotic eyes, shaped like huge green teardrops, had changed, as she had changed. Those expressive eyes, once sparkling with joy and mischief, now were cautious and wary.

And those eyes had looked right through him.

With a muffled curse, Jonathan jammed his hands in his pockets and walked briskly toward the lobby. In all the times he'd dreamed of this night, fantasized about seeing her again, not once had he ever believed that she would have forgotten him.

But it was painfully apparent that she *had* forgotten. No one could give a performance that convincing, even a woman with Catherine's talent for deception. She'd smiled at Jonathan with polite curiosity, greeting him as a stranger, without a hint of comprehension.

Angrily he pushed through the revolving door into the street. The cold night air was like a slap in the face. He took a deep breath. Hoping exercise could calm his pounding heart, Jonathan started to walk.

What had he expected? That she would run into his arms and apologize for betraying him and then disappearing without so much as a fond farewell? Of course not. All the bitter years and bitter tears had made Jonathan a realist.

Still, to discover that the closeness they'd once shared could be so easily dismissed, hurt more deeply than he could have ever imagined.

Raking his fingers through his hair, he walked faster as though speed alone could ease the stifling pressure in his chest. But nothing could slow the racing of his tormented mind.

Nothing could erase the flood of memories.

Jonathan lost track of time, wandering aimlessly until he realized that he was in an unfamiliar part of town. Sighing, he leaned against a sagging wooden fence and looked up.

The winter sky was extraordinarily clear, almost like the crisp, twinkling nights on the mountain. For a single heartbeat, the silhouette of the sleeping city was transformed into tall pines and distant peaks, outlined by silvery moonlight. The sweet remembrance soothed him, allowed his mind to function rationally.

Yes, Catherine had changed over the years, but so had he. Once Jonathan had been soft, blindly following his heart and ignoring the plea of reason. He'd been trusting and noble to the point of being a fool; but Jonathan had never been stupid. He had a sharp mind. He learned quickly. And Catherine had been an exceptionally adept teacher.

Part of him was grateful for the lesson. Because of Catherine, he was tough, strong and resilient, a man of considerable wealth and unlimited determination. Allies called him shrewd, enemies labeled him ruthless; but no one disputed that Jonathan Stone was a force to be reckoned with.

And Catherine *LeClerc* would soon realize that.

"Drink this, *chère*. It will soothe you."

Catherine accepted the steaming cup of herbal tea that Maurice offered. She didn't really want anything, but recognized his familiar, solicitous expression and knew the Parisian would give her no peace until she did as he asked.

She sipped the hot liquid. "It's wonderful. I feel better already."

Instantly, Maurice's frown of concern relaxed into a relieved smile. "*Bon*." He covertly glanced at his watch.

The gesture wasn't lost on Catherine. Although it was after midnight in Los Angeles, she knew that it was early morning in Paris. His wife Genevieve would be awake and waiting for her husband's call. Still, Maurice seemed reluctant to leave, and Catherine sought to reassure him. "I'm fine, Maurice. Please, call your wife before she begins to worry."

Maurice cleared his throat and edged toward the door to his room. "If you are certain you will not require me..."

Laughing, Catherine held up the teacup. "I have everything I need. Now go, please, and give Genevieve my love."

"*Oui*. I shall not be long." Before he'd finished speaking, Maurice disappeared into the adjoining bedroom. In a moment, she heard him speaking to the overseas operator.

Alone at last. Sighing, Catherine set the teacup on the coffee table and settled back on the plush sofa.

The three-room suite was small and sparsely furnished, but a one-week stay didn't require a mansion. Besides, her entire classical tour wouldn't provide the profits of a single rock concert, so economy had been a major consideration. Still, she and Maurice each had a private room adjoining a comfortable living area, complete with a tiny kitchenette.

From the far room, Catherine heard the Frenchman's voice take on an animated tone. He spoke rapidly in his native language, and she smiled, eavesdropping without a trace of guilt. The love between Maurice and his family had always comforted Catherine, a tangible reminder that such happiness really did exist. At least, for some.

Catherine glanced toward the window. High-rise buildings cast squared shadows against the clear night sky. She saw stars between the dark silhouettes. It was unusual to see stars from any city, but in Los Angeles it was almost unheard of. In the seventeen years Catherine had lived here, she couldn't ever remember such a clear night, except...

Except when?

The memory had been right on the brink of her mind, then skittered away into a black, hazy fog. Suddenly, Catherine felt agitated. She thought about the cocktail party and the dark-haired man. The strange daydream, or whatever it had been, still confused her. Nothing like that had ever happened to Catherine before—at least, she didn't think it had. There were so many parts of her past that lurked in her subconscious like the muddy bottom of a murky pond. Everything below the surface was obscure and oddly distorted.

This image had been especially bizarre. It was more than a dream. Catherine had actually felt an icy wind on her face, and her fingers had literally become stiff with cold.

The entire experience was eerie. After all, she'd been standing in an overly warm ballroom surrounded by a hundred people. Besides, Catherine simply didn't believe in psychic "visions" and had assumed such nonsense to be the realm of the unenlightened and the gullible.

Suddenly, her chest felt tight, as though an invisible band was squeezing her breath away. Standing quickly, she paced, rubbing her temples to exorcise the unwanted thoughts.

Vaguely, she became aware that Maurice had returned and was excited about something. With some effort, Catherine tried to focus her attention on what he was saying.

"...And before Christmas, I shall have a second grandchild to bounce on my knee. Is that not wonderful news, *mon amie*?"

"Ah, yes, of course it is. Wonderful." Frowning, Catherine massaged her aching forehead and wondered which of her manager's growing children was expecting. Claudia, his oldest daughter, was Catherine's age. Maurice also had a twenty-two-year-old son, but as far as Catherine knew, the young man wasn't even married. Yes, Claudia would be the best guess. "Is Claudia hoping for a boy this time?"

Maurice beamed. "If not this time, then the next. But I have other news, a message from Bradford about another tour."

At the moment, Catherine couldn't care less. Her head hurt, and every time she closed her eyes, she saw a world of white and heard whistling wind. The image or dream or vision or whatever the devil it was, had totally distracted her. She simply couldn't concentrate and wanted to postpone any business discussion. "I'm a bit tired right now. Perhaps we could talk tomorrow—"

Unable to contain himself, Maurice interrupted. "This news will allow you to sleep like an infant."

Catherine doubted that she'd ever sleep again. Still, she saw that the Frenchman was about to burst. She acquiesced. "I'm all ears."

"Sit, sit." Without waiting for her to comply, Maurice took Catherine's shoulders and ushered her to the sofa, then sat beside her. "It has been arranged," he said smugly. "You will be pleased."

Sighing, Catherine tried to swallow her growing impatience. She spoke slowly and distinctly. "*What* has been arranged?"

"Prepare yourself." With great dramatic flare, Maurice waved his arm as though conducting his own private symphony. "You have been invited to participate in a tour of Eastern European countries that have not hosted free world artists in many years." That said, he sighed, leaned back and looked absolutely delighted with himself.

Catherine stared at him. "I see."

Maurice's smile flattened. "You are not pleased?"

"Yes, of course I am. I mean, I guess I am." Frustrated, Catherine stood and paced the small room. "I don't want to think about the next tour, or even tomorrow night's concert. I don't want to think about *anything* right now, nothing at all." The poor man looked so crestfallen that it nearly broke Catherine's heart. "I'm sorry. I don't know what's wrong with me. I'm just . . . tired."

Standing, Maurice put his arms around Catherine, comforting her as he would comfort his own daughter. "I have been thoughtless," he said quietly. "Of course you are tired. Two months you have traveled and played your heart out. You must rest for a while. I will see to it."

Shaking her head, Catherine tried to explain. "No, that's not what I mean. I don't want you to cancel anything—"

"Shh." He touched his fingers to her lips. "We will talk no more tonight. Now, you will sleep."

Catherine sighed. "Yes, that's probably best. I'll feel better tomorrow." She didn't believe that for a moment, but suddenly she wanted nothing more than to be alone. She was grateful when Maurice affectionately kissed her forehead and wished her good-night.

In the privacy of her room, Catherine absently went about her nightly routine. She showered, dried her hair, then slipped into a silky nightgown and crawled into bed. The crisp sheets smelled clean, like fresh mountain air, and the pillows cradled her head like a soft, powdery snowbank. Eyes closed, her mind replayed the vision, and again, she wondered what it could mean.

Restlessly she turned over, pounding the soft pillow and telling herself that the white image had probably been triggered by a book she'd once read or a long-forgotten movie.

But she couldn't dismiss the memory of Jonathan Stone. His gaze had been potent and compelling, the proprietary look a man gives the woman who is *his*.

When Catherine finally drifted into a troubled sleep, she dreamed of white mountains and twinkling stars and of the man with Scorpio eyes.

Chapter Two

The following morning, Jonathan waited impatiently in the hotel lobby. He glanced at his watch, straightened his tie, then shoved his hands in his pockets and paced.

She'd be down soon.

A bell caught his attention, and he anxiously watched a harried man emerge from the elevator. Jonathan sighed and looked directly into the curious eyes of the desk clerk. The man was staring at Jonathan as though he was a cat burglar. That was just swell.

Having chosen an observation point that offered an unobstructed view of the elevators, Jonathan had hoped that a tall cathedral palm would offer some concealment. But he'd been lurking behind this stupid tree for over two hours, and the hotel employees were getting suspicious.

Jonathan smiled wanly at the skeptical clerk and felt like the world's biggest fool. Still, it couldn't be helped. Eventually Catherine would emerge, and he was damn well going to be here when she did.

And she would definitely be alone since Jonathan had arranged for her European paramour to be called away on a sudden "business" meeting. After toying with the idea of airfreighting the distinguished Monsieur Bouchard to Antarctica, Jonathan had reluctantly settled for simply having the Frenchman tied up—figuratively—until noon. That had been necessary. The Frenchman hovered around Catherine like a protective lover—which Jonathan assumed that he was.

Just thinking about Catherine and Bouchard tightened Jonathan's stomach into a painful knot. He tried to push away the unpleasant image. After all, it was none of his business whom Catherine slept with. He didn't give a fat fig about her personal life. As soon as she told him what he needed to know, Catherine *LeClerc* could bed the entire French Foreign Legion for all he cared.

Perspiration beaded Jonathan's forehead, and he irritably wiped it away. Lord, he wished she would hurry. All he wanted was to get this over with, chug a quart of antacid and get on with his life.

He didn't have much longer to wait. The elevator hummed, and Catherine stepped out. She was breathtaking, wearing a loose sweater and slacks, the casual clothing that Jonathan remembered her favoring. As she walked briskly across the slick marble foyer, her hair gracefully brushed her shoulders like strands of shiny sable.

The sophisticated elegance of last evening had disappeared, replaced by the natural, unadorned beauty Jonathan remembered. He was taken aback by the transformation, and Catherine was halfway to the lobby doors before he was able to react.

He managed to intercept her. "Good morning, Miss LeClerc. I trust you're feeling better."

She was obviously startled. "Ah, yes, thank you, I'm quite well." With a stiff smile, she regarded him warily. "I didn't realize that you were staying at the hotel."

"I had business here," he replied politely. It wasn't a lie. *She* was his business. "We didn't have time to talk last night. I'd hoped that you would join me for breakfast."

Her expression was skeptical. Jonathan wasn't surprised. Catherine was an intelligent woman. Still, he knew she was much too well-bred to create a public scene and he firmly grasped her arm. Ignoring her astonished gasp, he kept up a stream of casual conversation and guided her toward the lobby's restaurant.

After token resistance, Catherine simply followed his lead, watching him with an expression of curious amusement. Strangely, he found it annoying. He would have preferred her to be angry, or at the very least, supremely indignant. Instead, she looked at him with the tolerant gaze of a patient parent.

After they were settled in a quiet booth, Catherine folded her hands and leaned forward. Her eyes sparkled. "Now that you have displayed your forceful personality, what exactly do you plan to do with me?"

Jonathan handed her a menu. "I plan to feed you."

One slim eyebrow hitched quizzically, but she accepted the menu. After they had ordered, he leaned back and tried to appear casual. "Last night you told the reporter that you'd be going back to France soon."

"Yes, the tour will be completed next week, then I'll be returning to Europe."

"You lived in Los Angeles once. Aren't there any friends or family you'd like to see?"

"Since my parents died, Uncle Brad has been my only family and he's still in Paris."

Jonathan was relieved to hear that. Although he wouldn't have run from another confrontation with Bradford Madison, the prospect had given him little pleasure. Still, there was someone Catherine had obviously neglected to mention. "What about Mr. LeClerc? Surely you're anxious to return to your husband . . . and children."

She looked perplexed. "I'm not married."

Considering her obvious involvement with the Frenchman, Jonathan wasn't particularly surprised. "So you're divorced," he commented tersely.

"I've never been married."

"Never?"

"No, never. Why does that surprise you?"

"Since your maiden name was Greer, I naturally assumed—"

Catherine looked up quickly. "How did you know that my name was Greer?"

He shrugged and lifted his coffee cup. "I must have read it somewhere."

She frowned. "I don't think so. The press kit doesn't mention that LeClerc is a stage name—"

Jonathan squirmed and interrupted with a fast subject change. "So there are no friends you're planning to visit before you go home?"

"No." Catherine's expression was thoughtful, her eyes strangely sad. "But France really isn't 'home' to me, except that my uncle is there."

And your lover, Jonathan thought cynically. He cleared his throat and started to speak, then fell silent as the waiter appeared with their meal. The young man fussed at the table for what seemed an eternity before clicking his polished heels and disappearing into the crowd.

After a moment, Jonathan spoke quietly. "Do you have children?"

Surprised Catherine looked up quickly, her fork frozen in midair. "I told you that I've never been married."

"The two are not mutually exclusive."

She blushed and lifted her coffee cup. "To me they are."

Jonathan considered that. Her firm tone had dismissed the subject, so he tried a different tact. "Tell me about your uncle. He used to conduct the local symphony, didn't he?"

Brightening, Catherine leaned forward. "Yes, for several years. Now he's the maestro of the Versailles Philharmonic. I think he'd like to return someday, though. He misses the States."

"If he's so fond of the area, why did he leave?" Resentment tightened his voice.

Her eyes clouded, and Jonathan could have kicked himself. He knew perfectly well why Bradford Madison had fled this country, although he certainly wouldn't expect Catherine to admit it. For a moment, Jonathan was certain that he'd blown it. Her face contorted slightly, then she stared absently into space.

Finally, she sighed softly. "Uncle Brad went through a difficult period after his divorce. He started drinking heavily and it affected his work. Eventually, he lost his position with the symphony and that broke his heart. It was a desperate struggle, but he finally pulled his life back together. When he was offered the position in France, he accepted."

As Catherine spoke, Jonathan studied her intently. What she'd said was true enough, as far as it went, but her uncle's personal problems had little to do with the covert exodus to Europe, and he knew it. Yet as Catherine had talked, her gaze hadn't wavered and she'd managed to maintain an expression of genuine sincerity.

Jonathan realized that he'd sadly underestimated her expertise. Obviously lying was an art that Catherine had managed to perfect. And why not? After all, she'd had Bradford Madison as her teacher.

Leaning back, Jonathan crossed his arms and furrowed his brow. "So when your uncle took off, you decided to go with him." It was a statement, not a question, and he nearly spat out the words.

Catherine stiffened, bewildered by his tone. "I didn't have much choice at the time. He was my legal guardian, and I was only seventeen."

Jonathan stared straight at her. "Of course."

She fidgeted uneasily. "Have I offended you in any way, Mr. Stone? You seem to be rather, um, agitated."

Closing his eyes, he took a deep breath and decided to play out the entire scenario by her rules. Charades annoyed him, but this could be his only chance to answer the question that had haunted him for so many long years.

Finally, he sighed. "I apologize if I've upset you. It's just that... you remind me of someone I once knew."

She relaxed slightly. "I wondered about that."

"Why?"

"Something about the way you look at me—" She flushed prettily. "I mean, as though we'd met before."

"But we haven't?"

"No—at least, I don't believe so."

Shaking his head, he laughed softly. It wasn't a pleasant sound. "After all, a face like mine isn't easy to forget."

Her voice was surprisingly soft and trembled slightly. "No...a woman could never forget you." Then she looked quickly away, as though she'd inadvertently exposed a part of herself she preferred to keep hidden.

Suddenly, Jonathan felt an icy fear thread down his spine. Something wasn't right about this, not right at all. "Tell me about the year before you went to France," he commanded harshly.

She blinked. "Pardon me? I mean, why would you be—"

"I want to know. Please."

Catherine seemed perplexed, but shrugged and said, "There isn't much to tell. I was a senior in high school. I loved rock-and-roll and hated the piano. I was a very boring girl, actually."

"I doubt that." He pursed his lips. "Last night, you were ill. Has that happened before?"

"No, never. I'm as healthy as a horse. In fact, I've only been really ill once in my life. I had some kind of accident and ended up in the hospital. Other than a couple of scars there was no serious damage."

Jonathan went rigid. "When did that happen?"

"Umm? Right before we left the country, I think. Yes, I'm sure of it, because I remember Uncle Brad bringing a man into my hospital room to take passport photos." She paused. "Are you all right, Mr. Stone? You've gone quite pale."

Somehow, he managed to force the next question. "The weeks before you were...hurt...what do you remember?"

"Remember?" She frowned and fiddled with a half-eaten croissant. "Not much, I'm afraid. The doctors told me that a partial memory loss was common with head injuries. They said I might regain my memory slowly or all at once. Then again, I may never remember. Actually, that entire winter is still kind of a blur."

Air rushed from Jonathan's lungs, and he absently clutched his abdomen. Maybe he should be relieved to discover that Catherine's memory of those months had been obliterated, but he wasn't. All these years he'd searched, only to discover that the answers he so desperately sought were buried beyond reach. It was a cruel blow.

Across the table, Catherine watched Jonathan's tormented expression with bewilderment and alarm. His odd questions had been confusing enough, but his responses were absolutely baffling. He seemed to take each of her statements as a personal affront. Now his tan had faded to a sickly hue, and he looked like a man who'd just suffered a grievous loss. His misery touched her.

Reaching out, Catherine laid her hand on his. "Can I do anything for you?"

He looked up then, his gaze boring into hers, as though desperately trying to push thoughts into her brain. Catherine felt dizzy.

Suddenly, the dimly lit restaurant became a swirl of white. As the image surrounded Catherine, she felt smothered, numb with cold and sick with fear. Then she felt something else, something soothing. Strong hands seemed to be lifting her, carrying her out of the icy prison.

The vision transformed from frigid white to glowing flames. There was a crackling fire, warming and nurturing. Catherine felt safe again. And someone was with her.

"Catherine." A distant voice beckoned, faint at first, then louder, more insistent. "*Catherine.*"

Opening her eyes, she looked across the table and saw Jonathan Stone watching with obvious concern. "What is it, Catherine? You seem to be on the edge of...remembering something. Tell me."

Flustered, Catherine pushed away from the table. "There's nothing to tell. I don't know what you're talking about."

She scooted across the booth trying to leave but Jonathan quickly stood and grasped her wrist. "Tell me," he urged softly. "I can help you."

Desperately, Catherine tried to swallow mounting panic, but it was a losing battle. The white images, the strange numbing sensations—

Oh, Lord. She wondered if she was going mad.

With a burst of strength, Catherine pulled away. Her voice was ragged, breathless. "Leave me alone, please, just leave me alone." Then she whirled and ran out of the restaurant.

Jonathan watched, staring at the doorway through which she'd fled. He smiled to himself. There had been confusion in her eyes and fear, but there had also been a spark of perception. She was remembering. He was certain of that. Eventually, Jonathan *would* have his answers.

It was just a matter of time.

The second concert had gone well enough. In spite of Maurice's insistence that she'd performed admirably, Catherine hadn't been particularly pleased. The music simply hadn't had enough depth or feeling to suit her.

Consoling herself that no one was capable of daily perfection, she ignored the possibility that something...or someone...may have distracted her. Instead, she fell back on the most overused and convenient of excuses: fatigue.

Now, she lay in the dark solitude of her hotel room and stared at the ceiling. If she was so darned tired, why couldn't she sleep? Why did her mind race like a runaway sled over misty white images and elusive fanciful dreams?

The telephone rang. Grateful for the reprieve from her own muffled thoughts, Catherine answered and heard her uncle's voice crackle across the miles. "Did I wake you, kitten?"

"No, I wasn't asleep." Catherine clutched the receiver and fought a sudden rush of tears. "It's so good to hear from you."

The familiar raspy chuckle warmed Catherine to her toes. "You didn't think I'd let an entire week go by without checking on my favorite girl, did you?"

Wiping her damp cheeks, Catherine laughed softly. She was twenty-eight years old, yet Bradford still considered her a child. Once his parental attitude had been the bane of her existence. During her teen years, Catherine and her uncle had constantly been at odds. She had rebelled against his rigid control and her own deep loneliness without realizing that Bradford had been enmeshed in his own emotional turmoil.

Catherine could remember those early times vividly, and with the wisdom of passing years, she now understood that instead of turning *to* each other, they'd turned *on* each other. She and her uncle had become extraordinarily close since then but occasionally Bradford reverted to the authoritarian approach that Catherine found immensely irritating. At the moment, however, she found her uncle's parental attitude rather comforting.

Bradford abruptly changed subjects. "Did Maurice explain the itinerary of the Eastern European concerts?"

"Umm? Yes, I think he mentioned it last night."

He couldn't disguise his glee. "Your American concerts must have been absolutely marvelous, my dear. Every musician I know is desperate to be included in this tour but only the very best have been chosen."

"That's nice," Catherine mumbled, her mind drifting.

"'*That's nice'?* An invitation to participate in the most prestigious classical event in decades, and you say *'that's nice'?*" Bradford's voice softened. "Is something bothering you, Cathy?"

"Of course not." Catherine sighed, ashamed to have quelled her uncle's excitement. Still, the peculiar events of the past days plagued her. She needed reassurance from the one man who had always been there for her. "Actually, something has happened, something rather odd."

Instantly concerned, Bradford asked, "What is it, kitten? What's wrong?"

"It's probably nothing, but I've been having these weird, ah, images."

The line was silent for a moment, then Bradford muttered, "Images? You mean dreams?"

"No. Well, maybe. I mean, I'm not asleep when I have them." Frustrated, Catherine rubbed her head, then shifted the receiver to her other hand. Standing, she paced the limited length of the telephone cord realizing how foolish she must sound. Words rushed out. "I know this seems strange but it *is* strange and that's why it's been bothering me so."

Her uncle soothed her. "Calm down and start from the beginning."

And so she took a deep breath and told him about the peculiar images of swirling white and the frightening sensation of freezing. When she'd finished, the telephone line was silent. "Uncle Brad?"

"I'm here." His voice had a strained quality.

"Did I ever have a similar experience when I was a child?"

He sounded puzzled. "No, not that I remember."

"Are you certain that I never got lost on a camping trip or trapped in a meat locker or..." Her voice trailed off as her own ludicrous words echoed in her mind. "Good grief, listen to me," she moaned. "Jonathan Stone was right—I *am* on the edge of something. I'm on the edge of losing my mind."

Bradford suddenly sounded as tight as a coiled spring. "W—what was that name?"

"Jonathan Stone, a man I met on opening night. For some peculiar reason these images, or whatever they are, seem to happen whenever he's around. The man probably thinks I'm a serious loony tune, and I'm beginning to agree. Please, just forget everything I've said."

She heard a gasping sound, as though her uncle had sucked in a ragged breath. "This...Stone person. What do you know about him?"

"Very little, actually. He was introduced as being some kind of executive with Stone Securities Corporation and apparently he's rather generous with his endowments. I don't know much else."

As she spoke, she visualized those mystical eyes and shivered at the memory. Such a powerful gaze, so menacing yet seductive. Catherine had no doubt that Jonathan Stone could terrify a battle-scarred warrior or tame a quivering virgin with a single potent stare. Surrender would be imminent. The thought sent chills down her spine.

Catherine detected a note of urgency in her uncle's voice and dragged her attention back to the conversation. "Pardon me?"

Bradford repeated his statement with growing agitation. "I said to stay away from him."

"Who?"

"Stay away from Jonathan Stone. Just concentrate on your work, Catherine. You can't afford any distractions now."

She felt her skin heat. Brad was right. Jonathan Stone *was* a distraction. Still, she felt a rumble of annoyance at her uncle's commanding tone. "I'm capable of concentrating on my work without turning into a hermit."

"Cathy, please, listen to me." His plea was broken and desperate.

"I am listening but I still don't understand. What is it about Mr. Stone that upsets you?"

"Nothing, nothing at all," he replied quickly. His voice rose to an adolescent squeak. "I think you should cancel the remainder of your performances and return to France at once."

"What?" Catherine was so stunned that she could only stammer incoherently. "Why in the world—? That's absolutely imposs—I can't believe you would even suggest—"

"You must begin preparations for the East Bloc tour immediately," he insisted urgently. "It's far more important to your career than a few West Coast concerts. Catherine—"

She found her voice and cut him off. "No! I won't even consider it. It would be a devastating blow to my reputation, not to mention that what you're suggesting is completely unethical."

After a long silence, Bradford mumbled, "You're right, of course." He suddenly sounded tired, defeated and very old.

"Uncle Brad, are you all right? You sound ill." Catherine was alarmed by his odd behavior. It wasn't like Bradford Madison to panic or act rashly. "Is something wrong there?"

"No nothing. Don't concern yourself, Catherine. I'll...call again soon."

Before she could reply, the line went dead. Catherine replaced the receiver and fretted about her uncle's strange attitude. Despite his denials, she suspected that he'd been less than honest with her. She loved her uncle but wasn't blind to his faults. Bradford Madison had never been adverse to stretching the truth if it served his purpose to do so. Weird things were happening, and Catherine was certain that Uncle Brad knew more than he would admit.

One way or another, Catherine was determined to find out just what was going on and to unlock the secret of the mysterious images. She was convinced that the man with Scorpio eyes held the key and that frightened her.

Catherine was no match for Jonathan Stone.

Jonathan laid the magazine on his gleaming walnut desk, then swiveled around to stare out the window. From his plush office on the twentieth floor, the city was a panorama of glass and concrete spreading from the vast mountains to the blue shores of the Pacific Ocean. The view was a silent symbol of success, conclusive proof that Jonathan was no longer a poverty-stricken street urchin. Sometimes, he just needed that quiet reminder.

The intercom intruded with a raspy buzz, followed by the brisk voice of his efficient secretary. "The Lieutenant Governor is on line one."

Turning, Jonathan picked up the telephone, pleased to hear from his longtime friend and associate. "Howard, you old coot. Haven't they impeached you yet?"

Howard Dylan's rich laugh boomed into the receiver. "You always were an impertinent devil, although I'd hoped a few million in annual profits would civilize you a bit."

"Not a chance."

"That's what I like about you, boy. Never let money go to your head. Now power, that's another matter."

Jonathan smiled. "You ought to know. You're the second most powerful man in the state."

"Then why in hell do I have to brown-nose the house speaker every time there's a decent bill on the floor?" Dylan snorted.

"When are you going run for office and give me a hand up here?"

"Politics doesn't interest me, Howard. You know that."

"First time we met I recall you saying that you weren't interested in money, either. Funny how a little taste of something can give you an appetite for the main course."

Jonathan's smile faded. The reminder was chilling. Eleven years ago, Howard Dylan had been a respected attorney who'd galloped to rescue a destitute young man from being bulldozed by blind justice. That young man had scorned the trappings of wealth, preferring the solitude and independence of a simple life in a natural environment. But that young man was gone forever.

Dylan's voice broke into Jonathan's thoughts. "You may be a gambler, Stone, but I've always bet on you to win."

"I wouldn't have won a damn thing without your financial backing."

"Nonsense. I just invested a little capital in a sound business venture, that's all. You provided the guts and the talent and the brains. By God, you were something to watch, too, a financial daredevil playing the stock market like a Vegas crapshooter plays dice. I never saw a man so driven."

Looking out the window, Jonathan's mind replayed the events of past years. Yes, he'd been driven—driven by seething rage and a need to prove his own worthiness.

Until that winter, Jonathan had been an arrogant but sadly naive young man. Then his mother had died, and her death had affected him deeply. He'd fought guilt and suppressed silent rage at having been abandoned. Eventually, Jonathan had found solace on the mountain. He'd convinced himself that he could survive alone and live totally independent of a society he considered greedy and materialistic.

Then he'd met Cathy Greer, and the fallacy of that conviction had struck with a mortal blow.

Dylan's thick voice pulled Jonathan back to the present. "So what do you say, son? Give me a green light and the party will roll out the red carpet."

Jonathan closed his eyes. Howard Dylan had been more than a friend and mentor; he'd become the father Jonathan never had. "Howard, you know I'd do just about anything for you, but not this—"

"Why? Hell, the party is scrambling for candidates."

"I have something to take care of."

"Then take care of it and let's get this show on the road."

"It's going to require some time—"

"Hell, we'll just speed things along. Who do I call?"

"This is something I have to handle myself."

The line fell silent for a moment, then Dylan said, "It sounds important."

"It is." After a pause, Jonathan added, "Catherine is back."

Dylan emitted a long, long whistle. After a pause, he said, "Let it go, Jon. It's over."

"No, it's not over. It won't be over until I know everything."

"Then what?" Dylan shot back. "Haven't you learned that playing with matches can cause a hell of a nasty burn? Cripes, I know how long you've been waiting for this but—" Abruptly cutting off the tirade, Dylan sighed. "You'll be like a dog with a bone on this, won't you?"

Jonathan didn't reply. He didn't have to. Dylan was well aware of all the years Jonathan had worked feverishly, driving himself to earn enough money for the desperate search. Now, when everything was falling into his lap and the end was in sight, Jonathan couldn't loosen his grip even for a moment, fearing the elusive answers would slip away again. He wouldn't let that happen, regardless of the consequences. Not even for his old friend. And besides, as Dylan was also well aware, Jonathan could *never* run for political office—even with Howard Dylan's backing.

Recognizing Jonathan's turmoil, Dylan backed off. "You do what you have to, son. If there's anything you need—"

"I know. Thank you."

When the conversation ended, Jonathan hung up the phone and looked at the glossy magazine on his desk. Automatically, he turned to the dog-eared page where Catherine's photograph smiled up at him.

It seemed a sad irony that a weekly news magazine had accomplished what fruitless years and untold thousands of dollars could not. Jonathan reread the article that had finally led him to Catherine, again marveling at how much she had achieved in such a short time. His own accomplishments had also been significant but he had no doubt that his own motivation had been considerably different than Catherine's had been.

Still, they were equals now. Once, Jonathan had been a lovestruck young man, ignorant of feminine ploys. This time, things would be different. He understood women; he understood Catherine.

This time, Jonathan was protected.

Chapter Three

The theater was quiet in the afternoon. Without the bustle of backstage personnel, Catherine could rehearse in peace. During these hours even Maurice seemed comfortable enough to disappear and allow her some precious privacy. For the past few days, Catherine's life had been a rush of rehearsals, photo shoots and meetings. Maurice had stuck so closely to Catherine that she couldn't even turn around without bumping into his smartly tailored chest.

In spite of her manager's interference, Catherine had managed a few furtive telephone calls about the elusive Jonathan Stone. What she had discovered was at best interesting and at worst frightening. The mere mention of his name made some people gush with praise and others quake in their collective shoes. That alone was odd, but Catherine decided to worry about the enigmatic Mr. Stone later. Now, she needed to relax.

Instead of practicing the classical pieces she'd planned for tonight's performance, she amused herself with her favorite rock classics. Pounding out a rousing rendition of "Rollin' on the River," Catherine was laughing and giddy as she sang along with the music. When the final raucous notes reverberated through the empty auditorium, Catherine was struck by a feeling that she was no longer alone.

Behind the last row of seats, the lobby door was open. Daylight streamed into the darkened interior, silhouetting the figure of a man who stood quietly watching. She knew instantly that the man was Jonathan Stone.

She stared at the shadowy figure moving slowly down the aisle. His aura preceded him, a presence of raw masculinity enveloping the musty atmosphere of the auditorium.

"That was very nice." His voice was both husky and wistful, as though his mind had traveled to another time, another place.

Catherine's mouth went suddenly dry and she managed an acknowledging nod.

Folding his arms, Jonathan ignored the fate of his expensive Italian suit and rested casually against the elevated stage. He looked up, regarding her for several silent moments before he glanced toward the wings. "Where is your bodyguard?"

Catherine's eyes narrowed. "If you're referring to my manager, Mr. Bouchard is upstairs." *Talking to his wife,* she nearly added.

Jonathan's smile was sharp, his eyes unpleasantly hard. "Anxiously awaiting your return, no doubt."

She stiffened, but chose not to dignify his innuendo with a response.

His smile grew wider. "I was surprised to find you alone. Your *manager* could give secret service lessons. Does he support all of his clients with such personalized... surveillance?"

She ignored his double-edged question and concentrated on the ivory piano keys.

After a moment, he spoke again. "Did you at least get my flowers?"

The trace of anxiety in his question caused her to look up quickly. For a brief moment, she saw a deep vulnerability, an inner sadness that tore at her heart. She suppressed an urge to touch him. "The basket of Mountain Laurel," she said quietly. "There wasn't a card..."

"You knew that I sent them."

"Yes," she whispered, the word like a soft breath. "I knew."

Without taking his eyes from her, Jonathan nodded slowly. For several moments, their eyes were locked in a silent communication that seemed completely natural and oddly familiar.

Nervously Catherine broke the silence. "The flowers were lovely. Now if you'll excuse me, I have to finish rehearsing." Tension sharpened her voice, and Jonathan's expression instantly tightened in response.

His smile was taut and ungracious. "I've never reacted well to aristocratic dismissals. Don't make the mistake of confusing me with one of your fawning lackeys."

Annoyed by his arrogance, Catherine lifted her chin and conveyed her displeasure with a hard stare. "Since you're obviously not a fan, I don't understand why you're here in the first place."

"Purely business," he replied slowly, then stretched like a panther and sauntered lazily up the steps to the stage. He leaned against the polished piano. "I have a proposition for you."

"Somehow that doesn't surprise me."

He cocked his head and hitched one dark brow. "Actually, I'm involved in fund-raising for a local children's home. I'd hoped you would consider doing a benefit performance."

"Oh . . ." She felt her skin heat.

"I'm sorry if you're disappointed."

Catherine cleared her throat and managed to meet his amused stare with one of cool indifference. "Mr. Bouchard handles my schedule. You should discuss this with him. Now, if you'll excuse me—"

Jonathan lifted her hand and pressed a card into her palm. "This is the address. I invite you to see for yourself, then decide if the center is worthy of your time. Mr. Bouchard did not wish to be bothered by charitable requests." Jonathan spoke softly, but Catherine didn't miss the biting inflection he gave the words. "I think you're well aware of how many times I've spoken to your Frenchman, since he has been intercepting my calls."

Slipping the card into her pocket, Catherine avoided Jonathan's eyes. "I apologize if Maurice has been rude. There have been some unusual events lately that have made him a bit uneasy."

Catherine remembered the morning that Maurice had received notice of an urgent cultural committee meeting—the morning she'd had breakfast with Jonathan—only to find himself locked in a freeway gridlock on the way to a nonexistent address. That frustrating escapade, combined with Uncle Brad's sudden need for daily reports on Catherine's whereabouts, had turned the normally relaxed Parisian into a bundle of nerves.

Now, Catherine saw the knowing gleam in Jonathan's eyes and instinctively realized who had sent poor Maurice on the wild-goose chase.

Suddenly Jonathan's smile became a threat, his teeth bared in warning. "And are these 'events' the reason you've suddenly found my background so compelling?" he growled.

Catherine looked away.

Jonathan persisted. "Have the results of your discreet inquiries proved interesting?"

Forcing herself to meet his challenging gaze, Catherine said, "Yes, actually."

"Really? I'm flattered." He laughed. "If you were curious, all you had to do was ask. My life is an open book."

"Not all of it," she said, surprising herself with a burst of courage. "Actually, no one had even heard of Jonathan Stone until about seven years ago, when you suddenly burst into the financial scene. Insider scuttlebutt says you have a secret partner, some kind of big-money backing that's all very hush-hush."

His gaze narrowed, and Catherine suddenly wished that she'd had the good sense to keep her mouth shut. A man with such dangerous eyes could very well have dangerous friends. It was a sobering thought.

For several long moments, she met his intense stare, trying to ignore the rapid pounding of her heart. The air was thick with tension, a heavy shroud of electric anticipation that was both exhilarating and frightening.

Then the angry glint in his eyes faded, replaced by a spark of grudging admiration. His full lips twitched, then fell apart in a dazzling smile of genuine pleasure. Scorpio eyes and a Sagittarius smile—it was a devastating combination. He chuckled once, then laughed out loud, a deep, rumbling male sound that was infectious.

Catherine felt her own mouth twisting and couldn't suppress a giggle. She had absolutely no idea what was so funny, but the laughter burst forth from the very core of her. They both fought for control, only to sink into renewed spasms.

Clutching her aching sides, Catherine finally wiped at her damp eyes and tried to focus on Jonathan. There was something wrong. He looked . . . different.

She squeezed her eyes shut, then opened them and gasped. Suddenly, Jonathan was wearing worn blue jeans and a thick down jacket. His dark hair was longer, oddly mussed and dusted with snow. The entire theater was white, swirling with soft snowflakes, and Jonathan was still laughing, as though a snowstorm inside of an auditorium was an entirely rational occurrence.

When his lips moved, Catherine realized that he was speaking, but she couldn't hear him. Her ears were humming, filled with a soft droning roar that drowned out all other sounds. Then this strange new Jonathan seemed to be reaching out, opening his arms to her and mouthing the words, "Come to me."

She desperately wanted to do just that. Suddenly, she was overcome by an incredible yearning, a longing to hold and be held, to sink into the sweetness of his embrace. Her heart ached, swelling with the deepest emotion she had ever experienced.

Closing her eyes, Catherine took a deep breath, rubbing her eyelids until they burned. When she looked up, Jonathan Stone was again professionally dressed, his hair neatly combed in a sleek Wall Street cut.

Oh, God. It had happened again.

Terror swelled up inside and threatened to completely engulf her.

"Are you all right, Catherine?"

She looked away, perspiration beading her upper lip. "Yes, of course."

"Tell me what you saw," he urged softly.

"Nothing," she murmured weakly. "I didn't see anything."

Jonathan scrutinized Catherine carefully. He'd watched her laughter turn to wonder, an expression of awe as though she'd seen something incredibly beautiful. For a brief moment, he'd recognized warmth in her eyes.

Then she'd blinked, appearing dazed and bewildered before her confusion had turned to fear. She had remembered something; he was sure of it. Still, he couldn't afford to press her. If he pushed too hard, she would skitter away and disappear. She was frightened, he could see that. He had to go slowly or she might slip over the brink in a disastrous plunge that could bury the truth beyond reach.

That was a risk Jonathan simply couldn't take.

Suppressing his own desperation, he forced a casual tone. "Talk to me, Catherine. Trust me."

Agitated, she pushed a strand of hair from her face. "Why should I?"

"Because I know what you're going through. I'm the only one who can help you."

"What a pompous thing to say." Her laugh was tight, bordering on hysteria. "Who do you think you are, some kind of sorcerer?"

"No, Cat, I'm just a man."

Her head snapped up, and her lost, childlike expression tore at his heart. "My name is Catherine," she said in a tiny voice. "No one calls me Cat."

"No one?" he asked softly.

"I've never liked that name." She stared for a moment, her eyes glazed, then suddenly stood. "I have to leave now."

"Not yet, please." Jonathan took her wrist and she pulled away, as though his touch had burned her. He felt a slow panic rising. "Stay for a while. We can . . . talk."

"No." Shivering, she rubbed her arms and backed away. She extended her hand helplessly, then whirled and ran out of the theater.

Sighing, Jonathan sat on the piano bench, still warm from her presence. Time was running out. Catherine's final concert was two days off and she was scheduled on the next flight to Europe. Then she'd be back in Bradford Madison's clutches and the story of what had happened so many years ago might be lost forever.

Jonathan wouldn't allow that to happen.

Catherine glanced at the address, then read the sign hanging on the wrought iron gate. "Here it is, Maurice. The Children's Care Center."

Maurice came up beside her, grumbling. "I do not understand why we are here, *chère*. Your schedule could not permit the addition of another performance, no matter how worthy the cause."

"The benefit isn't scheduled until late spring," Catherine replied. "Besides, it wouldn't hurt to look."

Pushing open the heavy gate, she walked quickly up a winding path to the large two-story structure. Maurice followed, muttering irritably.

Her beleaguered manager would be even more annoyed if he'd known that it was Jonathan Stone's request that had brought them here. Catherine had chosen to keep that information to herself. She'd also omitted mentioning Jonathan's visit to yesterday's rehearsal. Poor Maurice had quite enough to worry about and besides, Catherine didn't want to explain these strange compulsions she'd been having.

She wasn't even certain that she *could* explain. But this brightly lit building held a clue about the enigmatic Jonathan Stone, and Catherine wanted—no, she *needed* to know more about him. It was important to her peace of mind.

When they reached the porch, Catherine rang the bell and turned to Maurice. His sour expression spoke volumes. "You didn't have to come," she said pointedly.

"I would not allow you to enter a strange establishment alone."

"Fine. Then stop sulking and be gracious."

Before Maurice could respond, the carved oak door swung open, and a smiling, apple-faced woman greeted them.

"May I help you?" she inquired politely, regarding them with bright, inquisitive eyes.

Nervously, Catherine cleared her throat. "I'm Catherine LeClerc and this is my manager, Maurice Bouchard. I understand that the center is arranging a benefit and, uh..."

And what? And by the way, please tell me everything you know about Jonathan Stone?

Suddenly she was struck by an overwhelming urge to run. She didn't know what to say or how to behave in this ludicrous situation.

Fortunately, the jovial woman was one step ahead. Her round face split in a grin of absolute delight. "Oh yes, Miss LeClerc! We've been expecting you."

"You have?" Catherine's stunned expression must have been choice. Apparently Jonathan had been confident that Catherine's curiosity would lead her here. That was a little scary.

"Please come in," the woman said warmly. "I'm Margaret Broughton, the center's director."

After a moment's hesitation, Catherine stepped into the large foyer. Childish voices echoed from distant rooms, and a small, curious face peeked from the hallway.

Margaret beckoned to the child, a boy of ten or eleven. "Bobby, this is Miss LeClerc. She's a very famous pianist."

Catherine flushed at the overstatement.

Bobby seemed unimpressed. "Do you know Milli Vanilli?"

"No, I'm afraid not."

"That's a drag." The boy made no effort to conceal his disappointment. "How about Mick Jagger?"

Catherine shook her head apologetically. "I met Leonard Bernstein once."

Dismissing that information with an impatient grunt, Bobby frowned. "Don't you know anyone important?"

Catherine blinked. Actually, she'd been thrilled to meet the world famous conductor. But then, she wasn't a ten-year-old wearing a T-shirt emblazoned with a giant tongue.

Margaret chastised the boy gently. "That's impolite, dear."

Bobby's expression crumpled, and he stared at the floor. "Sorry," he mumbled.

Catherine's heart went out to the miserable child and she absently stroked his soft hair. "That's quite all right. To tell the truth, I've often wanted to meet Mick Jagger myself. If I ever do, I'll get his autograph for you."

The boy's eyes widened. "No kidding?"

"Cross my heart."

"Wow. I've got to tell Kelly." With that, Bobby dashed away.

Margaret's dark eyes twinkled. "Well, you certainly made his day."

"He's a charming boy," Catherine replied, feeling oddly wistful. "Where are his parents?"

"Bobby's mother deserted him when he was barely three. His father was convicted of armed robbery last year, so Bobby will be staying with us until a suitable foster home can be found."

"How sad."

"Yes. All of our children have suffered some kind of abuse or abandonment but we do our best to give them love and security."

A childish whoop filtered from another room, followed by excited whispers and giggling voices.

Catherine smiled. "It sounds as though you're doing a fine job. The children seem quite happy. Is this a privately run organization?"

"Yes. We depend on the charity of the community but time is more dear than money. We're always desperate for volunteers, people to spend quality time with the children." Margaret's expression grew pensive, then she blinked as though remembering her manners. "Would you like to meet the other children?"

"We'd like that very much," Catherine replied, slanting a glance at the sullen Frenchman. "Wouldn't we, Maurice?"

"*Oui*," he replied glumly.

Catherine patted his arm approvingly, then followed Margaret into a large parlor. Several youngsters were sprawled on the floor with coloring books, and two older girls played in the corner with Barbie dolls. Against the far wall sat a battered piano, dormant and dusty with neglect.

Margaret followed Catherine's gaze. "One of our volunteers used to play for the children but she moved to Arizona."

Nodding, Catherine turned her attention to the introductions. One girl caught Catherine's attention.

"This is Kelly," Margaret said cheerfully.

Kelly stared at the intruders with wary eyes and somberly stepped back when Catherine extended her hand.

"Kelly is shy," Margaret said hastily, then took Catherine's arm and propelled her away.

Still, Catherine glanced over her shoulder and saw Kelly watching, her young eyes filled with distrust. The girl's obvious fear was distressing to Catherine, and she wondered what devastation the child had suffered.

But Margaret was chatting and there were other young faces to greet. There were children everywhere, all sizes and colors and age groups. Some were friendly and happy; others were guarded and distant. All touched Catherine's heart. Even Maurice seemed to be mellowing.

As Margaret enthusiastically explained her plans for expansion, the doorbell rang. Her round face puckered in consternation and she turned to the dark-haired girl with skittish eyes. "Kelly, will you please answer the door?"

Kelly eyed Catherine warily, then nodded and left the room.

"Where was I?" Margaret mused absently. "Oh yes! I'm hoping that the benefit will raise enough money for a nondenominational chapel here on the grounds. The children need to have their spirits nourished along with their bodies and—"

A delighted cry echoed from the foyer, followed by a rush of gleeful young greetings. Was that shy little Kelly's voice? Catherine wondered what had suddenly brought such a pleasure to the sober little girl.

"What did you bring?" Kelly squealed. "Let me see, please!"

Margaret lit like a Christmas tree. "He's here! How wonderful."

The woman disappeared, leaving Catherine and Maurice staring at each other in total confusion. From the foyer, chaos erupted as a dozen chortling youngsters converged to greet their visitor.

Suddenly, Catherine's skin turned warm and tingly. She walked slowly toward the entryway, knowing instinctively who she would find there.

When she saw him, she sucked in a quick breath, unprepared for the sight of Jonathan Stone surrounded by a dozen happy grasping youngsters.

"Hold on to your britches," he admonished laughingly as a tiny boy pawed the pocket of his expensive suit. "There's plenty to go around."

"Mr. Jon, Mr. Jon," pleaded a curly haired tot who tugged relentlessly on the hem of his jacket. "Did you bring caramels? I love caramels!"

"Of course I did, pumpkin. You know I wouldn't forget your caramels." Jonathan squatted and caressed the tiny face with such love that Catherine's heart twisted.

He seemed so different with the children, so relaxed and comfortable. His eyes gleamed and his entire face seemed softer, less foreboding.

This was not the dangerous man that sent shivers down her spine. This was a man who made somber children squeal with delight, a tender and gentle man with love radiating from his clear eyes like a beacon of hope in a dark night.

When those eyes turned on Catherine, they grew wary, then warmed. Jonathan smiled knowingly, tilting his head in acknowledgement. As their eyes met and held, the room might as well have been empty. For those moments, Catherine was oblivious to everything except the power of Jonathan's sensuous gaze.

Maurice swore under his breath, then grasped Catherine's elbow. Ignoring her startled gasp, he propelled her to the front door.

Margaret protested. "Must you leave so soon?"

"I'm afraid we must," Maurice replied tightly. "Miss Le-Clerc must return to the theater for the evening's performance."

"But we haven't had an opportunity to discuss the benefit," she argued weakly, wringing her hands.

"Please contact me at the hotel," Maurice said crisply. "We shall discuss it then."

Smiling cynically, Jonathan watched Catherine while Maurice mollified Margaret's distress. Finally, the Frenchman acknowledged Jonathan with a brusque nod and guided Catherine out the front door without allowing her to do more than wave a limp farewell.

During the silent drive to the theater, Maurice brooded, and Catherine was lost in thought. She was grateful to have seen the gentle side of Jonathan Stone. Surrounded by giggling youngsters, he hadn't seemed so formidable. The man she'd seen tonight had been caring and tender. Still, something was bothering her. Catherine ran the scene over and over in her mind, trying to isolate the source of her agitation.

Suddenly, she realized why Jonathan's loving expression had seemed so familiar. She had seen that same expression before.

And she'd seen it on Jonathan Stone's face.

With a small cry, Catherine was jarred from a restless sleep. She was trembling, shaking with fear and cold, yet her skin was overly warm and damp with perspiration.

Throwing off the covers, Catherine got out of bed and slipped on a warm velour robe. It was still dark but she pulled back the drapes to look out at the quiet city. The dream still haunted her, its images as crystal clear as a cold mountain sky.

She'd been running through a blizzard. The frigid wind had been howling like an animal in pain. Still she had struggled onward, panting and gasping, nearly exhausted. In the dream she had been desperate, crawling through deep drifts of freshly fallen snow until her aching legs had folded. Above her, a gray sky rolled and heaved. Snow whipped at her face in a constant barrage of stinging projectiles. Soon the trees were coated white, their branches bent and crushed against the frozen earth.

The dream had been so frightening, so vivid, Catherine could still feel each icy flake striking with the force of a fist. Again and again she'd been hit until she'd collapsed, shivering and numb. She had been dying.

Then she'd heard a man's voice, deep and comforting. "Hold on to me," he'd said. "I'll take care of you. Everything will be all right."

Catherine had believed the voice and had clung to his warm body with all her remaining strength. She had opened her eyes and seen a blurred face. Powerful arms had lifted her, carrying her away from the cold, away from certain death. The voice had been soothing. She'd felt safe.

In her dream, she'd tried to focus, squinting up until her vision cleared. Then she'd seen the man who had saved her. She'd seen Jonathan Stone.

Releasing the curtain, Catherine turned from the window and rubbed her forehead. She desperately wanted to dismiss the dream as nothing more than the illusion of a creative subconscious, but deep down she realized that her mind had been fighting to reveal a crucial truth.

Instinctively she knew that hidden message would change the course of her life. The dream and the strange images preceding it were not metaphysical visions or premonitions of the future.

They were memories.

Catherine stepped into the richly furnished lobby of Stone Securities Corporation and nearly lost her nerve. The atmosphere of quiet power and unyielding control was an intimidating yet accurate reflection of the man who had created it.

Drawing on the strength of her own determination, she squared her shoulders and walked briskly to the receptionist and announced herself.

"Do you have an appointment?"

Catherine lifted her chin. "No."

"I see," the woman said significantly. "Perhaps you would care to speak with Mr. Stone's secretary."

"I believe Mr. Stone will see me. Please tell him that I'm here."

The young woman eyed Catherine with amusement. She used a red-tipped finger to poke a phone button, then spoke softly into the intercom.

Stiffly Catherine waited, wondering why she had been compelled to humiliate herself in such a degrading manner. Judging by the receptionist's smug expression, women requesting an audience with Jonathan Stone were fair game for vulgar speculation.

By the time a trim, well-tailored woman escorted Catherine to the carved-oak entrance of Jonathan's private office, she was not in a pleasant mood. He sat behind an elegant desk in an office that was a blatant showcase of power and money.

Seeing Jonathan's satisfied expression, Catherine realized that he had wanted her to seek him out. This was the world of a man used to getting what he wanted. She felt manipulated and controlled.

Anxiety turned to anger, and if Jonathan's wary expression was any clue, Catherine probably looked like a woman prepared for a fast and bloody war.

"I have to speak with you," she announced forcefully in a voice that dared him to gloat.

Jonathan regarded her for a moment, then motioned to a thickly upholstered sofa. She sat tensely, extremely aware of his presence close beside her when he joined her on the sofa.

"I'm glad you came," he said simply.

"You were expecting me?"

"Not expecting, hoping."

The modest statement deflated her anger. She'd expected infuriating arrogance or a triumphant smirk. The fact she was even here offered mute testimony to his power over her, but he accepted her presence with an expression of relief and gratitude.

That stunned her. If she'd misjudged his motives, what else had she misjudged? Had her conclusions about the dream and the images also been wrong?

Suddenly unsure, Catherine shook her head. "I shouldn't have come," she said shakily. "I don't even know why I did."

"You know, Catherine. We both know." Jonathan laid his hand on her knee in a gesture that was reassuring rather than suggestive. "Talk to me."

"I'm not sure what I should say to you." She laughed self-consciously, feeling awkward and insecure. "I . . . have questions."

He nodded slowly, but said nothing.

She felt a flush rise up her neck. He wasn't making this any easier. Finally, she took a deep breath and met his intense gaze. "We've met before, haven't we?"

His eyes were guarded. "Yes."

She waited, then realized that he wasn't going to expand on his answer. "When? Where? What happened?" Her nerves were raw and her patience thin. "Why won't you answer? Do you enjoy tormenting me?"

Jonathan sucked in a ragged breath and looked as though she'd struck him. He glanced briefly away and when his gaze returned to her, he was composed. "Tell me what you remember."

"I don't really remember anything," she said, frustration clipping her words. "That's why I'm here."

He stood as though dismissing her. "I see."

"Wait!" Desperately she grabbed his sleeve, pulling him back onto the sofa. "Please . . . I'm so confused."

His rigid expression melted. "I know you are," he said softly. "When you've remembered everything, perhaps you'll understand."

His words sent a cold chill down her spine. She didn't want to *remember*; she simply wanted to *know*. There was something frightening about those memories, something best left in the past.

Jonathan offered soft encouragement. "Some recollections have returned. I've seen it in your eyes."

"Just bits and pieces, images that don't make any sense."

"At the cocktail party you remembered something. Describe what you felt."

She closed her eyes, remembering the vision. "I felt very cold. Everything turned white and I was suddenly freezing."

"Anything else?"

"Not much. There were trees and snow and the sky was dark with storm clouds." Her eyes flew open. "It was in the mountains, wasn't it?"

"Yes."

"But I never go to the mountains," she murmured. "I hate being cold."

"It was a very long time ago."

She looked deeply into his eyes. "I went to a ski lodge once, with a girlfriend."

He nodded slowly, but said nothing.

Catherine searched her memory, hoping that if she could dredge up a few scattered images, Jonathan would fill in the gaps. "My friend Liza knew some guy who worked at the lodge. My uncle was unemployed at that time, so he was frequently away on job interviews. One weekend Liza and I went up to Lake Arrowhead so she could see her boyfriend." Catherine hesitated, watching Jonathan's face for any subtle hint of affirmation. His expression remained unreadable and she asked, "Did you work there, too? At the lodge, I mean."

"No."

"Then where . . . ?" The question died on her lips as his jaw tightened. He wasn't going to answer. Frustrated, Catherine stood and turned away from his intense stare. "This is ridiculous. I'm tired of playing games."

"I don't play games," he replied quietly. He grew thoughtful and seemed to be struggling with a decision. Finally, he said, "On the day we met, you'd been on the slopes with your friends."

"But I don't know how to ski," she protested.

He smiled. "I know."

Standing, he walked slowly to his desk and opened the top drawer. He pulled out a calendar filled with snow scenes and colorfully garbed skiers, then handed it to Catherine.

As she looked at photographs Jonathan came up behind her, murmuring encouragingly. "The run was nearly deserted. A storm was forming. You were cold and blinded by blowing snow. It's all in your mind waiting for you to reach in and touch it."

His voice was soothing, hypnotic. As he spoke an image formed. White swirled around her like an icy shroud. Reflexively she tried to push the vision away, but Jonathan's mesmerizing voice brought the memories clearly into focus.

"There was a storm on the mountain. You were lost and frightened. Think, Catherine... remember..."

Catherine relaxed, allowing her consciousness access to the image. "Yes," she whispered. "Liza and I went to meet her boyfriend on the steepest run. They promised to help me get down the mountain, but they went off together and I was all alone. I tried to find my way back but I fell and broke a ski. The snow started falling. I was lost. It was so cold and the wind—" She shivered. "I—I couldn't see. Everything was white, so damned white. I—"

Suddenly, Jonathan's arms were around her, warm and comforting. "It's all right, Cat. Everything's all right."

Catherine felt the warm moisture on her face and realized that she was crying. Vaguely, she realized that she should be embarrassed by such an unseemly emotional display, particularly in front of a stranger. But he didn't *seem* like a stranger. He was the man in her dream. "Then there was a fireplace and I... saw your face."

Reluctantly Catherine looked up and saw satisfaction in Jonathan's eyes. Then she realized that his arms were around her and she was clinging to him for dear life. Forcing her stiff fingers to release his lapel, she awkwardly stepped away. He didn't try to stop her. She cleared her throat. "I still don't understand how you found me."

"You stumbled to a clearing by the cabin where I was staying. My dog started to bark, and when I opened the door, he ran straight to you."

A shaggy black face flashed through her mind. "Mackie," she murmured, smiling wistfully.

"You remember Mackie?" Jonathan asked anxiously.

Catherine tried to focus, then shook her head. "Not clearly. I remember that I liked him. He had wiry fur and loved to have his ears scratched."

"He liked you, too," Jonathan said quietly, and Catherine wondered about his suddenly sad expression. His eyes grew distant and filled with pain, a profound sadness that made her heart ache. She couldn't breathe.

With supreme effort, Catherine looked away. Although she didn't understand Jonathan's distress, she couldn't bear to see it. She didn't know why his pain affected her so deeply but she wanted desperately to ease his torment. This had to be ended, for his sake and for her own. Remembering was the first step.

Alternately pacing and massaging her eyelids, she struggled with the disjointed images. "This cabin... was it a part of the ski lodge?"

"No, it was someone's vacation home, boarded up for the winter."

"It didn't belong to you? You broke into it?"

"Let's just say I borrowed it for a while." His voice was tinged with sarcasm. "We all can't be born into wealth and privilege. Some of us have to work for it."

"Yes, some of us do." Catherine didn't understand his resentment, particularly since he obviously had enough money to buy a dozen mountain cabins. Apparently that hadn't always been the case.

As she pondered that surprising revelation, another thought struck her. She looked up, astounded by a sudden realization. "I'd be dead if not for you. Oh my God, no wonder you were so hurt that I hadn't remembered. You saved my life and I didn't even thank you—"

"I don't want your damned gratitude." Jonathan's eyes flashed. "Is that what you think this is all about?"

His transformation bewildered her. "Then I don't understand. What is it you want from me?"

Anger contorted his sharp features. For a moment, Catherine saw the danger bubbling beneath his polished surface and recognized a ruthlessness that made her shiver.

Jonathan's voice could have etched steel. "You know what I want from you, Cat. And you know that sooner or later, I'm going to have it."

Pride overcame caution, and she raised her chin defiantly. "Are you threatening me, Mr. Stone?"

He sucked in a sharp breath and his eyes blazed. "I don't make threats, Miss *LeClerc*. I make promises."

Catherine took a step backward, holding her chest as though trying to push her heart back inside. Jonathan Stone was a dangerous and strangely desperate man. She should be frightened of him—a sane person would be—but somehow Catherine knew that he wouldn't hurt her. Her own fear went much deeper, to a part of her soul that had been untouched for over a decade. Something was buried there, something fearsome; something she didn't want to know. But she had to know.

Their eyes met and held in a silent duel of wills. Then his anger died, draining away so slowly that Catherine might have missed the transformation had she not been spellbound by his intense gaze.

Jonathan blinked, smiled coolly and motioned to the sofa. When he spoke, the man on the mountain had disappeared, replaced by the poised and polished professional. "My temper doesn't always serve me well," he said calmly. "Please sit down, and we'll talk."

She hesitated. "We've *been* talking. It hasn't done much for either of us."

He watched her quietly for a moment, then shrugged. "As you wish."

The dismissal irritated her. "This isn't just some casual high-school reminiscence I'm asking about. This is *my life* and a big piece of it is missing. I have a giant hole in my past, as though for those few weeks I simply didn't exist. Do you know what that feels like? Do you have any idea how humiliating it is to beg a stranger for tidbits of information about your own experience? I have a right to know—"

He whirled on her. "You have no rights. You want me to hold your hand and sympathize with your confusion, but I'm not going to do it. You're not the only one who lost something that winter and if you weren't so self-absorbed, you might realize that. I don't owe you one damned thing, lady, but you owe me. You owe me plenty."

Frustrated, Jonathan turned away but not before Catherine saw the hurt in his eyes. His shoulders were rigid, but his fingers shook slightly as he raked his hair.

"I'm so sorry," Catherine whispered. "I do owe you, I owe you my life."

Sighing, he shook his head, and Catherine saw a shudder move down his broad back. "I told you, I'm not looking for your gratitude. I have my own selfish reasons for wanting your memory restored."

"What reasons?"

Turning, he fixed her with a hard stare and ignored her question. "You were lost in the forest during a blizzard. I found you and carried you back to my cabin. Do you remember what happened then?"

Catherine swallowed hard. "You called my uncle and he came to get me?" she asked hopefully.

"That could have happened."

"But it didn't?"

"There was more."

She shifted uncomfortably. "How much more?"

"You'll remember that for yourself."

"When?"

"When you're ready."

"I'm ready *now*. Don't you understand that I have to know what's happening to me? I came here for answers—I *need* answers."

"Then find them. Search your heart and your mind and find them." His voice dropped to a whisper. "It's important, Catherine, for both of us."

Finally, she gestured helplessly. "I don't understand why you can't just tell me..." The empty words slid into silence. She wouldn't beg. No matter how many dreams she had or how many visions clouded her mind, Catherine Greer LeClerc would never plead for answers.

A warm hand covered her own, and Catherine looked up into Jonathan's concerned face. When he spoke, his voice was soothing, familiar and surprisingly intimate. "I can't tell you because there is too much you have to tell me first. I don't know everything. You do, Catherine, and when you've remembered it all, you'll have the answers we both need."

"What answers?" Even as she voiced the question, a chill slid down her spine. Somewhere along the way, Catherine had begun to suspect that they weren't discussing a simple weekend in the mountains. There was more to it than that, much more.

The Scorpio eyes bored into her. "You have something that belongs to me. I want it back."

The hotel messenger handed Catherine the package, then patiently waited as she fumbled through her purse for a tip.

Maurice peered into the living room toweling his wet hair. "Has the coffee arrived?"

"Not yet." Catherine held the ribboned package reverently. She knew Jonathan had sent it.

Tying his robe, Maurice entered, saw the small box and frowned. "What is that, *chère*?"

"I don't know. The bellboy brought it."

Draping a damp towel around his neck, the Frenchman sauntered across the room. He examined the box suspiciously. "I did not order this."

"It's for me."

"A gift?" His eyes narrowed. "From whom?"

She managed a casual shrug. "A fan, I suppose."

"Shall I open it for you?"

"Last night's performance wasn't my best but I still doubt that any disgruntled ticket holder would resort to mail bombs," she teased, then changed the subject. "Tell you what. You get dressed, and I'll treat you to dinner before the concert."

"I do not think—"

"Hurry! I'm starved." With that she dashed into the privacy of her own room and shut the door.

Holding the small box like something fragile and precious, Catherine perched on the edge of the bed. There was a small envelope, and removing the card, she read the enigmatic message.

Remember us, Cat. I do.

On the back of the card was an address and the word "tonight." There was no signature. None was needed.

Catherine fingered the bright red bow, hesitating briefly, then pulled the ribbon away. Nervously, she lifted the lid and gasped.

Reaching inside, she carefully took out a glass sphere mounted on a small wooden base. The crystal globe contained a clear liquid and when shaken, simulated snowflakes swirled around a small porcelain cabin surrounded by tiny pine trees.

The miniature world blinked at her through a flurry of white, a welcoming warmth in the icy wilderness. As she stared into the sphere, her mind cleared. She felt warm all over and remembered the crackle of burning wood. A fireplace. There was a hearth constructed not of brick, but of random stones, the kind that were scattered throughout the rugged mountain canyons.

She remembered a rough wooden floor and a colorful braided rag rug. The images rushed through her brain—the sound of rich male laughter, the softness of a fleecy blanket against her skin. At her feet curled a shaggy black dog, sighing in contentment. She'd wiggled her toes against the animal's furry coat and watched the snow fall through clouded windows. And Jonathan had been there.

He'd knelt beside her, then touched her face with an almost reverent gentleness. Catherine had turned to him, her lips seeking and he bent to kiss her.

The memory shook her to the soles of her feet. Even now, Catherine could still taste him, still feel his breath brushing her skin. It hadn't been a kiss of desperation or of rampant passion. Their lips had touched so softly, with sweet familiarity and warm comfort.

The globe slipped from Catherine's numb hands and bounced softly on the carpet. Bittersweet memories flooded her, memories of the cabin, of the mountain and of Jonathan.

She was astonished. She was horrified. Finally, she couldn't bear it.

Moaning, she covered her face with her hands. Tears slid down her cheeks. She cried for forgotten days and forgotten lives, for lost innocence and lost youth; but most of all, Catherine cried for Jonathan Stone.

Because once she had loved him.

Chapter Four

Jonathan had always loved the ocean at night. There was something about the moon dancing across the cresting waves that soothed him, made him feel whole again. Absently he rubbed his aching shoulder, throbbing in the chilly air. The wound was long healed; still the pain remained, a bleak and constant reminder of all that he'd lost.

Now he sat on one of the rocks scattered below his beach house deck and waited. Would she come? And what would he do if she didn't?

He tried to tell himself that it didn't matter. Now that he knew where she was—and who she was—a detective agency would eventually track down his answers. But this time Jonathan would hire someone new and fire the jackass who'd spent years taking his money and giving him nothing but excuses.

All that incompetent boob had done was to consistently report that the social security numbers belonging to Bradford Madison and Catherine Greer hadn't seen I.R.S. activity in eleven years. Because of that, the whining idiot believed that they'd both gone underground by creating new identities. Although the investigator had constantly assured Jonathan about closing in on Catherine's whereabouts, the man had never returned with anything more concrete than vague promises.

Still, no detective worth his license could be *that* incompetent and Jonathan should have fired him years ago. The fact that he hadn't was somewhat telling. Perhaps deep down Jonathan had been afraid to find Catherine—afraid of what he might discover.

Pushing away the unpleasant speculation, he scooped up a handful of cold sand and allowed the grains to blow free in the wind. The beach was private and secluded in the winter. Sun-loving Californians retreated from chilly water and damp air. Jonathan enjoyed the seasonal isolation.

He pulled back the cuff of his bulky sweater to check the time. No, she definitely wasn't coming. He shouldn't feel so disappointed, but he was. A new investigator may eventually discover "what" and "where" and "how," but that would never be enough. In spite of his secret fears, Jonathan knew that he had to understand "why." That answer was buried in Catherine's mind.

Remembering that long-ago time, Jonathan absently curled his hands into angry fists. If Cat had told him then that she'd wanted to leave, he wouldn't have stopped her. It would have hurt like hell but he'd have let her go, and she knew that. Things happen. People change. Life goes on.

But Cat hadn't been content simply to leave; she'd taken something with her, something dear to him, something he desperately wanted. That, Jonathan wouldn't ignore.

His fists clenched more tightly, and his teeth clamped like a vice. He was tormented yet couldn't free himself from the insidious memories. All these years he had planned for this reunion, rehearsing every detail in his mind. But nothing had gone according to plan. Jonathan's carefully constructed strategy had blown up in his face, and he felt like a nervous teenager preparing for a prom.

Jonathan's body reacted to his turmoil. A throbbing ache spread from his jaw to the base of his skull, and his stomach burned like a firepit. Rolling his head, he massaged his neck and told himself that no damned woman was worth an ulcer, especially one who'd betrayed him so royally.

Somehow, he'd get through this. The end of his search was in sight, and all he had to do was hold on for a little while longer. God only knew how many times he'd had to do just that. Life was tough for a kid alone on the streets but Jonathan had pulled through then and he would pull through now. Jonathan Stone was a survivor.

A strange prickling sensation traveled down his spine, and Jonathan realized that someone was watching him. Instantly alert, he simultaneously spun and crouched. A shadow stepped from behind the deck railing onto the sand.

"I am sorry to disturb you, Monsieur Stone," came the crisp male voice. "Your servant directed me."

Straightening slowly, Jonathan felt the blood hammering angrily through his veins. He purposefully forced his body into a relaxed posture designed to lull adversaries into a false sense of security. Beneath the casual exterior, he was ready for action. Old habits die hard.

"I have no servants, Mr. Bouchard," Jonathan replied with deceptive softness. "Mrs. LaRue is an employee."

"As you wish. I meant no disrespect." The big Frenchman stood stiffly, hands clasped behind his back, but in the diffused moonlight, Jonathan saw determination etched on his face. Maurice spoke in clipped tones. "The time has come for us to speak honestly, *monsieur*."

Lazily hooking his thumbs in the pockets of his jeans, Jonathan coldly regarded the rigid man in front of him. So, Cat had sent a bodyguard to do her dirty work. How like her to take the cowardly way out. And how foolish of her to believe Jonathan could be intimidated.

He fixed Maurice with a hard stare and a mean smile. "By all means, Mr. Bouchard. Honesty is always the best policy."

Although Jonathan's first instinct had been rather primal, his mind churned with the same razor intellect that had propelled him from dark alley to corporate boardroom. It was Jonathan's experience that the more people talked, the more they revealed. Perhaps he could glean some useful information.

Maurice cleared his throat. "Your recent attention has been quite distressing to Miss LeClerc."

"Has it?"

"*Oui*. She has been distracted, and her work has suffered. Tomorrow night is her final concert and her performance must be above reproach. I must ask you to refrain from further harassment."

Jonathan's eyes narrowed. "I see. And this is, of course, Miss LeClerc's request?"

Shifting uncomfortably, Maurice met Jonathan's direct stare. "It is my request, *monsieur*."

"Of course." Jonathan rocked back on his heels. "Miss LeClerc is too grand a lady to sic her paramour on unwanted suitors. That's so gauche, don't you think?"

The big man took a sharp breath. "*Mon Dieu*! How dare you speak of Catherine in such a vulgar fashion. You will apologize at once."

"And for what shall I apologize? Calling you a paramour or calling her a lady?"

Anger sharpened Jonathan's tone and dulled his senses. He didn't see it coming. The blow landed on his jaw, snapping his head backward. He staggered once, then took a sharp left cross to the cheek before he fell to the ground.

Ears ringing, Jonathan felt fury bubbling through his veins and allowed it to boil. This is what he wanted. This is what he needed. For years he'd suppressed secret pain, suffering in stoic silence. Suddenly, he wanted to pass along the hurt, to share the agony of his heart. Anger touched a primal chord and his brain churned with predatory cunning.

Pretending to be dazed, Jonathan moaned deliberately then balanced on hands and toes like a sprinter in the starting gate. Once positioned he slid a glance upward and saw the Frenchman, half a foot taller and thirty pounds heavier, poised in classic boxing stance. The man was obviously trained in the gentlemanly art of self-defense. Bouchard would play by the rules and that would be his downfall—because Jonathan was a street fighter.

With the speed of a pouncing panther Jonathan attacked, springing upward and sending three killing blows into the Frenchman's abdomen. The big man stumbled backward, gasping for breath. It took only a moment for Maurice to regroup and raise his fists, but a moment was enough. Jonathan shot a wicked jab to Maurice's jaw then followed with another flurry of pounding blows into his ribcage.

Rage had taken over. In his mind, Jonathan saw Cat smiling and sated, lounging in front of a warm fire. Her naked shoulders were gleaming, her hair spilling across the mussed pillow as she raised her arms to welcome her lover. Her French lover.

The vivid image consumed Jonathan's concentration. He dropped his hands, stepping backward, stunned by the direction of his thoughts. Had he gone mad? Was he actually beating a man simply because the poor guy had fallen victim to a woman Jonathan had once loved?

Concentrating on his own silent question, he dropped his hands and the Frenchman landed a crushing blow.

Jonathan's head exploded in pain. He arched into the air, landing flat on his back with enough force to knock the wind out of him. Everything whirled in blackness punctuated by agonizing flashes of brilliance. He tasted blood and fought to stay conscious.

From a great distance, Jonathan heard a scream, a tormented cry that touched the deepest recesses of his memory. He had heard that sound before, a long time ago. That time he had lost the battle, falling unconscious before he could see the source of that horrible sound. Now he forced his eyelids open and willed himself not to succumb to the blinding pain.

The scream turned into a wail. "Oh my God, you've killed him!"

Jonathan couldn't decipher Maurice's garbled response. He rolled to his side and futilely tried to push himself up. Soft hands touched his cheek. He opened one eye and saw a blurred face. Catherine's face. He wondered if she was a dream.

"Jonathan, oh Lord, you're hurt."

She cradled his head on her lap and when his vision cleared, he saw tears gleaming on her face. It wasn't a dream. Catherine had come after all and she was holding him, rocking him, caressing him. Jonathan was dazed and perplexed by her concern.

Catherine shouted at Maurice. "How could you do such a thing?"

Fuzzily, Jonathan followed her gaze and saw Maurice sprawled on the sand with blood trickling from his mouth. The Frenchman gingerly touched his lip, then said, "It was necessary."

"Necessary?" Catherine's voice rose an octave. "Necessary to beat a man you don't even know half to death?"

Jonathan blinked. *Half to death?* The inside of his mouth felt like raw meat, and he had a couple of loose teeth, but certainly he'd survived worse. He was bewildered by Catherine's obvious distress and downright baffled as to why she'd run to him instead of her Frenchman, particularly since she'd sent Maurice here in the first place.

Or maybe she hadn't.

Jonathan's head was clearing and he concentrated on the conversation between Catherine and Maurice with growing interest.

"What in the world are you doing here, anyway?" Catherine demanded. "You stole the card, didn't you? I knew I hadn't misplaced it. Honestly, Maurice, I can't believe you would stoop to something so...so uncivilized."

Maurice sat on the sand looking bewildered and embarrassed. "I was simply trying to protect you, *chère*. It is apparent that this man has bothered you and I wished only to alleviate your dismay."

"So you sneaked into my room and stole something that belonged to me, then took it upon yourself to interfere in my life *without my permission*." Catherine's voice shook with cold anger. "This is none of your business. You had no right."

"But this man, he—"

"*This man* once saved my life."

Maurice's jaw sagged.

Catherine ignored his stunned expression and turned her attention to Jonathan. "Are you all right?" she asked anxiously. "Do you need a doctor?"

For a moment, he was torn. There was something warm and soothing about her unexpected concern. He enjoyed the feel of her arms around him, the softness of her lap beneath his head. If he admitted he was okay, she'd probably drop his face in the sand like a discarded rock. He briefly toyed with the idea of feigning a brave grimace, but that really wasn't his style.

Stiffly, Jonathan propped himself on one elbow and tersely muttered, "I'll live."

Catherine's palm lingered on his face for a moment, then she pulled her hand away and retreated behind strained formality. "Please accept my apology for this unfortunate incident." She gave Maurice a hard stare.

The Frenchman got the message and mumbled his own apology, then stood awkwardly and extended his hand. After a moment, Jonathan took the offered assistance and swung to his feet.

Catherine was not as charitable, ignoring her manager's outstretched hand as she stood gracefully. "I can't condone what has happened here tonight," she told Maurice quietly. "For almost two months, you have treated me like an incompetent child. I've tolerated it, because we've been friends for so long and because protectiveness is part of your nature. I've felt guilty, knowing how much you've missed your family because of this tour."

Jonathan was stunned by Catherine's quiet strength. This was not a woman dismissing a scorned lover; this was a woman firmly disciplining a respected employee. Had he misjudged their relationship?

Jonathan dragged his attention back to their conversation. Maurice wrung his hands and looked so dismal that Jonathan almost felt sorry for him.

"Words cannot express my regret, *mon amie*," Maurice told Catherine. "I blame only myself for this unpleasantness and I beg your forgiveness."

Jonathan thought it time to step forward. "The misunderstanding has been mutual. Under the circumstances, Mr. Bouchard had little choice. I asked for it, he obliged. It's over."

Catherine regarded Jonathan warily. "The fact remains that he had no business coming here in the first place. As a matter of fact—" She turned toward Maurice "—Why did you?"

"I was concerned for your safety. Bradford led me to believe that Mr. Stone was a dangerous man." Quickly, Maurice extended a conciliatory hand. "No insult is intended, *monsieur*."

"None is taken." Jonathan rubbed his sore jaw. "I'm not up to another lesson in manners."

Wincing, Maurice automatically shielded his stomach. "Nor am I."

But Jonathan was still mulling the revelation that Bradford Madison was behind this entire mess. The only surprise was that Jonathan had underestimated such a tenacious adversary; it was a mistake he wouldn't make twice.

Catherine cleared her throat and spoke to her manager. "Please leave us now."

"I shall wait and drive you back to the hotel."

Even in the dim moonlight, Jonathan saw her eyes flash with green fire. "No. You take the rental car, and when I'm ready to return, I'll call another cab."

"But *chère*, it is too late for a woman alone—"

"Has nothing I've said gotten through to you?" Hands on hips, Catherine squared off with the startled Frenchman.

He instantly retreated, clicking his heels formally and bowing his head. "Of course. *Pardonnez-moi*." With that, he spun and walked into the night.

Catherine watched silently and felt sick. Maurice was a proud man, and she'd hurt him. For that, she felt deep sadness. But there were too many emotions waging war inside of her, draining her strength.

Nothing made sense any more. When she'd seen Jonathan crumpled in the sand, her heart had leaped into her throat. Terror had overwhelmed her, and icy horror that she was at a loss to explain. She'd thought him dead and for one brief moment, Catherine had been suspended in time, lost in a whirlwind of emotion that had possessed her entire being. She remembered the scream, an agonizing, tormented lament that had been ripped from her very soul by something she couldn't comprehend.

For a moment, Catherine knew that in her mind she'd been somewhere else, in a distant place and time far beyond this moment. And it had been terrifying.

Cautiously Catherine looked at Jonathan. He stood quietly, arms crossed, his expression strangely pensive. Moonlight illuminated the ugly, swelling bruise on his cheek and she suppressed the urge to touch him. Instead, she knotted her hands together and willed them to stop trembling.

Finally, he spoke. "You came. I didn't think you would."

"I know it's late," she said quietly. "I couldn't find the card, so I had to look up your address. Then the rental car was gone so I had to call a cab..." Her voice dissipated into the damp air, and she shrugged helplessly.

Jonathan's gaze penetrated the darkness like a laser beam. "Have you remembered anything else?"

Catherine rubbed her arms, more to buy time than to guard against the night's chill. She didn't know what to tell him and finally settled on the truth. "I remember bits and pieces, disjointed images. And there are . . . feelings."

"What kind of feelings?" A subtle break in his commanding tone betrayed his anxiety.

"I . . ." Catherine cooled her face with her palms. God, this was difficult. "I think there was more to it than a single afternoon in the mountains."

Jonathan was silent for a moment, then whispered, "Yes, there was more."

She looked out over the inky ocean, unnerved by his potent gaze. "There are things going on inside of me that I can't understand. Every time I try to fill in the blanks I feel smothered, as though I can't breathe. There's a terror that swells up until I feel I'm going to burst. I want to run away from it all and pretend it never was."

Even as she spoke, the fear surged up from someplace deep inside. Tears threatened, and she angrily wiped them away.

Instantly, Jonathan was close behind her, his strong hands on her shoulders. "It's all right, Cat," he whispered, his breath soft against her hair. "I'll help you."

"I'm still afraid." Turning, she looked into his face and saw compassion. "I did something terrible, didn't I?"

Wariness veiled his eyes. "Why do you think that?"

"Because a part of me just doesn't want to remember. I mean, everything about that time in my life seems to be one huge emotional upheaval, as though whatever happened then was so traumatic that my mind couldn't deal with the reality." Stepping back, she looked deeply into his eyes and saw the truth reflected there. "Did I hurt you? Is that why you look at me with such pain and anger?"

His mouth tightened, and he spoke in clipped tones. "I'm not after revenge, if that's what you're worried about."

"What did I do to you, Jonathan? Please, I'll do anything I can to make up for it, just tell me what I've done?"

His closed his eyes, and his body shuddered. "I can't tell you anything more. You have to remember on our own"

Frustrated, she tossed her arms up and paced. "Are you trying to punish me? Fine, maybe I even deserve it, but I can't make things right if I don't know what's wrong."

"Cat, no—" He reached out and took her arm.

She shook him off, fighting panic. "Was I a thief? Tell me, Jonathan, did I steal something from you?"

"You're not a thief," he said raggedly, his face contorted by demons of his own making.

"You said that I took something. What did I take? I'll replace it, I'll buy you another." Catherine was shaking all over, losing her emotional battle. She felt out of control. "My God, help me deal with this. Please . . . or I'll go mad."

"Catherine," he moaned, pulling her into his arms. "I'm going to help you, honey. Trust me."

His body felt so warm, so safe. Catherine buried her face in the curve of his neck and clung to him, trembling violently, desperately trying to control the nameless terror. Uncontrollable spasms shook her and she battled for control of her mind and body.

Jonathan murmured nonsensical words of comfort that were strangely soothing and familiar. He stroked her hair gently, lovingly, as though she were precious and fragile. She shuddered once, then again. Finally a slow heat unfurled inside, as though the sun was rising in her belly. Her taut muscles relaxed, her fevered mind grew calm.

She felt cherished, cared for, secure. But those feelings were from the past. When the image began to form, Catherine made a conscious decision and allowed the memories to flow.

She remembered the cabin and the shadows cast by the flickering flames. It had been night, very late, yet she'd still been there. Fleetingly, she wondered why, then concentrated on the warm feelings swelling up inside of her.

Catherine tried to focus on details and recalled a small wooden table with two plain chairs. Books had been scattered on the table and two coffee mugs. As she remembered the scene, she felt heat emanating the length of her body. She'd been lying in bed, watching the fire, feeling contented and happy. Then she remembered a man's hand stroking her, caressing her with proprietary confidence and shocking intimacy.

Someone had been in bed with her.

Stiffening, Catherine pushed away from the comforting arms, stumbling backwards. Jonathan was surprised by her sudden movement and took a step forward. She held up her hand. "No, please."

His eyes narrowed. "I see you're feeling better."

"Yes, thank you." Confused and embarrassed, Catherine avoided his gaze. She couldn't believe what her mind had shown her. The image must have been an illusion, some kind of wishful dream caused by being in the arms of an attractive man on a romantic beach. It couldn't have been true. Good Lord, she'd only been seventeen years old. Catherine could understand a young girl having a crush on a man, even believing herself to be in love, but that's all it could have been. She was not a promiscuous person; she never would have fallen into bed with a man simply because he'd pulled her out of a snowbank.

But the image had been so vivid, so strikingly real—

Cutting off the thought, Catherine turned toward Jonathan. She saw longing in his eyes and the heat of remembered passion. Her heart thudded erratically. Silently, she prayed that she was wrong but realized that, one way or the other, she had to know.

Jonathan spoke softly. "You have questions."

"Yes." She took a deep breath. "Other than the day you found me, did we . . . see each other again?"

"Yes, we did."

Her nod was jerky and she clasped her hands tightly together. The one thing Catherine could remember about those months was that Uncle Brad had been away more than he'd been home. She'd been on her own. And what had she done with that freedom? "Were we—" The words caught in her throat. "—good friends?"

He smiled sadly. "We were very close."

Extending her hand in a pleading gesture, she struggled with the words. "Did we ever—I mean, were we—"

"Yes, Cat. We were lovers."

A tiny sob bubbled up from her very core.

Jonathan's eyes hardened. "We were young and single. It was hardly an adulterous union. Why are you so shocked? These things happen—"

"Not to *me*."

Frustrated, she fiercely rubbed at her eyelids and tried to understand the incomprehensible. This man, this stranger, was calmly standing there telling her that they had shared the ultimate intimacy. How was she supposed to respond to that? Did he expect her to throw herself into his arms and declare undying passion? Was he waiting for her to strip off her clothes and flop down on the sand?

Oh God. She couldn't handle this.

When Jonathan spoke again, his voice was cold. "Is the thought of sharing my bed so distasteful to you?"

Catherine whirled on him, hands clenched into tight fists. "*Yes!* Should I be happy knowing that a lifetime ago I did sordid things with a complete stranger?"

His jaw twitched, and he spoke through clenched teeth. "We weren't strangers and nothing we did together was 'sordid.'"

"How do I know that? How do I know anything?" Her breath came in ragged gasps. "It's not real to me. It never happened. It doesn't exist because I can't *remember*."

With a lightening movement Jonathan grabbed her arms and roughly pulled her against him. "I exist. I'm real. Feel me, feel my heart beating against you." He tightened his grip, pressing her against his body. He was strong, and her struggle was futile. In his eyes Catherine saw his anger, his pain at her rejection of the memories they shared. She pushed at his shoulders and he cupped her hips, pressing her against him. His voice was raw. "You can deny me, Cat, but you can't deny yourself, what you're feeling now, what you felt then. And you can't deny this."

Then his mouth crushed her lips with power and fury and deep, burning pain. Catherine stiffened against the assault but instantly his lips softened, moving slowly, tasting deeply. His palms cradled her face gently, sweetly and his kiss conveyed a depth of emotion that took her breath away. She responded to him without thought, clinging with her arms and her mouth. The desperate kisses, the intimate cupping of their bodies suddenly seemed the most natural thing in the world.

Catherine was dizzy with the taste of him, the feel of his maleness pressed against her. A warm whiteness melted inside, a buttery flow of passion and need. She wanted this moment to go on forever. Nothing had ever seemed so perfect, so right, nothing since—

Since when?

As Catherine regained sanity, her body stiffened. Jonathan groaned in protest, holding her even more tightly. When he tore his mouth away, Catherine saw passion mingled with bewilderment. He traced the curve of her jaw with his fingertip, then brushed a damp strand of hair from her face before shakily releasing her. He stepped back and raked his finger through his hair, staring over the water with an expression of confusion and pure misery.

"I shouldn't have done that," he said quietly.

She didn't know how to respond and simply nodded.

Finally he took a deep breath and crossed his arms as though shielding his heart. "You can't avoid the past forever, Catherine. Neither of us can."

"It was so long ago and it's over."

"Is it?"

"Yes."

"A part of your life is missing. Are you willing to live with that, always wondering when something or someone will appear with another fragment, another image?"

The thought unnerved Catherine. "Is there more?"

"When you've remembered everything, you won't need to ask that question."

A cold gust whipped at her face, and she shivered. In her heart, Catherine knew he was right. She couldn't live with the fear of not knowing. The truth might be painful but the emptiness was a torment that she couldn't bear.

Jonathan Stone was the key; she knew that instinctively, just as she now knew that there had been much more between them than she'd guessed. When he looked at her, his eyes were smoldering with remembered passion and hot with leashed fury.

Yes, there was more. Catherine had to know.

She looked at him, and her chest tightened. His sadness touched her yet she instinctively knew that she was the cause of his pain. "Jonathan?"

"Yes?" He didn't look at her.

"Why is it so important to you that I remember? Why can't you just tell me what I should know?"

He stared out over the inky blackness. "Because I have questions, too."

"These...questions. Am I the only one who can answer them?"

"Yes."

"When you find the answers, what will happen then?"

Sighing, he closed his eyes. "I don't know. God help me, I just don't know."

At that moment, Catherine saw the agony etched on his face and realized how very much he had suffered. She knew what she had to do.

Catherine found Maurice pretending to read a magazine in the hotel suite's living room. He looked up. *"Bonsoir."*

"Good evening," she said softly, returning the formal greeting. "I'm glad you're still awake."

He put down the magazine. "I wished to speak to you, to apologize."

"No, please, I should apologize—"

He interrupted. *"S'il vous plait,* I must speak. You were correct to reprimand my behavior. Sometimes I forget that you are not my own daughter. Because I care so deeply, I forget that our arrangement is a business and I push myself into your life." Maurice spread his hands dramatically. "Genevieve says that I have the head of a pig."

Catherine laughed. "Well I suppose you are a bit pig-headed, but so am I. Perhaps that's why we understand each other."

"*Oui.*"

"I never wanted to hurt you, Maurice. The things I said to-night—"

"Do not fret, *chère*. My skin is not so thin as a grape. I understand."

"No, you don't understand. *I* don't even understand. It's all so...so frustrating." Catherine saw his baffled expression and realized that he deserved more than vague double-talk. She sat on the sofa and patted the cushion. "Please sit down. I have a lot to tell you."

After a moment's hesitation, the Frenchman seated himself and Catherine took a deep breath. Over the next half hour, she told him of the strange images and the man who had caused them.

She did, however, exclude certain details. The specifics of her past relationship with Jonathan were much too personal to share, even with her dear friend.

Stunned, Maurice mumbled, "*Quelle bêtise!* What an absurdity. It is madness to believe such a man."

"I don't believe him," Catherine said softly. "I believe myself and what I remember."

"This man has eyes of power and pain. He is dangerous and I fear for your safety."

Catherine remembered Jonathan with the children and how he'd caressed the toddler so lovingly. She also remembered the man she'd known eleven years ago, the man who had held her and made her feel safe.

"He won't hurt me," she told Maurice firmly.

"How do you know this?"

"I know."

Frustrated, Maurice quickly stood and lapsed into his native language. He paced, alternately holding his own head and gesturing for assistance from above. Catherine listened quietly and waited. Finally he collapsed in a chair. "At least we shall be on our way home by this time tomorrow. Then, *chère*, your nightmare will be at an end."

Catherine swallowed hard. "That's something else that I need to tell you. I'm not going."

"*Pourquoi*? Have you been so blinded by this man that you would tear out your uncle's heart?"

"It's only for a few extra days, perhaps a week. Don't you understand that I can't just fly off and forget everything that's happened?"

"No! I do not understand. This is madness, it is insanity."

"You're overreacting, Maurice. This is something I must do."

Pursing his lips, he frowned. After a moment, he acquiesced. "All right. I shall change our flight."

"I couldn't ask you to do that. You've been counting the hours until you could be home with your family."

"I shall not leave you alone."

"I won't be alone."

Maurice made an unpleasant sound. "Catherine, *mon amie*, you must listen to reason—"

"Please don't make this more difficult than it already is." Reaching out, she took the Frenchman's hand. "There's a part of my life that is a complete blank. If I don't find out what happened then, I'll have to live with this fear forever."

"But why with this man?"

"Because Jonathan Stone is the only one who really knows about that time in my life. We were . . . friends." Catherine felt her skin heat at the memory of just how close that friendship had been. She avoided her manager's disapproving stare. "Please, try to understand. I have to find out what happened eleven years ago. It's important to me."

He regarded her thoughtfully. "You have not discussed this decision with your uncle."

"No."

"He will not be pleased. I do not understand the reason, but he fears this Jonathan Stone."

"I realize that, but I don't know why. It's one of the things I need to find out."

Standing stiffly, Maurice clasped his hands behind his back. After a moment, he asked, "Do you wish to terminate my services as your manager?"

Catherine was stunned. "Of course not!"

"Then may I assume that, as my employer, you are giving me a direct order to return to France tomorrow afternoon?" His expression was serious but Catherine saw a subtle gleam in his eye.

She understood what he was asking. "Yes, I am, and you may inform my uncle that those were my instructions."

"And when shall I inform Monsieur Madison?"

"I believe he plans to meet us at the airport. That would be an appropriate time."

Maurice smiled sadly. Lifting Catherine's hand, he kissed her fingertips and bid her good night.

Alone, Catherine closed her eyes and wondered if Maurice was right. Was this madness? Perhaps. But her dear friend would have been even more dismayed if he'd known that she planned to spend the next few days in a lonely mountain cabin.

And Jonathan Stone would be with her.

Chapter Five

The narrow highway circled the mountainside like a ribbon of pavement. As Jonathan steered the truck around the sharp banks and sloping curves, Catherine stared out the window into the plunging valley below. The road was sandwiched between fog rushing up from the flatland and a rolling cloud bank that enveloped the mountain peaks. The surrounding wilderness was magnificent and treacherous, a collage of trees and rocks and jagged cliffs.

Everything was beautiful; everything was familiar.

The trip had been quiet. Catherine had been nervous at first, then pensive and preoccupied. Jonathan had been formally attentive and polite, yet willing to allow her the solace of silence.

Now she slid a glance at him. His lips were pursed, and his brow furrowed in concentration. Then as though her gaze had been a touch, his expression grew wary and he looked at her.

Catherine managed a nervous smile. "I've never cared much for this road. It's like walking a tightrope in combat boots."

"It's familiar, then?"

"Yes. I've driven it dozens of times."

"Have you?"

Catherine wasn't fooled by Jonathan's casual tone. She noted the taut edge of his mouth and recognized the hidden question. "I used to get restless on the weekends when Uncle Brad was away looking for work. Since I had my own car, I took off a lot just to get away."

After a moment's silence, Jonathan asked, "What kind of car did you have?"

"A big blue gas-guzzler." She laughed. "My uncle believed that it was safer to drive a tank than a tin can, so he bought me the biggest and ugliest used car on the lot. Still, I didn't mind. It usually got me where I was going."

"And where was that?"

She looked out the window. "I know I liked the mountains. After we first met, I . . . continued to visit you, didn't I?"

"Yes."

The conversation had taken an unsettling turn. Catherine brightened her voice and changed the subject. "This is a nice little truck."

"You sound surprised."

"I thought you'd be more comfortable in a pricy import complete with wire wheels and cellular telephone."

He laughed. "That's a fairly accurate description of my city car."

"I thought so." Crossing her arms, she leaned back triumphantly.

"Don't look so smug. That car is strictly for my business image. This—" He patted the dashboard affectionately "—is my favorite."

"Why?"

"Perhaps it reminds me of the old days." His expression grew thoughtful and for a moment, he seemed miles away. Then he blinked, glanced at Catherine and smiled. "Actually, a four-wheel drive is the only way to get to the cabin during bad weather."

That surprised her. "It is?"

"Hmm. There's an old logging road cut through the forest that turns into a river of muck in the spring."

Catherine absently chewed her lower lip and mulled this. If she'd made frequent trips up here that winter, as Jonathan had led her to believe, how could she have driven that huge old sedan over such a road? Doubt gnawed at her, and she wondered if this entire charade was some kind of elaborate prank.

"Did you have a truck eleven years ago?" she asked on a hunch.

His eyes lit. "Yes, yes I did."

"Hmm." She stared out the window. It had been winter then, and Catherine had already remembered the snow. Even this paved highway was impassible during foul weather without tire chains, and the old sedan had none. "Did I ever leave my car down in the valley?"

Jonathan couldn't keep the anxiety from his voice. "When the weather was bad, yes. I'd meet you down the hill, and we'd drive up together in my truck." There was a new confidence in his voice that startled Catherine. His eyes glowed, and he smiled. "What else do you remember?"

Catherine knew that he'd misunderstood her curious questions, and her heart sank. "I didn't remember anything Jonathan."

"You remembered my old truck and where we used to meet—"

"I was guessing, that's all." Her voice was gentle, and she absently laid a comforting hand on his sleeve. "I'm sorry."

His jaw twitched, and his eyes veiled. "Perhaps when we reach the cabin—"

"Yes, of course," she agreed quickly.

Nodding, he slowed the truck as the turnoff appeared, and Catherine looked away. Jonathan's obvious disappointment affected her deeply. In spite of her own apprehension, Catherine had convinced herself that regaining her memory was necessary for her own peace of mind. Now, she wondered if that decision had been made as much to please Jonathan as for her own benefit.

Catherine pushed the thought away. This was something she needed to do for herself. She couldn't live with a hole in her life and no matter what the cost, that lost winter was a mystery she simply had to solve.

After a few moments, Jonathan steered between two huge pine trees and drove over what Catherine assumed to be the logging road he had told her about. The word "road" was a misnomer. All Catherine saw were two deep ruts winding into a thick forest. Nothing was recognizable, and she had absolutely no idea where they were. Still, she was aware of Jonathan's covert glances in her direction and not wanting to raise his hopes again, she maintained an impassive expression.

Then they turned into a clearing and there it was—the cabin. The small rectangular structure was shingled with cedar clapboards and fronted by a tiny covered porch.

Catherine, emitting a soft gasp of fascination and surprise, recognized it instantly. It was exactly as it had always been—the bulky stone chimney, the oblong propane tank beside the north wall—and she suddenly remembered every detail of the building with crystal clarity.

The moment the truck stopped moving, Catherine jumped out. She felt like laughing and didn't know why. Hands clasped beneath her chin, she walked slowly, comparing every nuance of what she saw with the fresh flood of memories.

Jonathan's voice broke into her thoughts. He sounded apprehensive and cautious. "Is . . . anything familiar?"

"Yes," she whispered. "It's almost exactly the same."

"Almost." He gave the word an unexpected harshness.

"There's no snow, not even patches," Catherine said, more to herself than to him. "The propane tank is new. The old one was all rusty— Oh look! The hummingbird feeder is still there! I remember how upset I was to find out that the hummingbirds wouldn't be back until spring and then I absolutely insisted that we hang it anyway, just in case they came early." Excited, she whirled to face him. "Do you remember?"

His sad expression shocked her to the core. "Yes, I remember."

"What's wrong?"

"Nothing," he mumbled. "I'll get the suitcases." With that, he spun and walked away toward the truck.

Confused by his sudden mood swing, Catherine watched him hoist the luggage from the bed of the pickup and wondered what had upset him. She looked back up at the bird feeder, a clear plastic cylinder that narrowed into a straw-like tube. But the one she remembered had a red stripe; this one didn't. It was similar, but not the same one that they'd hung together so many years ago.

Jonathan brushed past her carrying the suitcases, then started up the porch steps.

"This is a different bird feeder, isn't it?"

He paused. "Yes. The other one got broken."

"Oh." She felt strangely disappointed. "But you replaced it—why?"

"Because you like hummingbirds," he said simply, then unlocked the wooden door and disappeared inside.

Catherine hesitated, looked up at the bird feeder once more, then tentatively followed. At the doorway, she stopped, took a deep breath, then stepped inside.

Her gaze swept the single room. To her left was the bathroom and a tiny kitchen with a wooden table and two chairs. There was a dusty oil lamp on the table, and Catherine suddenly envisioned the soft golden glow that had been their only source of light after sundown. There was no electricity in the cabin. And there was no telephone. She was truly stranded here. Alone. With him.

Swallowing her attack of nerves, Catherine continued to scan the cabin's sparse interior. The rear door was directly across from where she stood. To her right was a worn sofa and in front of the massive fireplace, the braided rug she'd remembered. In the farthest corner of the room, a curtain separating the sleeping area from the main living quarters had been pulled back to expose a tiny dresser, a battered armoire and a double bed.

One bed.

Jonathan cleared his throat, and she jumped. "I, uh, put your suitcase on the bed. You can unpack whenever you like."

On *the* bed.

A slow heat crept up her cheeks. "Thank you."

He recognized her discomfort. Smiling, he knelt, reached under the bed and dragged something out. He stood, carried the object to the other side of the curtain, then quickly unfolded it. When he stepped back, Catherine laughed. It was a tiny cot.

Jonathan's eyes gleamed. "I'll flip you for it."

"No way."

"What if I was allergic to canvas?"

"Then you'd just have to itch. The mattress is mine."

He shrugged. "It was worth a try."

More relaxed, Catherine walked around the small room. She could feel Jonathan's anxious gaze following her. "At least there's no piano," she murmured. "I don't have to feel guilty about not practicing."

"You never did like practicing. Why did you make a career of something that you hated?"

She shrugged. "I like playing the piano. I guess it was just *having* to play that I hated back then."

Jonathan was silent for a moment, then said, "Whether you hate it or not, you're very good. Your final performance last night was extraordinary."

"You were there?"

"I was always there, Catherine, at every performance."

"Oh." She should have been surprised, but wasn't. Deep down, she must have felt his presence. But she wanted to change the subject to something safer, something impersonal. "I noticed that you had a key. Does that mean you got the owner's permission to use the cabin?"

"In a manner of speaking. I'm the owner."

That surprised her. "I thought you had 'borrowed' it."

"That was during my days of poverty. When I earned enough money, I bought it." As he glanced around, his mouth tightened. "The previous owner was damned glad to be rid of it."

"Why?"

His laugh was dry and humorless. "Let's just say it needed some major repairs."

Catherine frowned. The place had needed a little paint, sure, but she didn't remember it being all that run down. But her recollections were still pretty fuzzy. "If it was in such bad shape, why didn't you buy something else? There are so many beautiful vacation homes in the area, and I'm sure you could afford any one of them."

"I guess I'm just a sentimental kind of guy." He stared at her, and Catherine shivered. His eyes were so powerful that she felt paralyzed and trapped. There was a tingling sensation in the pit of her stomach, and she couldn't look away, couldn't move. She felt like a fly on a corkboard, helplessly pinned in place by the potency of his gaze.

Suddenly he took a ragged breath, muttered, "I'll get some firewood," then strode quickly out the back door.

It took a few seconds for Catherine to catch her breath, then she turned shakily and moved her suitcase to a chair beside the bed. She toyed with the idea of unpacking but decided that the casual clothes she'd brought didn't require the luxury of hangers. Besides, she wanted to be ready for a quick getaway.

She sat on the edge of the bed and scanned the room again, trying to remember. Her mind was blank. Closing her eyes, she rubbed her forehead fiercely, as though the pressure would force the memories. That didn't help either. Finally, she sighed and tried to simply relax.

As her muscles unknotted, peaceful sensations flooded her and she was aware of various scents surrounding her—crisp pine and aromatic cedar, the lingering spiciness of Jonathan himself. She smiled and absently caressed one of the soft pillows.

An image flashed through her thoughts, startling her. With a gasp, she stood and stared down at the bed.

She remembered.

In her mind she saw the mussed covers, heard rapid breathing and soft, passionate moans. Going back in time, Catherine recalled everything so vividly that she was reliving the experience. She felt Jonathan's warmth covering her and could actually taste his kisses. His muscled arms had been knotted by the strength needed to survive in a wilderness, yet his hands had been gentle, caressing her with infinite delicacy.

As Catherine thought back to those early days, she recalled how sweetly he had loved her. She remembered his firm weight pressing her into the soft mattress. He had been inside her, thrilling her with his passion and strength. She could remember his voice, thick with desire.

"My sweet little Cat," he had murmured. "God, I can never get enough of you."

Cathy had sighed with pleasure as the poignant spasms subsided. "Do you love me, Jonny?" she'd asked quietly.

"You know I do, honey." His mouth had brushed her ear and goosebumps had covered her arms.

"Say it, please," Cathy had begged. "I'll never get tired of hearing it."

Then Jonny had rolled over and chuckled softly. "And I'll never get tired of making love to you."

"Promise?"

"Cross my heart."

"Even when I'm old and wrinkly and my hair turns white?"

"Hmm." He pretended to consider the question. "Just *how* wrinkly? Ouch! Don't hit— Hey! No tickling—"

Cathy dived on top of him, running her fingers over his ribs as he fought to capture her wriggling hands. "Say it," she commanded, barely able to control her own mirth. "Say it or you'll die laughing."

"I give up," he shouted, nearly choking.

"Then say it!"

With a deft twist, Cathy was suddenly underneath him, her wrists neatly pinned by one of his strong hands. His voice was husky. "I love you, Cathy Greer. I love you now and I'll love you until I take my final breath on this earth."

Jonny's free hand caressed her body with slow, sensuous strokes. She closed her eyes, moaning softly as his touch became more and more intimate. Her head rocked feverishly against the damp pillow. She shuddered once, then whispered, "Again, Jonny. Please. Make love to me again."

And he had.

This wasn't going to work.

Jonathan stared at the stack of neatly split logs and realized that this entire idea had been a massive mistake. Even if Catherine were to remember everything, what good would it do either of them? The past was gone. It couldn't be erased but it couldn't be relived, either. What had he been thinking, bringing her up here?

Yes, he had questions, important questions that had tormented him for over a decade. But the answers might torment him for the rest of his life.

And destroy Catherine in the bargain.

Catherine couldn't remember because her mind was unable to handle the pain; it was that simple. If Jonathan forced those memories, would she be confronted with a truth too horrible for her to accept?

He didn't know. God, he didn't know anything and yet he was pushing forward as though his world and hers wouldn't be ripped apart by what they both might discover.

In spite of his reservations, Jonathan knew he'd never have a day's peace until he understood everything that had happened eleven years ago. He was torn by the conflict—destroy Catherine or destroy himself.

Angrily, Jonathan scooped up several logs and walked up the steps to the back door. Perhaps it wouldn't come to that. Perhaps he was just being melodramatic. After all, he honestly didn't know what had occurred on that final desperate day.

At the time Jonathan had been too busy answering other people's questions to pose any of his own. When he'd finally been freed, it had been too late. Catherine had disappeared and taken with her all that he'd held so dear—his love, his life, his future.

The icy wind increased, snapping him out of his mental sojourn. He looked at the dark clouds boiling overhead and realized that the temperature had dropped quickly. A storm was brewing. He may have had grave concerns about the wisdom of this trip but there would be no retreat until the weather cleared.

Balancing the logs on one arm, Jonathan pushed open the back door, quietly walked inside, then froze in his tracks.

Catherine stood beside the bed, eyes closed, head thrown back, cradling her own body with her arms. For that instant, she was the girl of yesterday, the child-woman who had loved him with all the passion of her young soul.

Smiling to herself, she moistened her lips with her tongue and her head moved slowly from side to side. Jonathan recognized her expression. He knew that she was remembering—no, reliving their lovemaking. An intense longing overwhelmed him, a sharp stab of desire that tightened his loins and made his arms ache to hold her.

Then Catherine's eyes flew open and she stared right at him. She flushed to the roots of her hair, then spun away and began to search through her open suitcase. Her voice was muffled with embarrassment. "I, uh— It's getting cold." She pulled out a sweatshirt and with her back still to him, shrugged into the garment.

Jonathan tested his voice. "A fire will help."

She hesitated, then peeked over her shoulder. "That would be wonderful."

He nodded, then somehow managed to move across the room. Kneeling, he rolled the logs onto the stony hearth, then stacked a few on the fireplace grate. Sweat beaded his forehead as the image of Catherine in the throes of remembered passion rolled through his mind. He'd have to tie himself to the cot tonight or he'd pounce on her in his sleep.

A crinkling sound captured his attention. Looking over, he saw Catherine searching the lower cupboard where the newspapers had always been kept. Fascinated, Jonathan watched as she wadded each sheet, then tossed it over so he could position the starter fuel beneath the log stack.

It was a chilling déjà vu. As Jonthan stuffed each paper ball under the fire grate, he remembered the day he'd climbed onto the roof to install a double screen on the chimney to protect against burning embers. Catherine had stood below, her small fists pressed against her mouth in fear. She hadn't relaxed until he'd climbed down again. Then she'd hugged him so tightly he thought she'd never let go again.

And here they both were, as though the intervening years had never happened. Catherine was tossing paper balls, and Jonathan was starting the fire. He wondered if she realized what she was doing.

After a few moments, Catherine's eyes widened. She stared at the crumpled wad in her hand, then looked questioningly at Jonathan.

He managed a stiff smile. "You haven't lost your throwing arm. Do you remember where the matches are?"

She chewed her lower lip for a moment, then said, "I think so." Standing, she walked into the kitchen, opened a drawer and took out a box of matches. She stared at them for a moment, then grinned. "Head's up," she called, then threw a fastball pitch over the counter and directly into Jonathan's waiting hands.

She looked so pleased with herself that he just had to laugh. He ignited the newspaper, then followed the script from their past, tossing the box up and batting it with his hand. Catherine was waiting for it and squealed as she jumped to grab the matchbox sailing through the air. "Aha! Good hit, Stone, but you can't beat a golden-glove shortstop. You're out!"

Face glowing, Catherine dropped the box back into the drawer and snatched a rusted coffeepot from the stove. After filling it with water, she opened a top cupboard, stood on her tiptoes and pulled down the dented metal canister of coffee.

As she went about her task, Jonathan could only stare, painfully aware that at this very moment Catherine was as comfortable in the tiny kitchen as she had been so many years ago. His chest tightened.

Catherine reached for the knob to turn on the stove, then suddenly stopped. She straightened, took a step backward and stared at the appliance.

"Is something wrong?" he asked.

"No—I mean, I don't think so." She turned toward him. "It's just that the cupboards seem different and this isn't the same stove is it?"

"Why do you ask?"

"The other one... well, wasn't there a big chip on the top? And the oven door didn't quite close, but this one is nice and tight." She looked up anxiously. "Am I remembering that right?"

"Yes, you are. It's not the same stove."

She glanced pensively around the small kitchen. "The bird feeder, the cupboards, the stove—a lot has changed, hasn't it?"

"Yes."

Jonathan watched warily as she frowned, then rubbed her forehead. Suddenly, he didn't want her to remember what had caused all those changes. The memory would hurt Catherine deeply, and his turmoil increased tenfold. He wanted to stop her, yet knew that the pendulum was now in motion and would continue in a steady rhythm until the arc was completed. All he could do was to help her through it, easing her pain as much as he could. He held his breath.

Catherine regarded the stove thoughtfully. Finally, she shook her head, shrugged and turned on the burner. Jonathan exhaled slowly, gratefully. Whether she was ready to handle the memories or not, he realized that *he* wasn't. Not yet.

"Jon?"

He looked up, surprised by her use of his informal name. Since he'd introduced himself to her at the theater, Catherine had always called him Jonathan. Everyone did, except Howard Dylan.

"Yes?" He swallowed hard and watched her carefully.

She was smiling, looking at the rusty old pot. "Do you remember the first time I made coffee for you?"

"I don't know..." His voice trailed off as his mind recaptured the past. Oh, God. Yes, he remembered, and the image made him shudder. It had been their first morning together. Cat had jumped out of bed and slipped on one of his plaid flannel shirts to cover her nakedness.

He could still see her long legs dashing across the cold floor, could still hear her squeal as the icy air buffeted her body. Jonathan smiled. "Yes, Cat. I remember."

"I almost killed you."

"I'll say," he muttered wistfully, still thinking about her half-naked dash across the room. Startled, he looked up and saw mischief in her eyes. "Uh, you meant breakfast?"

"What else?"

"Never mind." He cleared his throat. "What about it?"

"You were very gallant," she told him. "You actually tried to eat the eggs I fixed, even though they were harder than Frisbees."

Jonathan chuckled. "I remember. Even Mackie wouldn't eat them, but the eggs were gourmet compared to your first pot of coffee. Didn't we finally use it to strip paint or something?"

"Very funny. You told me to use three scoops of coffee and then put eggshells in the pot. That's exactly what I did."

"I didn't think you'd use a measuring cup instead of a tablespoon," he pointed out. "And I certainly didn't tell you to crush the damned shells up so that the coffee had to be chewed."

"Then you should have been more specific," she replied primly. "I take instructions quite literally."

His smile was slow and sexy. "I always liked that about you."

She blushed furiously and turned away, busying herself by pulling out utensils. "Are you hungry?"

"Yes, but I hesitate to admit that."

"I think you'll find my culinary skills have improved."

"That's a relief." He stood, walked to the kitchen and opened the refrigerator. "My secretary had the place stocked for us, but I'm not sure what she ordered— Oh, this looks great."

Catherine peered over his shoulder. "Ham and bacon, fresh fruits and vegetables and, your personal favorite, eggs. Want an omelet?"

"Omelet's are my specialty. I'll cook."

"Ye of little faith."

"I'm trying to be a gracious host."

"You're trying to save your stomach."

"That, too."

Her eyes gleamed. "Tough. You tend the fire, I cook the grub. Those were the rules, remember?"

Jonathan winced. "Rules can be changed."

"Out." She put both hands on his back and pushed him from the kitchen.

Tossing his hands in the air, Jonathan acquiesced and went quietly. He crouched in front of the fire, alternately poking at the burning logs and covertly glancing at Catherine. As she puttered in the small kitchen, she hummed softly. Her face was serene, her expression one of pure contentment.

Whether she was aware of it or not, Jonathan knew that she was reexperiencing their time together, remembering their love. Perhaps she was even experiencing those feelings all over again.

The realization should have pleased him. Isn't that what he had wanted? After all the lonely years he'd lived with the memories, both sweet and bitter, he had wanted Catherine to feel the same things. Deep down, perhaps he'd even wanted her to fall in love with him again.

But something else was happening, something Jonathan had never considered. He, too, was reliving that time and his own burgeoning emotions scared the hell out of him.

Catherine was his weakness, and weak men were destined for failure. He couldn't let that happen—not now, not when he was so close. No matter how sweet the memories, this woman had betrayed him.

Jonathan would never forget that.

Later that evening, Catherine sat in front of the fire and watched flames lick the blackened stone. She pulled the worn afghan around her, tucking the ends over her chilled legs.

In the kitchen, Jonathan was finishing the dishes, and she was comforted by the familiar domestic sounds. For the first time in more years than she could remember, Catherine felt at home. Why had she given this up? It didn't make sense.

The cabin had been the one place on earth where she could be herself and Jonathan had been the one person who'd accepted her as she was. He had loved Catherine when not much about her had been lovable. During her teen years, she remembered being selfish and immature, rebelling against her uncle's authority with adolescent zeal. She had been pouty and sullen one minute, silly and excitable the next; yet Jonathan Stone had loved her.

And she had left him?

No. She couldn't have. The memories were still patchy, but she'd recalled enough to realize that she never would have willingly walked away.

Jonathan's voice startled her. "Are you warm enough?"

"Umm? Oh yes, thank you."

"Are you sure? I could put another log on the fire—"

"No, really. I'm fine."

"Good." He stood awkwardly, jamming his hands in his pockets and rocking back on his heels, as though trying to decide whether he should sit beside her or allow her some space.

She patted the cushion. "Please sit down. The fire feels wonderful."

He hesitated, then warily complied, seating himself on the far side of the couch.

A strained silence fell between them. Finally, Catherine said, "Thank you for cleaning up the kitchen."

"Those were the rules. You cook, I clean." The fire's glow illuminated his smile. "Somehow, I always thought that was a bit backward."

"It probably was but I was determined to be a proper little wi—I mean, I was determined to learn how to cook."

She looked quickly away but not before she saw that Jonathan had noted her slip of the tongue. Thankfully, he didn't comment on it.

Wife? Why had she nearly said that?

Then she remembered one cold winter night. Jonathan had knelt nervously, his face shining with perspiration. Then he'd taken Cathy's hand and slipped on a tiny ring made of woven grass.

"Someday, I'll buy you diamonds," Jonny had told her. "But I love you, Cat, so much that I can't even imagine my life if you weren't a part of it. Say that you'll marry me, that you'll be my wife."

She remembered how she'd kissed him and hugged him and promised that she would never marry anyone but him.

And she never had.

Was this why she'd never married? she wondered. There had been opportunities, fine men who'd wanted her, but Catherine had always discouraged them. She'd never been interested and she'd never spent much time considering why.

"Catherine? Are you all right?"

She blinked and saw Jonathan's concerned expression. "Yes," she said, reassuring him. "I was just remembering... things."

"Good things?"

"Of course." Something in his tone caught her attention. "Why do you ask? Were there bad things, too?"

He looked away. "There were good times and bad times, like everything else in life."

She considered this. "I've remembered quite a bit about our time together, but I really don't know anything about you. Why were you living here? Didn't you have any family?" His mouth tightened, and Catherine stared down at her lap. "I'm sorry. It's none of my business."

Finally he spoke tiredly. "I dragged you up here this morning, so I guess that makes it your business."

"If you don't want to talk about it—"

"It's all right." He took a deep breath. "My father died when I was young, and my mother worked two jobs to feed me. We lived in a pretty rough part of town, so survival meant learning how to think on your feet."

"And how to fight?" Catherine asked, remembering his altercation with Maurice.

Jonathan smiled sadly. "Yes, I learned how to fight and how to conceal weakness so enemies couldn't use it against me. As I look back, it was pretty good training for the business world."

Catherine remembered the newspapers and books that had always covered the kitchen table. "The stock market," she mumbled suddenly. "You used to play the stock market, not for money but for fun. I remember being so impressed that you could actually understand all those odd abbreviations and fractional numbers." She laughed. "You made a hundred thousand dollars from a thousand-dollar investment in two months."

"Only on paper," he reminded her. "I didn't even have a thousand pennies at the time."

"But you were so clever. I don't understand why you weren't in the city climbing the ladder of some big brokerage firm."

"Because I dropped out of college when my mother died."

She sobered. "I forgot. I'm sorry."

"It was a long time ago. My mother and I didn't spend much time together during her last years."

"Why?"

He stared into the fire. "I worked nights and went to school during the day, planning to make a bundle of money someday so I could buy her a nice house and give her the kind of life she deserved. For a couple of years, we hardly saw each other, then suddenly she was gone."

"But that wasn't your fault."

"Maybe not, but I should have spent more time with her."

"You wanted to make her life easier. That wasn't a crime."

"No matter how noble the motive, the fact is that I abandoned her and left her to die alone." Standing quickly, Jonathan crossed his arms tightly, avoiding Catherine's empathetic eyes. "Suddenly, there wasn't any reason to work toward being rich. I packed a bag, jumped in my truck and ended up here trying to sort out my life."

Catherine felt the sting of tears. "That must have been a terrible time for you."

His voice was taut. "I've had worse."

"But you pulled yourself up and went on. You've made a success of your life."

"Have I?"

"Of course you have. You own a respected brokerage firm and you obviously have enough money to live comfortably."

"Is that your definition of success—money and respectability?" He picked up the poker and jammed it into the fire, lifting the logs so they would burn cleaner. "Money can't buy happiness, or so they say."

Catherine again noted the strange sadness in his eyes. "Aren't you happy?" He avoided her gaze, and she persisted. "You chose your own path. It took years of hard work to build what you've achieved. If it wasn't what you wanted, why did you do it?"

"Perhaps I had the proper motivation," he replied dully. "I needed the money."

"Why? I mean, you just said that after your mother died there was no reason to work toward being rich—"

"Motivations change," he growled.

"Still—"

Cutting off her words, he looked straight at her. "So how about you?"

"Pardon me?"

"I've told you my story. Now it's your turn."

Catherine saw pain etched in every line of his taut face. Instinctively, she knew that Jonathan's terse manner was simply his way of dealing with a hurt too deep to acknowledge.

Jonathan's expression remained rigid but his eyes held a silent plea. "Do you remember anything more?"

She looked into the fire. "Yes."

Catherine was reluctant to admit just how much more she *did* remember. Still, she felt a deepening kinship with Jonathan and a secret understanding of his anxiety. Despite the missing pieces of her past, one memory had become all too clear.

"What?" he asked urgently. "What else have you remembered?"

"I remember us." She hesitated, then met his direct gaze. "And I remember how much I loved you."

Chapter Six

"Did you hear what I said?" Catherine asked softly, bewildered by Jonathan's unchanging expression. "I remember how much I loved you."

His jaw twitched, and his shoulders vibrated as he clenched his fists. "Yes, but have you remembered anything *important?*"

He might as well have slapped her.

Catherine gasped, touching her throat as though his words had cut off her very breath. She stared in disbelief. Before her very eyes, a man of compassion had suddenly turned to granite. "That . . . was cruel."

Jonathan's eyes hardened. "I'm a cruel man, Catherine. Ask anyone."

"No," she whispered. "No you're not. I saw you with the children and I remember your kindness, your gentleness—"

"Your memories are flawed," he snapped. "That's why we're here." His mouth softened but only for a moment, then he jammed his hands in his pockets and spoke tersely. "I'm not looking to rekindle an old flame. If it pleases you to weave a fantasy out of a meaningless childhood fling, fine, but I won't be an accomplice to your delusions."

Catherine went rigid. She had admitted loving him and was deeply hurt by his coldness. "I see."

"You don't see anything, not one damned thing." Jonathan took a deep breath and turned away, but not before his face contorted with anger and pain. "Your memories are clouded by romantic delusions. You see the past through the eyes of a girl."

"Are you saying that what I remember didn't really happen?"

His shoulders slumped, then he faced her with an impassive expression. "It happened but there was more, much more."

Catherine met his gaze and shivered. "How did it end between us?"

He didn't respond.

She sat stiffly, staring into thin air. "Once I repaid my debt by sleeping with you, did you get tired of me?"

Jonathan's eyes narrowed. "What?"

Catherine stood, anger and humiliation surging inside her. She was certain that he must have rejected her then, just as he now rejected her tender memories. "Come on, Jonathan. I was a starry-eyed kid, but now I'm all grown up. I know the score. It was probably a real ego trip for you, being the first and all, but after the initial thrill of conquest you must have found me a bit unimaginative."

"That's not true."

"No? Did I learn fast, Jonathan? Did you teach me how to do all the delicious little things that made you crazy?"

"My God, Cat—"

"Well I've got a news flash. You weren't all that wonderful." The words rushed out through ragged gasps, and Catherine angrily shoved her hair from her face. "After all, whatever we had together wasn't even worth remembering, was it?"

He stared in stony silence, only the rapid spasms of his jaw betraying his inner turmoil.

"So how did it end?" Her fists clenched, and she fought for control. "Did you find some nubile ski bunny to replace me or did I just show up one day and find you gone?"

"Don't do this," he said quietly. He stood close enough to touch her yet kept his hands rigidly at his side. "You're just hurting yourself."

The pity in Jonathan's eyes drove Catherine over the edge. The emotion, the intensity of the past days simply exploded.

"Tell me!" Catherine screamed, pounding his chest as tears spilled down her face. "Tell me everything I did, every dirty little thing, then tell me how you laughed in my face and sent me away."

She was vaguely aware that Jonathan winced under the assault of her small fists but didn't try to stop her. The ineffectual blows diminished. She sobbed and clung to him, sinking into his comforting embrace.

His lips brushed her face. "I never laughed at you, honey. I never sent you away."

Catherine couldn't stop shaking. "I—I'm sor—" She hiccupped and tried to pull air into her convulsing lungs.

"It's all right. Go ahead and cry." Jonathan brushed a damp strand of hair from her cheek, then murmured soft words until her violent sobs subsided. Scooping Catherine into his arms, he carried her across the room and laid her gently on the bed.

Catherine closed her eyes, turning her face away as she clutched the pillow. She was shocked and mortified by her behavior and wondered if she had gone completely mad. Never in her entire life had she said such vile things, never had she wanted to hurt anyone the way she had wanted to hurt Jonathan.

But never had Catherine *been* so deeply hurt. When he had coolly dismissed the love she'd remembered as unimportant, she'd been devastated.

"Get some sleep," Jonathan whispered, brushing his palm across her forehead.

She heard the curtain swish and in a moment, the cabin fell dark as Jonathan turned off the oil lamp. The wood-paneled walls flickered, illuminated by the still-warm fireplace. Time passed, uncounted silent minutes. Catherine stared at the ceiling through eyes that would not close.

The glow dimmed, the flames died. From the darkness, she heard quiet footsteps, then the cot squeaked. She heard breathing, his and hers.

Then he spoke, so softly she barely heard. "I loved you, too, Cat. You were my life."

The morning air was cold enough to freeze meat. Jonathan pulled the blanket back and took a deep breath. His lungs revolted at the icy intrusion. Swearing softly, he burrowed back under the covers. He didn't want to move; he didn't want to think. The last time he'd looked at his watch, it had been four in the morning. Three hours sleep wasn't enough, but it was all he was going to get.

He had to stoke a fire and warm the cabin before Catherine woke up. Moaning, he dangled one foot over the edge of the cot, feeling for the floor. Finally, Jonathan heaved upward into a sitting position and numbly fumbled into his boots. Shrugging into his down jacket, he moved silently across the room and somehow managed to get a small blaze ignited.

With a sigh, he collapsed on the hearth and held his hands over the tiny flame. As a young man, Jonathan had thought this primitive existence an exhilarating challenge. Now, he just thought it was stupid. After all, a man with a six-figure income could certainly afford a few luxuries and at the moment, a propane heater was at the top of his list.

He made a mental note to have his secretary take care of that, then slid a glance toward the bedroom curtain. Catherine must be sleeping soundly not to have been awakened by his clumsiness. Even when the log had rolled off the hearth with a resounding thud, he hadn't heard a peep out of her.

At least she was getting some much-needed rest. This entire weekend had been an emotional roller coaster for them both, and he had spent half the night wondering what kind of man he really was. He couldn't seduce Catherine while she was confused and vulnerable, yet he wanted her so badly that his teeth ached.

And she wouldn't have refused him. Jonathan had seen the light in her eyes as she'd remembered what they'd shared so long ago. After all the years, all the betrayals, he had underestimated the effect she would still have on him. When she'd looked at him with an expression of love and utter trust, he'd nearly come apart. Then to fight his own weakness, he'd brutally lashed out.

At the moment Jonathan didn't like himself much. He and Catherine were playing a game. This time, he wouldn't be the loser. He didn't want to hurt Catherine, but knew that when she'd found her answers, she'd simply disappear from his life again. When that happened, his only protection would be to steel against the sweet emotional assault. Jonathan would never allow himself to be hurt like that again.

Stiffly, he stood and was aware of a bubbling noise in the kitchen. Investigating, he found the coffeepot filled and hot, steeping on a low flame. He frowned, looking toward the closed curtain. "Catherine?"

There was no reply. Fear twisted his stomach like an icy hand, and he strode across the room, ripping the curtain aside.

The bed was neatly made and quite empty. Swallowing the sour taste of panic, he ran to the front door and threw it open. The landscape was blanketed with fresh snow. Jonathan saw no footprints, and the truck, frosted white, was still parked in the clearing. "*Catherine!*"

Had she sneaked out last night before the storm? Was she on foot somewhere between the cabin and the village?

He panicked. What had he done? She could never have survived the night in subfreezing temperatures. Oh, God.

Whirling, he ran straight through the cabin, then burst out the back door. "Catherine!" he shouted into the silent, white woods. "*Cath—*"

The snowball hit him mid-chest.

Jonathan's arms flew out like flapping wings, then froze as he stared dumbly down at the wet snow clump clinging to his jacket. Blinking, he looked over the porch rail and saw Catherine, grinning brightly. Her mittened hands were busily forming another white ball.

"Arm yourself, Stone!" she hollered. "I take no prisoners."

Before he could react, she went into a major league windup and another snowball splattered against his shoulder. His astonished expression must have been comical because Catherine grabbed her stomach and hooted with glee.

Laughing, she fell back into the soft snow and wiped her pink cheeks. "Honestly, Jon, the look on your face is positively priceless."

"I'm glad you're amused," he muttered, brushing snowball remnants from his chest. "What in the hell are you doing out here?"

"I really don't know. I just had the overwhelming urge to be silly." She tilted her head. "It snowed last night."

"I've noticed," he said tartly. "I thought you didn't like the snow."

"I love snow. It's the cold I'm not fond of."

He shook his head and walked down the steps. "Call me crazy but I always thought of snow as being relatively cold."

"Not when one is wearing two pairs of socks, three shirts, a sweater and a jacket."

He hitched a brow. "Thank goodness. I thought you'd gained twenty pounds in your sleep."

"Cute." One hand snaked out and scooped up a pile of fresh snow.

Jonathan saw the movement. "Two free throws is all you get, Cat. You'd better think carefully about your next move."

"Is that a threat?"

"I never threaten, remember?" he replied drily. "Now come into the cabin and dry off before you turn into a green-eyed Popsicle."

She emitted a sound of disgust. "When did you become such an old fogy?"

"And when did you regress to infancy?"

"I'm immune to your insults, sir." She patted the pile of snow in her lap, squeezing it into a round shape. "If you can't keep up, go put on your little slippers and sit by the fire."

Folding his arms, he rolled his eyes and wondered just when he'd lost control of this ridiculous situation. But this was an image of the playful girl he remembered. Then, her eyes had flashed fire one moment and twinkled with mischief the next. He'd always loved that unpredictability. Now he discovered that he still did.

"Do you have a hat?" she asked suddenly.

"A what?"

"A hat. You know, that piece of cloth that covers one's head." She jerked her thumb, gesturing behind her. "It's for my snowman."

Jonathan stared at the lumpy column of snow and barely suppressed a snort of laughter.

Catherine looked at the ugly mound with affection. "I know he still needs some work, but I'm not sure exactly what's missing."

"A shape?"

Catherine smiled sweetly. "Why, yes! How clever of you to have noticed."

Her arm shot out. This time, Jonathan was ready. He ducked and the wad of snow flew harmlessly over his head. Catherine's eyes widened and she scrambled to her feet.

He grinned maliciously. "Well, we do want to play, don't we?"

Catherine edged toward the steps.

Jonathan blocked her way.

Catherine backed up, her eyes searching for escape.

Jonathan crouched, advancing.

Catherine spun and ran.

Jonathan leaped forward with a flying tackle.

In a tangle of arms and legs, they plowed a wild furrow in the fresh snow. Squealing and laughing, Catherine struggled against Jonathan's superior strength. For a brief moment, he carelessly loosened his grip and before he could recover, Catherine shoved a handful of snow down his neck.

He bellowed like a wounded stag, then snagged her ankle as she tried to escape.

"Release me, you cad," she hollered, then her laughter turned into a soft whoosh as he pinned her on her back.

"Not until I've wreaked a proper vengeance." Straddling her, Jonathan smirked and made a production of scooping snow. He balanced the pile in one palm, then smiled politely. "Do you have a preference, or should I just surprise you?"

She covered her eyes with her hands. "Go ahead. Do your worst."

"I plan to," he replied silkily, unzipping her jacket.

The mittens slid apart, revealing one startled eye. "You wouldn't—Ahh! Stop!" Rolling and kicking, Catherine screamed as another pile of icy snow was dumped under her thick clothes. When Jonathan stood, she jumped up instantly and yanked her shirts loose, shaking out the remaining snow. "Oh Lord, that's cold."

Bending at the waist, Jonathan shook the snow off his head. "You still play dirty."

"I thought just this once, you'd be gracious enough to let me win."

"I would have, if you'd stopped in time. You always did have to press your luck."

"Nothing worth having comes without risk." She tucked her shirttail into her jeans and shivered. "You taught me that."

He raked his hair. "Caught up by my own philosophy."

Suddenly, Catherine sat down in the snow. "Are you going to help me finish my snowman?"

"Later. I need coffee." He sat beside her. "You should warm up first. I don't want you to get sick."

"Umm." She took a deep breath and looked contentedly out at the woods. "It's so beautiful. I remember that Mackie just loved fresh snow. He'd run and run until his little paw prints covered every inch of the clearing. I use to throw snowballs for him, and he'd try to catch them, only to come up with a mouthful of wet ice. He'd be so disgusted, poor thing."

Jonathan smiled sadly, remembering. Cat had been crazy about that dog. The two of them had been inseparable, romping and barking and laughing. Catherine had teased that if they ever broke up, she wanted custody of the dog.

But it hadn't turned out that way.

"Jon?"

"Umm?" He turned and saw Catherine's apprehensive expression.

She licked her lips. "I wish Mackie was here. He would have loved being back in the snow."

Jonathan looked away. "He's gone, Cat."

"Oh." Her voice broke slightly. "Did he . . . run away?"

He shook his head, then took a deep breath and met her gaze. Her eyes were wide and somber, glistening with unshed tears. "No. Mac died a long time ago."

Catherine swallowed hard, then nodded jerkily. She tried to smile but it didn't come off. "I—I guess he would have been pretty old in dog years by now." Her laugh was tight and humorless. "I haven't thought of Mackie in a long time, but suddenly I miss him so much. It's strange, isn't it?"

An annoying lump wedged in Jonathan's throat. Abruptly he stood, then reached down and helped Catherine up. "Can you still make cornmeal pancakes?"

She wiped her damp face. "I don't know but they sound horrible."

"They are," Jon replied, steering her up the back steps. "They taste like soggy sandpaper."

"Yuk." Catherine grimaced and looked at Jon as though he'd lost his mind. "Then why on earth do you want them?"

"I don't really know," he replied wistfully. "But for some strange reason, I have a craving for cornmeal pancakes."

At the door, Catherine paused and smiled knowingly. She knew damn well what Jonathan was craving. And it had nothing to do with breakfast.

Catherine scooped up the sticky plates and piled them in the sink. She peered over her shoulder. "Well, were they as awful as you remember?"

Jonathan winced. "Absolutely."

"Good. I wouldn't want to disappoint you."

Responding with a low moan, he grimaced and turned away as though trying to conceal his distress. "Do you have any antacid?" he asked casually.

"I don't think so." Turning off the water, she walked over and touched his hair. "You're really sick, aren't you?"

"I'm fine," he lied, clutching his stomach.

Instantly concerned, Catherine knelt beside him. "What's wrong? Do you have ulcers?"

"Not yet," he muttered irritably, then pushed back his chair and tried to stand. "A couple of chalky tablets and I'll be good as new."

"Sit down, I'll get them." Catherine stood and headed toward the bathroom, assuming the antacids would be in the medicine cabinet.

Jonathan stopped her. "They're in the truck," he said apologetically. "In the glove compartment."

Catherine slipped on her jacket and offered her brightest smile. "I'll be right back," she told him cheerfully, then went out the front door.

Pausing on the porch, she gazed out over the clearing. The truck was parked on the far side, about a hundred feet away. Beyond was the forest, thick and green, lightly dusted with fresh snow.

Suddenly, she was exhilarated, unable to contain her excitement at just being here. Running down the steps, she dashed across the clearing reveling in the feel of icy air whipping her hair.

Halfway across the clearing something odd happened. Before her eyes, the fresh snow transformed into crusted patches, iced over by days of thaw and refreezing. As she ran, the soft squishing sound of footsteps in new powder was suddenly replaced by the crunch of packed ice. She stopped, confused.

It was another image, another vivid memory.

But a memory of what? It wasn't what Catherine was seeing that upset her; it was what she suddenly felt. There was fear, a deep terror surging up with such power that she thought she might explode. She stared at the forest and saw the trees appeared to be moving.

Impossible. Rubbing her eyes, Catherine looked again. The forest was quiet again but all was not as it seemed. Something lurked in that pristine beauty, something dangerous—something deadly.

Catherine felt a choking sensation. She couldn't breathe. Although she knew Jonathan was safely inside the cabin, she was inexplicably afraid for him.

In her mind she heard a dog barking, a series of frantic yelps. It was Mackie, warning her. But of what? What was happening? Why did she feel captured, like a prisoner held in the arms of terror?

Because someone was holding her. Cathy couldn't breathe. Jonny was in danger.

With a gasp, Catherine pushed at the empty air as though fending off an invisible attack, then staggered backward.

When she looked up again, the horrible image had disappeared. The snow was fresh and powdery, the forest was still a frosty white. The paralyzing fear subsided. Her heartbeat slowed and her legs no longer trembled. Catherine was safe again.

Stunned, Catherine stood quietly and wondered if the memory would return with another sneak attack. She couldn't trust her own mind and felt helpless in the face of the sudden traumatic memories that were so frighteningly unpredictable.

After a few minutes, she walked cautiously to the truck and completed her task. But the image haunted her not only because it had been so terrifying, but because she had instinctively realized that it held an important clue.

Catherine knew that whatever had happened here eleven years ago had been terrifying and dangerous. And deadly.

"Are you feeling better?" Catherine asked.

Jonathan turned from the window and blinked. "Yes, thanks."

Catherine had been absently scanning a magazine. Laying it on the sofa, she joined Jonathan at the table. "How long have you had these stomach problems."

He shrugged. "A few years. It's nothing serious."

"Not yet, but if you don't slow down, you're liable to find yourself in the hospital."

"It's a hazard of the profession." He leaned back in the chair and regarded her thoughtfully. "You've been awfully quiet for the past hour. Is everything okay?"

Catherine scratched at the marred tabletop. She hadn't told Jonathan about her latest memory because she didn't understand it. And because it had scared her half to death.

Finally, she said simply, "Everything is fine."

The Scorpio eyes narrowed, but he didn't press the issue. "Speaking of hospitals, have you remembered anything about the accident that caused your memory loss?"

She wasn't fooled by his casual demeanor. Jonathan's questions usually had some hidden meaning. He'd been so careful not to reveal anything she hadn't remembered on her own that Catherine had given up asking. Still, it occurred to her that it could be advantageous to employ his technique. Perhaps she could deceive him into offering information.

"Actually I have," she lied brightly. "It happened here, didn't it?"

Jonathan's expression was unreadable. "Did it?"

"Yes. I remember everything."

"Tell me."

She squirmed. "I'm sure you already know."

He steepled his hands. "Do I?"

"Of course. After all, you were here." He wasn't taking the bait, and Catherine was feeling a bit desperate. She tried something vague and plausible, hoping for confirmation. "You took care of me and brought me to the hospital after I... fell and hit my head."

After a moment, Jonathan's mouth tightened. "It's not going to do either of us any good if you're just going to lie to me."

"What makes you think I'm lying?" She tried to look innocent, but finally gave up and shrugged. "All right, I haven't the foggiest notion how I hit my head. I was hoping you'd tell me."

He rubbed his forehead. "Haven't you figured out by now that I don't have all the answers?"

"But I thought—"

His fist hit the table, startling her. "This isn't a game to me, Catherine. This isn't just some enjoyable little romp down memory lane." Cursing under his breath, he stood so quickly that the chair fell over backward. Jonathan paced the length of the cabin, then turned and gestured helplessly. "My impatience isn't going to help. I'm sorry."

"So am I," she whispered. "I won't lie to you again, Jonathan."

He nodded, then picked up the chair and sat down. "Let's start with something easy. Tell me about Europe."

"But that was after—"

"Please, humor me."

"All right. When we first moved to France, we had a small flat in Versailles. Uncle Brad had been hired as conductor of the local philharmonic and later on he was in demand as a guest maestro throughout the country."

"And what did you do?"

"Monsieur Jean-Luc Souliers accepted me, so I moved to Paris and studied with him for a couple of years."

"Who is this Souliers guy?"

"A highly respected music teacher. He never gained much of name as a pianist, but his students have garnered acclaim all over the world. I was very fortunate."

"Were you?"

His question surprised her. "Of course. Why do you sound so skeptical?"

"Because you seem to be parroting something you've been told instead of expressing your feelings."

The observation unnerved Catherine because it was true. She hadn't been enthusiastic about studying with Souliers; in fact, the entire ordeal had been pure torture. Still, results counted, and Catherine had managed to turn that unpleasant experience into a respectable career.

"I admit that I've never been fond of constant practicing. It's too restrictive and repetitive, I guess, but it's also an absolute necessity to reach concert proficiency."

"And that's what you wanted, to be a concert pianist?"

The question was casual enough, but it sparked a long-concealed doubt deep inside her. "No, it wasn't exactly what I wanted, but it was the way things worked out."

Jonathan's voice was deceptively soft. "What did you really want, Catherine?"

She suspected that he already knew. "I just wanted to raise a family. Ever since I was a little girl, all I ever wanted was to have a dozen kids and bake cookies every day."

"Why didn't you?"

Catherine sighed. "I honestly don't know. Once I was in France, things just seemed to happen. I completed my studies, and when Maurice took an interest in me, my career began to take off."

Jonathan's voice hardened. "Good for Maurice."

"What is with this feud between you and my manager? Good grief, you don't even know each other."

Shrugging, Jonathan smiled sheepishly. "Maybe I'm jealous."

That stunned her. "Jealous? Of Maurice?" She laughed in disbelief. The notion was ludicrous. "Even if I was interested in him, which I'm definitely not, Maurice is wildly in love with his wife."

"I didn't know that," he muttered defensively.

"So ignorance gave you the right to crack two of his ribs?"

Jonathan shifted uncomfortably. "He hit me first."

"Maurice has admitted that, but what I don't understand is why. He's the gentlest, sweetest man in the world, and I've never even known him to kill a bug. It doesn't make sense that he'd show up on your doorstep with the sole intent of punching your lights out unless he had a darn good reason."

Clearing his throat, Jonathan studied the floor. "Actually, he just wanted me to leave you alone but I was in a pretty sour mood and said some things that were rather unflattering."

Catherine frowned. "About whom?"

"About you."

"Oh." Catherine didn't ask for specifics. Given what she'd already remembered, she didn't really want to know. "Maurice is very protective of his clients."

"So I discovered."

They sat in silence for a few moments, each lost in thought. Catherine mulled over what she'd just learned. Jonathan had gone to great lengths to convince her that he had no feelings for her, yet he'd fought a much bigger man because he'd been jealous.

Regardless of what he wanted Catherine to believe, Jonathan still cared for her. The realization pleased her immensely.

Suddenly, Jonathan changed the subject. "What's the last thing you remember before you went to France?"

She considered the question. "Being in the hospital, I guess."

"Anything in particular about the hospital?"

She sighed. "Nothing specific. Everything was white and fuzzy. I remember whispered conversations between my uncle and the doctors. I remember having my picture taken and being told that as soon as I was well, we were going to Europe."

"Do you remember what month it was?"

"Not really."

"Think, Catherine. Was it cold or hot outside? Was it Christmas time or the fourth of July?"

"It was raining the day I was released. "I remember, because I slipped getting into the cab. It was winter, I'm sure of it."

"Okay, that's good. You're in the cab. What happened then?"

Catherine looked at Jonathan's intense expression, and a realization hit her. "You're not just trying to jog my memory, are you? You honestly don't know either." Suddenly, she felt giddy. "I thought you must have left me or sent me away, but you didn't, did you?"

He closed his eyes. "No."

She sobered. "Did I leave you, Jonathan? Is that why you are so angry with me?" He said nothing, and his silence frightened her. The fear came back, the same growing terror she'd felt during the last image. "No. I loved you more than anything in the whole world and no matter what, I *know* I couldn't have done that. Please tell me it didn't happen that way."

His anguished expression was her answer, and she emitted a small sound of pain. What horrible thing could have caused her to willingly walk away from the only man she'd ever loved? It must have been unspeakably vile.

Catherine shook her head, trying to throw off the unwanted thought. No wonder Jonathan was so angry with her. For some unknown reason, she had left him and he still didn't know why. The worst part was that Catherine didn't know either.

And she didn't want to know.

Jonathan took a ragged breath, then spoke calmly. "You were in the cab, Catherine. Where did you go?"

She felt numb. "To the airport."

"And on to France?"

"Yes. I remember that I was still very weak and I got ill on the plane. Too many chocolates, I suppose."

"Chocolates?"

"Umm. Uncle Brad bought me a box of valentine chocolates at an airport gift shop." The impact of her words finally sank in. "That's right, it was Valentine's Day and I'd been in the hospital a little over a week so that means—"

Jonathan interrupted, finishing her thought in a voice that was strangely broken. "The accident happened the first week in February."

Like a sleepwalker, Jonathan stood and walked to the window, arms crossed tightly across his chest. Catherine was bewildered by his obvious dismay.

"What's wrong?" she asked. "Now we know when the accident happened—"

"No." He sounded choked, as though the word had stuck in his throat. "You could have lost your memory a year after we met, or two years, or six."

Catherine considered this, still baffled as to why Jonathan was so upset by such seemingly innocuous information. "But it wasn't."

He whirled around, impaling her with the force of his gaze. "How do you know?" he demanded. "Everything before the accident is all jumbled up in your mind. You can't know how much time passed between the winter we spent together and the winter you went to France." Then he made a tormented sound and turned back toward the window.

Catherine went to him and gently touched his sleeve. "It was the same year, Jonathan. The date is stamped in my passport."

He shuddered and before he turned away, Catherine saw his eyes fill with tears. She had no idea what had caused his emotional reaction but his pain nearly broke her heart.

Chapter Seven

Jonathan stared through the frosted window and wondered how everything could be so white and pure when he felt so black and empty. Catherine's hand was on his arm, and he heard her whisper his name. He shook off her comforting touch and turned away, squeezing the bridge of his nose as though to exorcise demons.

He couldn't panic. He couldn't give up, not now, not when he was so close.

Closing his eyes, he fought the turbulent emotions by logically sorting through what Catherine had just told him. That February, eleven years ago, had been a time of severe trauma, an emotional upheaval that had forever changed the course of their lives. When Jonathan had discovered that Catherine's memory of those events had been obliterated, he'd naturally assumed that she'd also forgotten the months immediately following their ordeal.

But now she stood there calmly telling him that although her recall was hazy, she remembered much of that time. She remembered going to Europe and studying music.

Music, for God's sake, as though nothing worth mentioning had happened that following summer. But something *had* happened that summer. Jonathan knew it with a desperate certainty. How could Catherine *not remember*?

Jonathan felt as though everything he'd clung to all these years had just crumbled into ash but tried to get a grip on himself. Squeezing his eyes shut, he focused on exactly what Catherine had said. The first few months in Europe were still unclear to her. He consoled himself that she was obviously confused about dates and times. Eventually, everything would be revealed. He just had to wait and be patient. It wouldn't be easy.

With a shuddering breath, Jonathan grabbed his jacket from a hook by the front door.

"Where are you going?" Catherine asked in alarm. "Please tell me what's wrong. Did I say something to upset you?"

"I just need to be alone for a few minutes." He zipped the jacket and took a step toward the door.

Catherine blocked it, her hands outstretched in a pleading gesture. "At least let me go with you."

"No."

"But—"

"No! Now move or be moved," he commanded gruffly.

Catherine's hand fell away and she staggered back as though she'd been struck. Her eyes filled with confusion and fear and something deeper. Jonathan's chest grew tight. Lord, after all the years and all the torment, he still loved her.

The realization hit him like a fist.

This simply couldn't happen. If he loved Catherine, he wouldn't be able to do what had to be done. He'd be condemned to relive the horror and heartbreak of the past, over and over and over, until his mind snapped and his soul shattered.

He wouldn't be able to bear it.

Swallowing a bitter taste, Jonathan grasped Catherine's shoulders, effortlessly lifting and moving her from the doorway. Exotic green eyes regarded him with a silent plea. Unable to stop himself, he reached out and gently caressed her face.

"I'll be back soon," he said softly, then spun and walked out the door.

For several minutes Catherine stared at the closed door. Something seemed out of place. For a moment, she studied the empty space by the front door, then realized what was missing.

Years ago there had been an old hunting rifle propped against the wall. Jonathan had teased that the weapon was for bears, but both of them knew that the rusty old gun would probably explode if fired. Besides, there weren't any bullets for the dumb thing and she suspected that the rifle belonged to whoever owned the cabin. But it was gone now.

A lot of things were gone now.

At the window, Catherine wiped away the condensation and looked out but Jonathan was not in sight. Trembling, she went to the kitchen and sat down, trying to sort out what had just happened between them. Nothing made sense. Everything was going according to Jonathan's plan. Her memory of that lost time was flooding back—hadn't that been what he'd wanted? Yet he'd turned away from her with a bereaved expression, as though he'd suddenly lost a loved one.

Catherine didn't understand any of this. She hated it when they argued. In fact, she couldn't really remember them ever arguing; at least, not over anything serious. They'd always been so in tune with each other, except—

She pursed her lips and concentrated. There had been something, a problem between them that she couldn't quite pull into focus.

Standing, she paced absently and forced her mind into the past. A vague remembrance stopped her mid-stride. Uncle Brad. They'd fought about Uncle Brad. Catherine had been adamant that her uncle not know about their romance. She specifically recalled being terrified that Bradford would do something terrible, something that would separate her from Jonathan forever. Her uncle had been a controlling man with powerful friends. As defiant as she'd been back then, Catherine had still been afraid of him.

But Jonathan hadn't been afraid—not of Bradford Madison, not of anyone. Her mind went back in time, visualizing the small tract home that she had once shared with her uncle.

The streets had been dampened by recent rain. Cathy had been looking out the front window when Jonny's battered pickup had pulled into the driveway. She'd gasped, stunned to see him in front of her uncle's house in broad daylight.

When he reached the front door, she opened it quickly and yanked him inside. "Are you crazy?" she asked, then ran to close the front drapes. "What if Uncle Brad had been home? That would have ruined everything."

Jonny's jaw twitched stubbornly. "I'm tired of sneaking around like a thief in the night. Are you ashamed of me? Maybe you think I'm not good enough to meet your precious uncle—"

"No! That's not true!" Cathy took a deep breath. "Listen, Uncle Brad is going to Europe next month and he'll be gone a whole week. By the time he gets back, we'll be married and there won't be a thing he can do about it."

"He's the only family you've got, Cat. You can't just exclude him from the biggest event in your life and pretend he doesn't exist."

"He'll . . . try to stop us."

"But he *won't* stop us."

"How do you know? You've never even met him. You don't have a clue as to what he'll do." Cathy felt panic surge up inside and tried to make him understand. "Listen to me, please."

Jonny folded his arms. "I'm listening."

Nervously, Cathy cleared her throat and wrung her hands. "You know that Uncle Brad was my mother's brother and that my dad was one of the best violinists in the world."

"What has that got to do with us?"

"I'm getting there." She took a deep breath. "After Mom passed away, Daddy and I were very close. My earliest memory is of Daddy telling anyone who'd listen that someday we would tour as father-daughter duo. When my father got sick and knew he was dying, Uncle Brad promised that I would carry on the family's musical legacy." Smiling brightly, she finished in a rush. "So you see why we can't tell him."

Jonny fixed her with an intense stare. "You're not making any sense at all."

Frustrated, Cathy retreated behind adolescent temper. "Then you're not listening! Uncle Brad will never let us get married because he promised my father that I'd be a famous pianist someday."

"He had no right to make that promise. It's your life."

"That doesn't make any difference, don't you see? My uncle would never break that promise."

"I'll talk to Madison." Jonny sat calmly on the sofa. "When will he be home?"

She suppressed a frantic urge to scream. Jonny couldn't be bullied and she knew that, but his stubbornness could destroy their entire future. "Please, trust me on this. You've got to leave."

He looked at his watch. "I'll wait."

"No! He's in San Francisco. He won't be back until tomorrow. Please, Jonny—"

"I'll wait."

Cathy lost it. All the tension and fear building over the past weeks exploded. She grabbed a throw pillow and flung it across the room. A brass lamp tilted under the blow, bounced off a padded armchair, then rolled onto the floor.

Ignoring the damage, Cathy whirled on Jonny. She fought hysteria, knowing that if their secret was revealed something terrible would happen. "Get out! Get out this minute or I swear that I'll never marry you. I'll run away, and you'll never see us again—"

He rose from the sofa like an angry phoenix, bumping the coffee table with his knee. An ceramic dish fell off, shattering on the hardwood floor. Ignoring the broken glass, Jonny grabbed Cathy's arm. "Don't threaten me. I'm not some pimple-faced kid who can be cowed by a tantrum and I'm not going to build my family on the ruins of someone else's."

Cathy pushed him away. "There won't *be* a family unless you listen to me."

His voice was low and deadly. "I won't let you go, Cat."

With a tiny cry, Cathy ran into his arms. Tears streamed down her face. "I love you so much," she sobbed. "I'm so scared, Jonny."

He held her tightly, kissing her wet face and murmuring words of comfort. Finally, he said, "Let's go to the cabin, honey. We'll figure something out."

Cathy sniffed. "Uncle Brad will be home before noon tomorrow."

"You'll be back by then." He brushed his lips over her forehead. "Get your coat, okay?"

"Okay," she mumbled, then hiccuped and wiped her face.

As though he couldn't bear not to touch her, Jonny kept hold of her arm as she grabbed her jacket. Still fighting tears and convulsing sobs, Cathy allowed him to steer her to the waiting truck. He opened the door and she stumbled getting into the cab.

"Damn," he muttered.

Cathy glanced up and saw Jonathan staring at the house across the street. "What's wrong?"

"There's some woman watching us."

Squinting, Cathy saw a white-haired lady peeking between the drapes. "It's only Mrs. Fabbish. The old busybody watches everybody. She had the police out here twice last week because she thought the neighbor's gardener was a Peeping Tom. No one pays any attention to her."

Jonny swore under his breath, then climbed into the truck and they drove away...

The memory faded.

Catherine blinked, glancing around the empty cabin. Jonathan hadn't returned, and she realized that she'd been lost in thought for almost an hour. Her stomach was knotted painfully, and she felt dazed, inexplicably frightened by what she'd just remembered.

Instinctively, she knew that something else was buried deep inside her, recollections that were irrevocably moving from the realm of her subconscious. Those memories would emerge soon. That realization scared her stiff.

The cabin door flew open, and Catherine jumped as though shot. When Jonathan stepped inside, relief flooded her and she ran to hug him.

He held her tightly, kicking the door shut with his foot. "What's wrong, Cat? You're shaking all over."

She pressed her face against his chest and shook her head. "I'm fine now that you're back."

Jonathan didn't buy it. He gently tipped up her chin, forcing her to meet his gaze. "You've remembered something. Tell me."

Catherine turned away, rubbing her icy hands to warm them. "When I talked to my uncle last week, he was very upset. He recognized your name. Have the two of you ever met?"

Jonathan was silent for a moment, then said, "No."

She glanced over her shoulder. "But you were at his house once, weren't you? You came to get me."

His jaw tightened. "Yes."

"You wanted to talk to Uncle Brad, to tell him that we were getting married."

"Do you remember what happened?"

"I didn't want you to. We argued."

He nodded slowly—eyes guarded, expression wary. "And then?"

"And then..." Her voice trailed away, and she frowned, concentrating. "And then we got into your truck and we drove to the mountains. That's all I remember."

For a moment, Catherine was overwhelmed by the intensity of Jonathan's steady gaze. The breath caught in her throat, and she experienced a swelling sense of foreboding. Even when he looked away, the horrible fear continued to grow.

She was vaguely aware that Jonathan had removed his jacket and was talking to her, but she couldn't focus on his voice. A premonition haunted her, a fear of impending doom expanding from her very core, then exploding with frigid fury.

New images pressed into her brain, ricocheting through her skull with rapid-fire intensity. It was too much. She couldn't sort them out, separate the memories from the terror that overwhelmed her.

"Jonathan, help me!" she finally croaked. In a split second, she was in his arms clinging to him desperately.

"What are you seeing?" he asked tensely.

"I don't know. It's all jumbled up but I feel so frightened."

"Think back, Cat. We argued at your uncle's house, then we came up here. That afternoon, we made plans—and we made love. Let the thoughts come. They can't hurt you, they're only memories."

Covering her face with her hands, Catherine tried to focus her mind. This was important. She felt tension in Jonathan's muscles, heard the desperate edge to his voice. She was close, she knew it. But something blocked her efforts.

Jonathan spoke urgently, his voice a raw whisper in her ear. "Please, honey... please."

Feelings surged through her, warm and loving, an overwhelming need to give Jonathan what he sought. She calmed herself, squeezing her eyelids until colors flashed in blinding profusion. She saw the image. A metallic taste flooded her mouth. Terror. She shook it off, focusing on the memory as Jonathan's soft voice encouraged her.

"I was feeding Mackie his dinner," she whispered. "It was late afternoon and the sun was going down." She paused, glancing at him for confirmation. When he nodded, she continued in a halting voice. "We were arguing again, actually yelling at each other. We were both so angry."

"Do you remember what the argument was about?" Jonathan asked anxiously.

"No." She tried, then shook her head. "But I remember the awful things we said to each other. I said you were a selfish bully, and you called me a spoiled brat and there was more..." Her voice trailed off and she looked up helplessly. "Why, Jonny? Why did we say such hateful things to each other?"

Although Catherine saw the hurt in Jonathan's eyes, he ignored her question. "Go with it, Catherine. Then what happened?"

"I don't rem—" Abruptly, she pressed her lips together and massaged her temples. "I cried."

He took a deep breath. "Yes, you cried."

"I said I never wanted to see you again."

"I told you that you could never leave, that we were bonded together . . . forever."

Tears rushed into her eyes and her voice broke. "I was crazy, screaming that you'd be sorry, that you'd pay for what you'd done to me. Then I ran out the front door."

With a sob, Catherine looked at Jonathan. He was staring into space, and his eyes were red.

Suddenly, Catherine knew why this particular memory had been so traumatic. That day had been their last, and it would be eleven long years before they would meet again.

"Drink this," Jonathan urged softly. "It'll make you feel better."

Catherine loosened the knitted afghan, extending her hand to take the steaming cup he offered. "What is it?"

"Chamomile tea." Jonathan sat beside her on the braided rug and used the sofa as a backrest. "My mother used to swear by it. She said it had magical powers."

Smiling her thanks, Catherine lifted the cup and sipped the hot liquid. "It's nice. Thank you."

"You're welcome."

Jonathan looked away, staring into the flickering flames while Catherine quietly studied his strong profile. He wasn't touching her but she could feel his nearness like a gentle caress. His presence was more warming than the heat radiating from the fireplace. She felt safe. The throbbing pit of fear still lurked inside her. That confused Catherine but as long as Jonathan was with her, everything would be all right. He would protect her. He always had. The horror only started after she'd left him.

Catherine felt all of these emotions and something more; there was a gentle swelling in her heart, filling the emptiness that she'd lived with all these years. She was whole again. She was with the man she'd once loved.

And the man she still loved.

Overcome with the depth of her feelings, Catherine brushed her fingertips across his strong jaw. A tiny muscle twitched, then his mouth tightened as though he'd reached some momentous decision.

"I'm going to take you back to the city tomorrow," he announced.

The cup nearly slipped from her hand. "Why?"

"This was a bad idea." He picked a wood sliver off the rug and tossed it into the flames.

"I want to stay."

"You've been through enough. I didn't realize—" He bit off the words and shook his head. "I never should have brought you here."

"But you *did* bring me here," she pointed out quietly. "And I'm grateful."

His laugh was dry and humorless. "Grateful for being forced to relive memories of another lifetime while half-frozen in a primitive hut?"

"Yes. Most of the memories are beautiful." Catherine set down the cup. "First you saved my life, then you made it worthwhile by loving me—and by allowing me to love you."

Jonathan looked at her, his eyes filled with pain and passion. He started to speak but the words seemed to stick in his throat and he turned away.

"I've remembered it all," Catherine whispered. "The joy and the love and the happiness we shared. Now I realize that a part of me never really forgot. The memories were blurred but they were there, locked up and waiting to be freed."

"No. You haven't remembered it all," Jonathan said grimly. "And now I don't want you to."

That surprised her. "But I remember the beginning and I remember the end—at least, I think I do. When I ran out that afternoon, was that the end for us, Jonathan?"

His lips flattened into a hard line. "Yes."

"Why did I do that? I still don't understand—"

"It doesn't matter any more." Turning, Jonathan looked deeply into her eyes, then touched her face with exquisite gentleness. "I never wanted to hurt you, Cat. I never wanted revenge."

"What did you want, Jonathan? Why did you seek me out and bring me here?"

"Maybe I was trying to prove something to myself, maybe I was trying to recapture the past. A week ago, I was so certain, but now—" he sighed "—I don't know. I just know that I can't watch you suffer any more."

"I'm not suffering." Resting her palm against his taut jaw, she urged him to look at her. "For the first time in years, I feel like I belong. I don't understand everything yet, maybe I never will, but I remember what I felt then and what I wanted then."

The Scorpio eyes captured her with an intensity that took her breath away. "We can't go back."

"We can go forward," she said huskily. "I ran away once. I don't know why I did but I know I lost everything in the world that I cared about."

"Don't, Cat—" The ragged words were choked off and he slowly shook his head. "You're still confused. You...you don't know what you're saying."

"I know that I loved you more than life itself. Maybe I still do."

Hope flickered in Jonathan's eyes, mingled with a hot flash of desire that thrilled Catherine to her toes. His shoulders shook slightly, as though he was fighting to keep from reaching out. He still cared for her; he still wanted her.

Then he closed his eyes and when he looked at her again, the passion was still there, but he'd regained control. "I was nineteen when my mother died. It tore me up inside because I hadn't had a chance to give her the life she deserved. I felt that I had let her down and been unworthy of her love."

A lump wedged in Catherine's throat. "I know. When my father died I was so angry with him. I thought that if I'd been a good enough daughter, he wouldn't have abandoned me. Those feelings are very painful, but they're also very normal."

"Perhaps, but after you left, I felt all the same things—unworthiness, fury, self-doubt. Now I realize that everything I've built since has been fueled by a secret need to prove to you and to myself that I wasn't a failure." The husky timbre of Jonathan's voice betrayed his deep emotion. "For years I've searched for answers, basing every decision in my life on feelings of rage and betrayal. I hardened myself to the pain of others and was ruthless in the pursuit of what I wanted. My compassion became a business liability, a weakness that had to be cured like a disease. Then one day I looked in the mirror and saw the reflection of everything I'd once reviled. I was immune to love."

"No," Catherine whispered. "You're a strong man but strength is not cruelty. I know that you care for people, that you experience their sorrows and agonize because you can't solve their problems."

"You know the man I was, Catherine. You don't know the man I am now."

"Yes I do. As you've pointed out, I've done my homework on you. I researched your charitable contributions and found the paper trails of subsidiary corporations founded for no other reason than to provide anonymous help for people in need. You're a good and decent man, Jonathan Stone. That's why I fell in love with you." Swallowing hard, Catherine lifted Jonathan's hand, cradling it as she brushed her lips across his fingertips. "And that's why I still love you."

He shuddered. "After everything I've put you through, you can say that to me?"

"I have no choice," she said quietly, pressing her cheek against his palm. "It's what I feel."

He took a harsh breath, then gently lifted her face and wiped her damp eyes with his thumb. "I don't deserve your tears, Cat. All these years I've searched for you, driven by my own pain without considering yours. I've given you nothing but grief—"

Catherine laid her finger against his lips to stop the heresy. "Don't ever say that," she said shakily. "You gave me back my life. You made me feel cherished and adored and I was transformed by our love. You said that I was reliving the past through the eyes of a girl, but that's not true. I'm grown up now, with a woman's eyes and a woman's heart."

She brushed her fingertip over his full mouth and felt his lips quiver beneath her touch.

"Don't play with me, Catherine," he warned hoarsely. "I'm not made of steel."

"On the outside you are," she whispered, then laid a hand on his chest. "But in here, you're soft and warm and filled with love."

He groaned and took hold of her wrists. "If you don't take those sweet hands off me, there won't be anything soft about what you'll find."

She smiled. "I'm counting on that."

For a moment, Jonathan simply stared at her. Emotions twisted his face, and Catherine saw a smoldering passion locked in his potent gaze but she also saw doubt and fear. A fierce battle seemed to be raging deep inside of him, an inner combat that Catherine recognized but didn't understand. Finally, he spoke in a voice heavy with conflict. "I didn't bring you here for that."

"I know."

Closing his eyes, he took a deep breath, then pressed his lips against her open palm. "Are you sure?"

"Yes."

"So much has come between us, I don't want to add new regrets to the tally."

"That isn't going to happen," she murmured. "Even when I couldn't remember, you were always with me—a face in my dreams, a voice in my heart. The only thing I will ever regret is all the years we've lost—because I love you, Jonny. I always will."

Jonathan groaned and pulled her into his arms, burying his face in the silky sweetness of her hair. "I've missed you so much. I felt like a part of me had been torn away." Lifting his head, he cupped her face with one hand and tilted her chin. "I never stopped loving you, Cat, and that scares me to death. If I lost you again, I don't know what I'd do."

"You won't lose me," she said softly, then gently brushed her lips against his. "You couldn't pry me out of your life with a crowbar. I'm here to stay."

Jonathan kissed her then, a slow, sweet kiss that built in intensity until both were breathless. He pulled slightly away, with an expression of awe and wonder, then his mouth covered hers with an almost desperate urgency.

Catherine responded instantly, her heart pounding wildly as a liquid warmth unfurled deep inside. She captured his face in her hands, her mouth seeking his fervently. She tasted him and wanted more. She couldn't get enough and wound her arms around his neck, pulling him closer.

Jonathan moaned, and his body flexed and shuddered as passion mounted to a fever pitch. His skin was hot, nearly searing her probing fingers, her searching mouth. She explored his face, from his silky-soft eyelids to the coarse roughness of his cheeks. She memorized the sharp contours and the gentle hollows until his face was indelibly etched into her memory. This time, she would never forget. Never.

He urged her head backward, exposing her soft throat to his hungry lips. Between moist kisses and feathery flicks of his tongue, he whispered her name with such loving inflection that it nearly made Catherine sob with joy.

She wanted to get closer, but the afghan tangled around her twisting body, thwarting her efforts. Frustrated, she kicked it away and fell back on the braided rug.

Jonathan loomed above her, then brushed a strand of hair from her face with incredible tenderness. "I want to love you as though it were the first time," he whispered. "I want every part of your body to cry out for me as mine is crying for you right now." As he spoke, his hand glided the length of her. Heat radiated through her clothing, scorching her tingling skin from throat to thigh.

Desire surged through Catherine like a hot flood. She felt wild with it, out of control. Just when she thought she would explode, Jonathan's hands were stroking her body, and a tiny cry of pleasure bubbled from her throat. His finger hooked the top button of her shirt, then paused as his lips moved down the V-neck of her top.

She arched her back, giving him access, begging for his attention. Air brushed her fevered skin as the shirt fell open, then his mouth was on her, loving her, caressing her swollen breasts until she cried out in pure joy.

Reaching up, she tugged at his sweater until he smiled lazily and shrugged it off. Then she sighed in contentment, rubbing her hands across his smooth chest. Her fingers brushed over a roughened area just below his collarbone. Opening her eyes, she saw a spidery web of scar tissue radiating from a puckered circle of withered skin.

She gasped. "Good Lord, what happened to you?"

"It doesn't matter," he whispered, bending to kiss her.

She pulled away, unable to comprehend what could have caused such damage and horrified by the pain he must have suffered. "Ohh..." Tears flooded her eyes and she gently kissed the ugly scar. "My poor Jonny."

Jonathan shuddered, groaning with pleasure as Catherine brushed inquisitive fingers from his shoulder to his belly and lower, until crisp hairs tickled her palm. She felt the tiny spasms as his abdomen contracted beneath her touch.

Awkwardly, she struggled with the buttons on his jeans. She couldn't have been clumsier if she'd been wearing mittens. Taking pity on her bumbling efforts, Jonathan deftly removed the obstacle. Then he whispered, "Your turn."

She gamely tried, but her fingers were stiff, and her brain was fuzzy, and her entire body seemed to have a life of its own. "I—I can't."

"Shall I help?"

She managed to nod. The zipper hummed and in a moment, Catherine lifted her hips as Jonathan smoothly slid the garment over her long legs. She gasped, realizing that except for a silky slip of fabric, she was lying nude in front of the fire while Jonathan made love to her with his eyes.

She didn't feel a twinge of modesty or shame. All she felt at this moment was a surge of love and desire. Raising her arms, she whispered, "Make love to me, Jonny. Please, make love to me now."

Then he bent to kiss her, and Catherine's world swirled into a vortex of dizzying color. She felt his hands slide over her hips and when she opened her eyes, the final silky barrier to their lovemaking lay atop their pile of discarded clothing.

Jonathan was stretched out beside her. He touched her cheek as though she was fragile and precious. "My sweet little Cat," he murmured. "In my dreams, I've touched you like this. Your eyes would light with love, and I'd know it was for me. Part of me is afraid that you're not real, that I'm still dreaming."

"Does this feel like a dream?" She touched his chest, then allowed her fingers to brush downward until he shivered under the intimacy of her caress. "I'm real, Jonny, and this moment is real. Our time together is so precious. Let's not waste it."

With a hoarse cry, he moved over her, smothering her face with his kisses as he pressed against her. Catherine felt a surge of passion that shook her to the soles of her feet. She lifted herself to him, wanting him so desperately that she was beyond thought, reacting only to the rhythm of her pounding heart and her throbbing body.

But Jonathan held back, continuing to stroke her with feathery caresses until she was nearly wild with need. He murmured her name, kissing her damp face, then taking her mouth.

Just when she thought she would die of frustration, he whispered her name and entered her slowly, powerfully. She cried out, clinging with her body, bonding with her soul.

He withdrew and thrust as she arched to meet him again and again and again, until she felt she might explode with the mounting passion. Then, when she could bear no more, the crescendo peaked and crashed in a shattering mutual climax.

Minutes passed, or perhaps hours; Catherine didn't know. Afterward, she was nestled in his arms, sated and happy. Gently, he stroked her hair and from what seemed a great distance, she heard his voice. "Regrets, Cat?"

"Never," she murmured sleepily, then tossed an arm over his chest and sighed.

When he started to sit up, she moaned in protest.

"I guarantee if we sleep on this floor all night, we'll have plenty of regrets by morning." He slipped his arm around her and tucked the afghan over her shoulders. "Up we go. That's a good girl."

Catherine was too drowsy to argue and allowed Jonathan to help her into bed. He lifted her arms and pulled a sweatshirt over her head. "So you don't freeze anything valuable," he murmured.

Catherine smiled lazily, and Jonathan kissed her forehead chastely, then started to move away. When she realized he was simply going to tuck her in and leave, her eyes flew open. Rolling over, she pulled back the sheets in silent invitation. He hesitated.

"We can both sleep on the cot if you'd rather," she purred.

Smiling, he slid beside her, pulling her close and holding her as she drifted into a deep, contented sleep.

Jonathan's arm was numb but he would have rather cut it off than move it. Even in the predawn darkness, he could see Catherine's satisfied expression as she nestled closer to him. The blanket slipped from her shoulder, and he covered her. His hand lingered against her throat, then he brushed his knuckles over her soft skin.

How could she still be so beautiful? he wondered. How could she still have such a powerful grip on his heart?

And how had he let this happen?

God knows he hadn't meant to let things get so out of control, but when she'd looked him straight in the eye and calmly said that she still loved him, the war had been over. As Catherine had already warned, she took no prisoners. Even if his heart hadn't already thrown up a white flag, Jonathan realized that he'd never really had a chance. He'd been in love since the first day he'd pulled Catherine out of the snow. She'd been the most beautiful woman he'd ever seen; she still was. All Catherine ever had to do was look at him, and he'd melt like a spring thaw.

Some things were apparently not destined for change.

A movement caught his attention, and he quickly looked down at Catherine. She was frowning, tossing her head restlessly. Then she gasped and kicked at the blankets, moaning and mumbling.

Jonathan tried to cover her. "It's all right, honey. Go back to sleep."

Face contorted, she made a series of pitiful sounds that reminded him of a mewing kitten. Her skin had paled three shades, and an icy dampness beaded her forehead. Jonathan's stomach knotted up. He knew it was just a dream, but seeing her in distress of any kind upset him.

"Shh," he whispered, touching her wet forehead.

With a hoarse croak, she jerked away. "Stop," she mumbled. "Jonny... Jonny..." More frantic now, she rolled her head back and forth as though trying to escape something. Her breathing was ragged and she clawed at her own face.

"Don't, honey, you'll hurt yourself." Jonathan grasped her wrists, and she fought him.

"No," she moaned, kicking at some invisible enemy. "Don't hurt... please don't—"

Suddenly, she bolted upright, eyes wide and glazed with terror. She scrambled to her knees, reaching out to the darkness. Stunned, Jonathan grabbed her waist to keep her from leaping out of bed. She struggled violently, hands outstretched as she screamed, *"No! Jonnnnny!"*

Catherine went absolutely rigid and gave an agonized cry, a scream of pure torment torn from the deepest part of her soul. Then she fainted.

Chapter Eight

Something wet and cold touched Catherine's face. She moaned and turned away, then heard Jonathan's voice calling her name. He seemed very distant, and she was confused. Why was he waking her up in the middle of the night? Why did she feel so . . . disconnected?

A slow terror built deep inside her. Something horrible had happened, but she couldn't focus on exactly what it had been. There had been an awful noise, then fire and smoke and—

And what?

Again Catherine heard Jonathan's voice, soft yet insistent. He was repeating her name, but he seemed so far away. The icy dampness brushed her cheek again, and she shivered, then painfully opened her eyes.

Jonathan was bending over her, sponging her forehead with a damp rag. "It was just a dream, honey," he said quietly. "You're all right now."

A dream. She closed her eyes, visualizing the horror that had invaded her sleep. "It was so real," she murmured, then rubbed her eyelids and shakily sat up. "I've never been so frightened in my life."

The mattress sagged slightly as Jonathan sat beside her, pulling her close. Gratefully, she laid her head on his shoulder. He felt so solid, so comforting.

"Can you tell me about it?" he asked.

Catherine concentrated until pieces of the vivid image flashed through her mind. "I was running toward the woods and someone grabbed me."

She shuddered and gave herself to Jonathan's warm arms.

"It's okay now," he murmured. "You're safe. Think back, tell me what you dreamed about."

Absently, Catherine rubbed her knotted neck muscles as she tried to recall details of the nightmare. Like a technicolor filmstrip, the image unrolled through her mind. Then she saw everything as crisp and realistic as though she'd lived the experience mere moments ago.

She spoke hesitantly, more to herself than to him. "I was scared to death, trying to scream but there was a hand over my mouth. Then I heard a man's voice and I knew he was going to take me away from you..." The words trailed away and Catherine frowned.

Something wasn't right about what she'd just said. Everything was just too vivid, the details too clear. She could remember ice crunching beneath her feet, and a dog barking frantically. Someone had grabbed her from behind, twisting her upper body and pulling her head back. Catherine could actually feel the rough gloved hand crushing her mouth and smell the rancid odor of cheap leather. Her heart had leaped into her throat, and she'd kicked violently, terrified.

Then there had been the voices, male voices surrounding her with agitated shouts and authoritarian commands.

"Wait a minute," Catherine mumbled.

"What is it?" Jonathan asked anxiously.

"Something's wrong. I remember sounds, shouts and barking and male voices, but—"

But in her dream, there had been no voices, no barking dog. That had to mean—

"Oh my God." Catherine felt ill. She clutched her stomach and moaned, shaking her head as though she could throw off the horrid image.

"Cat, what's wrong?" Jonathan's voice, thick with alarm, penetrated her mental fog. His hands cupped her face. "You're all right, honey, I won't let anyone hurt you."

Pulling away, Catherine looked at him. "It wasn't a dream, was it?"

Jonathan didn't answer. In his eyes, Catherine saw concern and compassion; and she saw the truth.

Her lips formed the word "no," but she didn't make a sound. Shoulders slumping, Catherine stared at her knees, slowly shaking her head. It *had* happened, all of it. She could remember as though it had been yesterday. All the terror, all the anguish had been horribly real.

In a broken voice, Catherine looked at Jonathan through a blur of tears. "He found us, didn't he? Uncle Brad found us and came to take me back."

"Yes."

"It happened when I ran out of the cabin that last afternoon. My uncle took me home and wouldn't let me see you again."

Pursing his lips, Jonathan regarded her for a moment, then said softly, "In a manner of speaking, yes."

"Why did I go with him?" Catherine asked. "Why didn't I stay with you?"

Jonathan's eyes hardened, and he looked away. "That's a good question."

The impact of his statement made her heart sink. "You don't know?" She looked into his eyes and cringed at the sudden bitterness they reflected. Trembling, she denied his silent accusation. "I wouldn't have done that. I don't remember everything that happened but I remember my feelings. I loved you. I wouldn't have left you—*I just couldn't have done that.*"

"You would, you could and you did." He took a sharp breath and spoke through clamped teeth. "As to why? I've asked myself that question a thousand times. I still don't have the answer. Do you?" His eyes impaled her.

"No," she whispered. "But I know that there must be something else, something more than what I've already remembered."

Jonathan's expression softened, melting from leashed anger to extraordinary sorrow. "Yes, there's more."

"Please, tell me," she implored as panic bubbled up inside her.

He sighed. "I can't."

"But I don't understand—" Her eyes widened. "There were other men in the woods. They were hiding behind trees and they had guns." Turning, she clutched at Jonathan's shirt. "Who were they? What did they want with us?"

"Shh." Jonathan took her wrists to keep her from clawing him, then delicately kissed the back of each rigid hand. "They were from the sheriff's department."

She blinked. "Policemen? Did we rob a bank or something?"

"No."

"Then why did they surround us like we were some kind of criminals?" Her voice rose. "Why did they point guns at the cabin? Why did they—" Her fist flew to her mouth. "I remember gunshots. Jonathan, they were shooting at us."

"Not at us, Cat, at me. You were safe with your uncle."

Numb with disbelief, Catherine could only stare. What was Jonathan saying? Good Lord, they don't send SWAT teams out to rescue lovestruck teenagers. Something else had happened, something Catherine couldn't even begin to fathom.

"But why?" she finally managed to ask.

Jonathan brushed Catherine's hair back, then kissed her forehead. "Tell me everything you remember, then we'll talk about why."

She shrugged helplessly. "I remember running and being grabbed. I remember Mackie yelping, and my uncle's voice saying that I was all right. Then I remember men behind the trees, pointing guns at the cabin." Catherine looked up, seeking Jonathan's confirmation.

"Yes, that all happened. Then what do you remember?"

"Nothing. I mean, there were gunshots, and I was trying to scream, but I was being pulled away and I couldn't see you and—" An image formed in Catherine's mind, cutting off the words. Dazed she allowed the vision to take over and saw everything as though in slow motion. There were shouts and screams and shots.

Then—

"There was an explosion," Catherine mumbled, partially in shock from what she was remembering. "A deafening blast, and parts of the cabin were flying through the air along with dust and smoke. I—I broke away from my uncle and I ran toward the cabin, screaming for you over and over, but you didn't answer me. When I was almost to the front door—or where the front door had been—then it was like the sun blew up in my face and everything went black."

Jonathan listened to Catherine in stony silence, but his eyes registered shock and surprise.

Tears streamed down her face. "I thought you were dead," she whispered. "They told me you were dead."

The corner of Jonathan's mouth twitched, and his eyes narrowed. "What did you say?"

"I remember opening my eyes. Everything was blurry but I think I was in the hospital." Catherine wiped her face. "I was on a gurney. People in green were pushing me, and my uncle was running alongside. My stomach hurt, and I kept asking for you and—" A sob racked her. "—I remember Uncle Brad telling me that you were gone, that you'd never hurt me again."

For a moment, Jonathan simply stared at her. In his eyes, Catherine saw disbelief and anger and finally, burning hatred. Then he turned away, raking his hair as he walked across the room. When he spoke, his voice was thin and distant. "Anything else?"

"Only what I've already told you—the hospital room, the photographer, going to the airport. It's all pretty vague." Shakily, Catherine stood and went to Jonathan, laying her hand on his arm. "What happened to you, Jonny? Why didn't you come for me?"

He took a shuddering breath. "I couldn't, Cat."

"Why? And why did the police come if we hadn't done something awful?"

Jonathan stared thoughtfully out the window. "Madison came back from San Francisco a day early. He showed up at your house right after we left. He found you missing and the house a wreck."

"Oh, no." Catherine remembered the broken glass, the overturned lamp, and her stomach twisted. "He must have been worried sick."

"You could say that," Jonathan replied drily. "When he saw your car still in the garage, he called the police. Since they'd already had a report of a man forcing a crying girl into a pickup truck—"

"Mrs. Fabbish," Catherine muttered, interrupting. "I never even considered that she'd be taken seriously."

"Ordinarily she might not have been, but the house showed signs of a struggle, and Bradford Madison was down at the station pounding desks, so they put out an APB on my truck." Jonathan saw Catherine's questioning expression. "Mrs. Fabbish was quite thorough. She gave them the license number, and they tracked it to my post office box in Lake Arrowhead."

"Oh, Lord." Catherine rubbed her forehead, then walked shakily over and sat at the table. "My uncle thought you had kidnapped me."

"That's about the size of it," Jonathan said coolly.

Catherine closed her eyes and tried to make sense of what she'd just heard. Never in a thousand years would she have believed that so many coincidental events could have led to such tragedy. "Even with all of that, how did they track us to the cabin? We weren't renting the place. Who knew we were there?"

"Just about all of the locals," Jonathan said. "Most of them figured it was none of their business, until the cops started sniffing around. Since they didn't want criminals in their quiet little community, they were more than willing to draw the deputies a map."

Jonathan joined Catherine at the table. She avoided his gaze; he avoided hers. They sat in silence, pondering what they'd learned. Finally, Catherine took a deep breath. "So they swarmed around the cabin, guns drawn, thinking this was some kind of hostage situation?"

"Apparently. When you bolted out the front door, everyone thought you had escaped."

"But why did they shoot at you?"

"Because I didn't understand their little scenario," he said bitterly. "All I knew was that some man jumped out from behind a tree and grabbed you. I didn't know who the hell he was but I saw you struggling, and something just snapped inside of me. I was blind with rage. I got the rifle and went after him."

Catherine couldn't stand it. Propping her elbows on the table, she covered her eyes and tried to erase the image Jonathan's words had conjured. It didn't help. She knew exactly what had happened next. The deputies had seen Jonathan holding a gun and had opened fire.

Then the world had exploded.

Lowering her hands, she looked at Jonathan. He was staring into space, jaw taut, eyes dark with fury. She remembered the scar, the horrible jagged hole in his shoulder. "You were hurt," she whispered. "They shot you."

He nodded, never meeting her gaze. "Yes. The blow knocked me back inside the cabin and halfway to the back door."

Her eyes widened. "The explosion . . . ?"

"One of the bullets either severed the gas line or hit the propane tank."

"How did you survive? My God, Jonathan, the entire kitchen was blown off—"

"I'd already crawled onto the back porch. The first explosion tossed me down the embankment. I guess I blacked out, because I don't remember a second blast."

Squeezing her eyes shut, Catherine choked back a sob at the image of Jonathan, broken and bleeding. The memory of the horror flashed through her mind again and again, the pungent smell of gunpowder, the shouting and barking and—

Barking.

Her head snapped up. "What happened to Mackie?"

Jonathan's expression remained hard as rock.

She reached across the table and grabbed his arm. "Right before the explosion, he was on the front porch. He was growling and barking at the men. What happened, Jonathan? *What happened to Mackie?*"

Jonathan looked at her then, his eyes filled with pain. With an anguished whimper, Catherine released his arm and felt fresh tears rush down her face.

"I'm sorry, honey," Jonathan said. "It happened quickly—he didn't suffer."

Jonathan watched Catherine's face as the realization seeped into her mind. Her eyes glazed, her skin paled and for a moment, he feared she might faint again. Slowly, she stood and swayed, then steadied herself on the table.

"He was just a little dog," she mumbled dully. "They didn't have to kill him."

Her voice was hollow, and Jonathan feared she'd go into shock. Standing quickly, he slid his arm around her shoulders and felt her tremble at his touch. She stared sightlessly into space and he spoke in a soothing voice. "No one wanted to hurt Mac, honey. The explosion was an accident."

A long, slow shudder racked her body, then she looked at Jonathan with a vacant, bewildered expression. "They hurt you." She touched his shoulder, caressing the scar through his sweatshirt. "You could have died because of me."

"No, Cat—"

She interrupted, speaking in a flat monotone that made the hairs on Jonathan's nape prickle. "It's my fault, all of it. Mackie is dead, and you were almost killed, all because of me and some stupid argument that I can't even remember." She emitted a sound that was halfway between a dry laugh and a choking sob. "It was like being in some kind of Twilight Zone. I remember thinking that if I could get to you, the men and the guns would just dematerialize and everything would be the way it was. Only my legs felt like lead, and I tried to scream, but no sound came out."

"Don't think about it any more." Jonathan hugged her close, caressing her face and kissing her soft hair. Terror overwhelmed him, the terror that he'd pushed her too far, too fast. Oh God, what had he done? "It's all over, Catherine, put it out of your mind. Everything's all right, everything's fine now."

Only everything wasn't fine at all. Catherine's eyes were blank and even as Jonathan held and comforted her, he knew that he'd opened a flood of horror that couldn't be stopped.

"It was so odd," she murmured. "Everything was happening in slow motion, you know? Shingles and pieces of wood just kind of sailed through the air, hanging in the sky as though they would never touch earth again. It was like being in a dream and you're trying to run, but your feet are stuck to the ground."

Her dazed expression cut him to the core. He'd realized that remembering that terrible time would be difficult for Catherine, but never in a million years could he have anticipated the devastation he saw in her face. At the moment, Jonathan doubted that Catherine was even aware of his presence. She spoke in a flat, unemotional voice, as though she were watching a performance and calmly relating what she saw.

All Jonathan could do was hold on to her and pray that her mind was strong enough to survive.

"I saw the hummingbird feeder," she said suddenly. "It flew up and circled, like it had grown wings and was flying away. I watched it for a long time, but it never came down. Then there was a terrible sound, a loud moaning scream that went on forever. I—I think it was me."

Jonathan remembered that scream. After the explosion, his ears had been ringing and his mind was growing dim, but he could still hear that soul-wrenching cry of anguish. It had been his final memory before he'd awakened to the pain of rough hands dragging him across the icy ground.

Catherine touched his face, bringing him back to the present. He looked at her, saw awareness in her eyes and nearly cried with relief. She was back.

"I'm so sorry," she said quietly. "I thought you were dead. That's probably why I lost my memory in the first place, because I couldn't face losing you. But all these years, you thought I'd simply walked away from you. You must have felt so betrayed."

Closing his eyes, he forced himself to release her. "I assumed that you'd discarded me because I had become an inconvenience and an embarrassment."

She gasped. "How could you ever believe that? Didn't the doctors tell you what had happened?"

"No one told me anything. I didn't even know you'd been hurt."

"Surely after the truth was known—"

"No one was interested in the 'truth,'" Jonathan said harshly, then instantly regretted his tone. "There's no reason to go over this, Cat. It's just going to upset you, and you've been through enough."

"I need to know what happened to you."

"It doesn't matter any more."

"Doesn't it?" Catherine touched his face, urging him to meet her questioning gaze. "Is that why you've been searching all these years, because it doesn't matter any more?"

He didn't have to answer. They both knew that nothing in their entire lives mattered so much to either of them as what had happened during that winter so long ago.

"Please," she urged softly. "Tell me."

"All right." Jonathan took a deep breath. "When I regained consciousness, I was sprawled halfway down the embankment behind the cabin. There were deputies all around. One of them handcuffed me—" Involuntarily he winced at the memory. He'd been so weak and when his arms had been pulled back, the pain had been blinding. The icy ground had been strewn with cabin debris and stained with his blood.

As he continued to recount the story, scenes of it screened vividly through his mind.

He remembered waiting for Catherine, knowing that she'd suddenly appear and soothe away the pain with her loving touch. He'd whispered her name, over and over until he'd been silenced by rough hands dragging him mercilessly up the embankment.

Jonathan recalled the rapid-fire questions assaulting him, a machine-gun staccato of gruff voices and angry words. Even in the ambulance, the ceaseless inquiries had continued: Why had he kidnapped the girl? Had he planned to demand a ransom? Did he have accomplices?

Jonny hadn't understood the odd questions. He'd been confused, weakened by loss of blood and fighting the seeping blackness pushing at the edge of his mind. Where was Cathy? he'd wondered groggily. Why had she run away?

When he'd finally looked up, a uniformed man was glaring at him with hard eyes and an expression of utter contempt.

"W-Where's Cathy?" Jonny had asked.

The deputy had sneered. "Thanking her lucky stars that she got away from you, buddy boy. Right now she's probably giving a statement that'll put you away for a long, long time."

At that moment, Jonny hadn't fully grasped the implication of the ominous prediction that would haunt him throughout the endless months to come.

Catherine's anxious voice broke into his thoughts, and Jonathan realized that she'd been speaking to him. He dragged his attention away from the tormenting memories.

"What happened then?" she asked tensely.

He decided to soften reality for her. "I was taken to the hospital."

"The same hospital that I was in?"

"No." Jonathan walked into the kitchen and filled up the coffeepot. He was trying to buy time, trying to decide how he could tell Catherine what had happened then without shocking her into a coma.

Catherine followed him, wringing her hands. "Were you badly injured?"

"I had a good surgeon and a disgustingly cheerful physical therapist who subscribed to the 'no pain, no gain' philosophy," he replied casually.

There was no sense telling Catherine that he'd been on the critical list for over a week. According to the doctors, only his determination and fighting spirit had brought him through. But Jonathan knew better. He had survived for Catherine, because he couldn't bear the thought of not seeing her again.

Catherine delicately caressed his arm, then kissed his shoulder. "It must have been horrible for you to go through that alone," she whispered. "I should have been there for you."

Jonathan's mouth was suddenly dry as a desert. "Do you really think your uncle would have allowed that?"

At his sharp tone, Catherine took a step backward. "I'm sure he didn't know. I mean, he thought you had been killed."

"That's bull and you know it." Whirling on her, Jonathan cursed violently, and a hot fury washed over him. Even knowing what Madison had done, Catherine was still protecting him. "Bradford Madison knew exactly where I was and what I was going through."

"But he told me—"

"He told you lies, Cat, deliberate lies." Clenching his fists, Jonathan saw Catherine's bewilderment and was even more enraged. "Do I have to paint you a picture? Why do you think he rushed you off to Europe like that? He knew I was alive and he knew I was still a threat to his control over you."

She stared in astonishment. "But he didn't even know that I was with you of my own free will."

"He found out soon enough."

"How? I couldn't have told him. I didn't remember anything."

Instantly Jonathan went cold. The discussion had gotten out of hand and was veering perilously close to an area that Catherine wasn't yet ready to handle.

Her bewildered expression begged for answers. "The police told him, didn't they? As soon as you were better, you cleared everything up . . . right?"

Relieved that her speculation had given him an out, Jonathan simply nodded. It wasn't exactly the truth, but it was close enough. Jonathan *had* told the police the truth, and they *had* informed Catherine's uncle. Even if Madison hadn't wanted to believe it, the facts would have been indisputable by then.

But truth meant nothing to Bradford Madison. After all, the man had a reputation to protect, and Catherine's partial amnesia had provided the perfect opportunity to leave Jonathan twisting in the wind.

And that's exactly what Madison had done.

"Perhaps Uncle Brad was trying to spare me." Catherine nervously licked her lips. "I mean, he might have just been waiting for my memory to return before he . . . he—"

"Told you that I hadn't really been blown into human hamburger?" Jonathan's jaw clenched. "Of course, I can see that he only had your best interests at heart."

Catherine watched Jonathan's expression cloud. Anger flashed through his gray eyes like lightening ripping a stormy mountain sky. Fear gripped her. His fury was so real, a throbbing, tangible presence between them. She didn't understand it.

Just moments before, Jonathan had seemed so relieved, so grateful to realize that she hadn't consciously left him. But something even deeper was going on inside of this mysterious man. Catherine had loved him once and still loved him; yet he remained an enigma.

As Catherine contemplated Jonathan, her mind replayed all that she'd learned over the past few days. There were still holes in the logic, blank spaces that defied rational explanation.

A thought occurred to her. "After you were released from the hospital, where did you go?"

Jonathan regarded her sullenly. The coffeepot started to boil, and he turned down the heat without responding to her question.

"You didn't have any friends or family that I knew about, and the cabin had been destroyed." Catherine persisted. "You would have needed someone to care for you while you recovered."

Reaching into the cupboard, Jonathan pulled out two cups and filled them with steaming coffee. He handed Catherine one, then took his and walked into the living room.

Catherine set her cup on the counter and followed him. He was sitting on the floor, using the sofa as a backrest, staring into the cold fireplace. She stood facing him, then crossed her ankles and sat down.

"Jonathan, please. Talk to me. Where did you go? Why didn't you come after me?"

"Why didn't *I* come after *you*?" His eyes narrowed, and his voice was chillingly soft. "It was months before I could look for you and by then your precious uncle had covered your tracks so that the CIA couldn't have found you."

"*Months?*" she croaked. "Is that how long you were in the hospital?"

"I was in the hospital for a few weeks," he said coolly, setting the cup down with enough force to slosh its contents over the hardwood floor. "Then I spent some time as a guest of the state."

"Pardon me?"

His mouth twisted in a macabre smile. "I was in jail."

"Jail?" Catherine's lungs emptied instantly, and her hand flew to her throat. She fought for air, first to breathe, then to speak. "But...you were innocent."

He laughed unpleasantly. "Society doesn't want to believe that innocent people can get shot."

Catherine stared in shock, trying to assimilate what Jonathan had told her. "You went to jail because of me?"

"I went to jail because no one believed what I had to say and because—" He cut off the words and looked away.

An icy chill slid down Catherine's spine. "And because I wasn't there to corroborate your story?" When he didn't answer, she leaned forward and took his wrist. "Is that the reason? Because I didn't tell what really happened?"

Caressing the slender hand on his arm, Jonathan avoided her gaze. "It wasn't your fault, honey. You couldn't remember anything."

"But you didn't know that, did you?" Her voice trembled in anguish. "All those weeks, you waited for me and I never came. You must have felt so abandoned and so hurt...no wonder you hated me."

"I never hated you, Cat," he said quickly. "I was hurt and angry and confused. I *wanted* to hate you, but I couldn't."

Catherine felt sick. She could imagine Jonathan in a cold cell waiting for the woman he loved to set him free with the truth. How many sunsets had he counted before he realized that she would never come? How much pain had he endured alone, without the comfort of a loving touch, a soothing word?

Her soul cried for him, a wrenching flood of agony that went beyond mere tears. Jonathan had saved her life. He had loved her and trusted her, and she had abandoned him. Perhaps he could forgive her, but Catherine wasn't certain she could ever forgive herself.

Jonathan's expression of profound sadness tore at Catherine. She gently touched his face and whispered, "You must have been so alone."

Jonathan blinked and managed a thin smile. "Actually, I wasn't completely alone. As it turned out, that experience introduced me to the man who changed the course of my life."

That surprised Catherine. In the days they'd been together, Jonathan hadn't mentioned anyone else. "Who was that?"

"His name is Howard Dylan and eleven years ago he was a partner in an established law firm as well as L.A.'s elected City Attorney." Jonathan smiled sheepishly. "He was also the owner of this cabin."

"Oh dear," Catherine murmured.

"Indeed. Mr. Dylan was not happy to hear that his mountain retreat resembled the remnants of a military bombing range." Jonathan leaned back and sipped his coffee, smiling. "The first time I met Howard, he was on the other side of a glass partition, fuming and huffing into the jail's visitor phone. I wasn't particularly receptive to having a big-bellied blowhard threatening to sue. At the time, I was an angry young man viewing the entire legal system as twisted and unjust, so my response was, ah, rather crude."

"I can imagine," Catherine mumbled. "What did he do then?"

"He laughed." Jonathan's eyes grew wistful. "It seems that old Howard was more used to people polishing his boots than telling him where to get off. He said he admired my gumption and asked me what in hell I was doing in jail."

"So you told him."

"Yes. Howard said that I'd never be able to make restitution for blowing up his cabin as long as I was behind bars, so he convinced one of his law partners to take my case. I was out in a week."

"How?"

"The rest of the charges were dropped."

"'Charges?' As in more than one?" Catherine swallowed hard. "I don't understand."

"The original arraignment was for everything from kidnapping to assault with a deadly weapon. I found out through my attorney that the one thing your uncle did do was to try to drop the kidnapping charge, but the state prosecutes criminal actions so the victim has little say in the matter."

"There *wasn't any victim*!"

"The state said that there was, but the case was too weak to prosecute. You apparently hadn't given them a deposition and when you disappeared, they had no witness."

"So the District Attorney had to drop the charges?"

"Yes, but there was still the matter of assaulting police officers and resisting arrest—"

"What? You didn't assault anyone and you didn't resist anything. *They* shot *you!*"

"Hmm. Well that's a picky point. I had a rifle and I pointed it toward law enforcement officers." Jonathan shrugged. "At any rate, the entire case was pretty shaky so all it took was one high-powered lawyer making a few waves, and the D.A. dropped all the charges."

Catherine was massively relieved. "So you were proved innocent."

"Not exactly. They simply didn't have enough hard evidence for a conviction. The arrest and the charges are still on record."

Catherine could only stare. It wasn't fair. Jonathan had done nothing except try to protect her. "I'll get a lawyer," she said suddenly. "I'll take them to court and tell what really happened."

Jonathan sobered. "No."

"Why not? They'll have to clear your name and restore your reputation."

"I don't need it, Cat. I own a corporation with subsidiaries in everything from computer chips to coffee imports and have enough money to last the rest of my life. To dredge up the past now would only damage my credibility and it's my stockholders who would suffer."

Mulling that over, Catherine could see the logic. Jonathan was right but that didn't alleviate her guilt. "I feel so helpless. Everything terrible that has happened to you is because of me, and I can't do one single thing to make it right."

Reaching out, Jonathan lifted Catherine's chin with his fingertip. "Don't cry for me, honey. I've done all right."

"Yes you have, no thanks to me." She sniffed. "How did you manage? I mean, you've come so far in these past few years."

"I had a little help from my friend."

"This Howard Dylan?"

"Yes. He greased the skids for me. With his endorsement, I landed a job at a small brokerage house, and things worked out from there."

When Catherine had been researching Jonathan Stone's career, she'd discovered that a few years back he'd engineered a leveraged buy out of a blue-chip corporation. That coup had shocked the business community and put Stone Securities on the financial map. Remembering the rumors of secret money, Catherine hesitated, then asked, "Is Mr. Dylan the man who financed your, uh, business ventures?"

He tilted his head, regarding her thoughtfully. "It's no secret that Howard and I have a close business association, but anything else is strictly between the two of us. It wouldn't be prudent for a man in his position to have undeclared financial interests."

"Exactly what is his position?" Catherine frowned. "I've heard that name somewhere."

"He's the Lieutenant Governor." Catherine's eyes widened, and Jonathan laughed. "Impressed, Cat?"

"Surprised."

"You'd like Howard. For all of his bluster, he's a down-to-earth guy with a good heart."

"I already like him." Catherine moved over to settle herself in Jonathan's lap. "He was your friend when you were alone. He helped you and cared about you and as far as I'm concerned, that makes him the greatest man on earth."

Catherine nestled against Jonathan's shoulder and felt his soft breath on her hair. For several moments he was silent, then he whispered, "Are you all right, Cat?"

"Yes."

"Then why the tears?" His thumb moved across her damp cheeks. "Why are you crying?"

"I'm crying for all that we've lost," Catherine said softly. "And for all that we've found."

Then Jonathan cupped her face in his hands, kissing her with silent promise and quiet passion. When their lips reluctantly parted, they held each other until dawn crept softly over the mountain.

Then they slept.

Chapter Nine

The snow was melting. Icy patches clung to shaded ground, crunching under Catherine's feet. The sound reminded her of that black day so long ago. Now she stood outside the cabin, envisioning how the tiny structure had appeared then and how much had changed.

The renovations had been done well, new materials blending subtly into old until only the sharpest eye could detect the variance. But Catherine could see the differences. She'd noticed them the moment she'd stepped out of the truck but hadn't realized the significance. There had been so much she hadn't realized then.

Life was so fragile. The events of a single day could change history and alter the entire future. Catherine had lived through one such day eleven years ago and she'd just survived another. She would never be the same.

"Cat?" Turning, she saw Jonathan on the front porch. He looked tense. "Is anything wrong?"

"The sun is shining, the air smells fresh and there's still enough snow for a decent snowball. What could be wrong?"

He frowned, then slowly moved down the steps. "You sound upset."

She avoided his gaze. Of course she was upset. Look at the grief she had caused Jonathan. Because of her, he had been seriously hurt, unfairly accused and imprisoned.

It didn't matter that she'd never intended for those terrible things to happen; they *had* happened. She couldn't erase that and she couldn't make amends.

Jonathan walked up behind Catherine, not touching her yet so close she could feel the warmth of his strong body. His voice was soft but edged with anxiety. "Do you regret what happened?"

Stunned, she turned toward him. "My God, of course I regret it! I would give anything—*anything* if it had never happened, but there's nothing I can do. Just thinking about it tears me up inside."

Jonathan looked absolutely stricken. He started to speak, then turned away and seemed to be fighting a surge of emotion.

For a moment, Catherine didn't understand, then she realized that they had been talking about two different things. He had been asking if she regretted their lovemaking and she had said—

"No! That's not what I meant." Frantic, she pulled at his arm until his expression changed from hurt to bewilderment. "What we shared last night was special and beautiful, a moment I'll cherish forever."

His eyes narrowed. "But you said—"

"When you came outside, I'd been thinking about everything you've suffered because of me, all the torment and the injustice you had to endure. That's what I regret, Jonathan, that's what tears me up inside."

"Oh." His embarrassed smile was endearing. "I was afraid you might be having second thoughts."

"No second thoughts. In fact I was even thinking about a second helping." She batted her eyes demurely. "Would that be gluttonous of me?"

"I like a woman with a healthy appetite." His smile twisted into a teasing leer. "Are you hungry?"

"Ravenous."

Wrapping her arms around his neck, Catherine brushed her lips over his mouth and was rewarded by his low groan of pleasure. He pulled her close, skillfully stroking her soft contours with intimate knowledge that was both comfortable and exciting. Like an affectionate kitten, Catherine rubbed her cheek against his neck. The skin was rough, unshaven and infinitely arousing. She flicked her tongue hesitantly and felt him shudder. Bolder now, she tasted him again, then lightly nipped his earlobe.

Instantly he made a growling sound low in his throat, cupped her bottom with his hands and held her tightly against him. "Honey if you do that again, I guarantee that we're going to shock the fur off every squirrel in the woods."

"Umm." She rubbed her lips down his flexing neck muscles. "Any squirrel worth its acorns has already bedded down for the winter."

"Now there's a thought," Jonathan mumbled, then scooped her into his arms. "Have you got any plans between now and April?"

She laughed softly and twirled a dark strand of hair curling over his collar. "I'm open to suggestions. What did you have in mind?"

"I think a demonstration is in order," Jonathan said huskily, then carried her up the steps and into the cabin.

He stood her in front of the fire, then took her hands and stared into her eyes. For several moments they simply gazed at each other, only their hands touching. Beside them the fireplace crackled with a golden warmth that paled in comparison to the love glowing in Jonathan's eyes.

Releasing Catherine's hands, Jonathan cupped her face with such gentleness, such tender reverence, that she nearly cried. Then he kissed her softly and whispered, "I've dreamed about loving you like this for such a long time. It doesn't seem real. I'm afraid to close my eyes for fear you'll disappear."

"I won't disappear, Jonny." She slid her palms over his chest, caressing him through the soft flannel, then slowly unbuttoned his shirt. When she'd completed the task, she brushed her lips over his bare chest. He groaned.

Then he lifted her sweater and softly caressed her breasts. He rubbed his tongue on her sensitive nipples until they stood erect. Catherine closed her eyes, tilting her head back to allow him full access to her body. His touch inflamed her. Heat radiated like tiny electric shocks from her breasts to her belly and beyond until she couldn't bear the tortuous delight for another moment.

With a soft cry, she stepped back. Jonathan straightened and watched her intensely. His eyes were hot with passion but cautious, as though he feared a forceful move, a thoughtless gesture, would send her skittering away.

Meeting his gaze, Catherine took the hem of her sweater and lifted it over her head. Without taking her eyes from Jonathan's face, she tossed the garment aside and slipped out of her slacks.

As she stood before him, bare breasts shining in the glow of flickering flames, his lips fell apart, and his shoulders tensed a moment before he shrugged out of his shirt.

Catherine could only stare. God, he was gorgeous. Every muscle gleamed in the firelight, accentuating the strong contours of his upper body. His arms had shape and substance; his smooth chest curved into a well-formed waist, where a line of dark hair pointed downward. Catherine's gaze followed.

Slowly, almost teasingly, Jonathan unbuttoned his jeans and lowered the zipper. Then he stopped, waiting.

Alarmed, Catherine quickly looked up wondering if he'd changed his mind. Then she recognized the smoldering heat in his eyes and what he wanted. She smiled.

Kneeling, she leisurely worked the denim over his hips and down his legs. She took her time, knowing that every feathery touch of her fingers against his bare skin made his muscles quiver in anticipation.

When the jeans were crumpled at his ankles, Jonathan pushed them away and dropped to his knees. He took Catherine's face in his hands, his mouth seeking hers with an urgency that sent them both into a frenzy of need. She memorized his body with her hands, touching him everywhere, needing to feel his ardent response. Catherine's skin was on fire, and her blood pulsed through her veins with frightening force.

Then they were lying on the braided rug in a tangle of slippery limbs and searching hands. The room was alive with sounds, pounding hearts and whispered words, soft gasps of pleasure and tiny frantic cries.

Spurning a gentle union, they were consumed by the fury of their passion. Their bodies joined with searing heat and explosive hunger, as though the power of their lovemaking could replace the lost years.

Afterward, they fell back exhausted. Jonathan cradled Catherine in his arms and stroked her softly.

She breathed a satisfied sigh. "You're such a beautiful lover, so powerful yet so tender that you take my breath away."

"You inspire me," he murmured, brushing his lips over her silky hair. "You give me strength, Cat. You always have."

Catherine went still. "I've given you heartache and pain. I never wanted to, but I did."

"That's in the past."

"Is it?" She turned toward him, wrapping the afghan around her body. "What about the future, Jonny?"

"What about it?"

"Do we have one?"

He regarded her for a moment then asked, "Do you want one?"

"Yes. I don't know if I can make up for all the grief I've caused but I want to try."

His expression was unreadable but his voice tightened. "Penance is poor motivation for establishing a relationship, Catherine."

"Is that what you think? That I'm willing to sacrifice myself out of some misguided sense of guilt?" Rolling off his lap, Catherine grabbed her sweater and angrily pulled it over her head. Muttering under her breath, she slipped on her pants, then got to her knees and indignantly put her hands on her hips.

"For all your famed intellect, you are one of the most frustrating creatures God ever put on this earth. Do I look like a human doormat?"

Her vehemence startled him. "Of course not."

"Good," she snapped. "Then listen closely because I'm not going to say this again. We both survived a tragedy but my suffering has been nothing compared to what you've endured. I wish I could snap my fingers and change history, but I can't. I can't change what happened to you, and you can't change the fact that I was responsible for a lot of it."

"Cat, it wasn't all your fault—"

She interrupted. "Whether it was or it wasn't isn't the point. I love you, Jonathan Stone. I think I've always loved you, even when your memory was simply a shadowy presence in my dreams. You were *with me* and subconsciously, I knew that."

"And what you feel right now, is it enough for a lifetime commitment?"

She hadn't really thought about her feelings in such universal terms. "We both need the chance to find out."

"Life isn't a snowy mountaintop and a warm cabin. Our lives are in different worlds. Are you going to throw away your career, dismiss all you've achieved for yourself? Or shall I?"

"Why are you trying to make everything sound so impossible? If we care for each other, we'll make it work." Catherine's voice broke. "Do you still care for me?"

"You know that I do." But his voice was tinged with sadness, and he stared into the cooling fireplace. "I have to be sure that we're not trying to relive the past by mistaking emotional memories and a weekend romance for something deeper."

That hurt. Dazed, Catherine sat back on her heels. "Is that all we had?"

Her stunned expression cut Jonathan to the quick. He hadn't meant to sound so cynical and he'd never wanted to hurt her. Things had simply spiraled out of control between them. He felt like he'd been strapped into a roller coaster and pushed over a cliff.

Now as he looked at Catherine, Jonathan wanted only to haul her into his arms and make love to her until the confusion in her eyes turned into heated passion. He longed to kiss away her pain, loving her sweet body until she called his name in that choked little voice that drove him insane. And then he wanted to lock them both in this damned cabin so that reality would never tear them apart again.

He wanted to do all that; instead, he crossed his arms protectively and forced himself to avoid her gaze.

"What we have is a history together." Jonathan struggled for words. "But for you, this weekend has been like watching a movie for the very first time. You're enthralled with the scenery and the emotion and you've become swept up in the story because you wonder how it will end. Once the final credits roll up the screen, the mystery is gone. The movie is over. You'll walk out of the theater and go back to your life."

Catherine sat back, hugged her knees and gazed thoughtfully into space. "You must think me quite a fool."

Startled, he looked up quickly. "No I don't."

"Then stop using quaint little metaphors and talk to me like an adult. I've grown up, Jonathan, a fact that seems to have eluded you." She stared right at him. "Are you certain this isn't some kind of vendetta? Bringing me here, bombarding me with memories until I fell into your bed, was it all a charade so that you could reject me to salve your bruised male ego?"

"You know better than that."

"Do I?" Catherine turned away. "I didn't reject you eleven years ago and I'm not rejecting you now."

"The movie isn't over, Cat. You still don't know the ending."

"What? There's . . . more?"

Her eyes filled with fear, and Jonathan could have kicked himself for that slip of the tongue. "It's just that your first few months in Europe are still hazy, that's all."

"But that was afterward, after everything had happened between us." Catherine's voice was thin and hesitant. "You said you had questions, too. Haven't I answered all of your questions?"

Jonathan felt icy perspiration bead his forehead. "It doesn't matter any more."

"It matters to me. My mind is totally blank—no images, no flashes, nothing. I thought I'd remembered everything. If I haven't, tell me . . . please."

"No." This was getting out of hand again, and he felt a surge of panic. "If I'd known what you would go through, I never would have brought you here. I never wanted you to be hurt, Cat, and God knows I never wanted—" He bit off the words as the completed thought rolled through his mind. *I never wanted to fall in love with you again.* But he had. Heaven help him, he had.

And as for the answer he'd so myopically sought all these years, suddenly Jonathan didn't want to know. Instinctively, he now realized that his futile search had been compelled by pure fantasy.

The realization was deflating. He'd accused Catherine of deceiving herself while he'd blithely pursued his own fictional happy ending.

Catherine's touch startled him. Her eyes were filled with compassion and concern. "What is it that you never wanted?"

He cleared his throat and wiped his forehead. "I never wanted you to feel guilty. That was never my purpose."

"What was your purpose? You say you don't want revenge, but I feel your anger. You say I'm not responsible for what happened, yet I hear accusation in your voice." Her words grew softer. "And you reject me, but I see my love reflected in your eyes."

The impact of her quiet words struck a killing blow. He covered his eyes and tried to compose his thoughts. She was right, but she was wrong. That didn't make sense, but at the moment there wasn't much that did make sense to him.

Finally, he managed to speak. "The anger you feel, the accusation you hear is directed toward myself, Catherine, not toward you. I took advantage of your confusion and your vulnerability. That wasn't my intention but as the proverb goes, 'the road to hell is paved with good intentions.' I feel like I'm on that road in a fast car with no brakes. I can't stop hurting you and I can't stop hurting myself."

After a moment of silence, Catherine took a deep breath. Her voice was clear and steady. "Then let's jump out, Jonny. Let's jump out of the car and start walking."

He looked up. "I don't understand."

"There's another old proverb—'a journey of a thousand miles begins with a single step.' Neither of us knows what the future will bring. If we had the gift of prophesy, none of this ever would have happened in the first place. All we can do is to go on, one step at a time. I don't know where our journey will end, but I do know that I want to walk with you as far as we both can go."

Jonathan wanted that, too. Deep down, hope still flickered like a dying flame. But the years had taken their toll. Hope was a weakness, and weak men didn't survive.

"I used to believe that we had free will and complete control over our lives," he said. "Now I know that the world can step in at any moment, and everything you love can be destroyed in a heartbeat." Jonathan clenched his jaw and looked away. "I can't go through that again, Cat, not even for you."

Catherine picked her way carefully through the woods. The sun was shining, although the forest foliage deflected most of the warming rays. She shivered, then zipped up her nylon jacket to protect herself against the crisp breeze.

Standing still, she glanced around and listened, trying to get her bearings. If her memory served her—and it frequently didn't—the creek should be over that knoll. Jonathan would be there, she was certain. It was a place where he'd always found solitude when struck by one of his pensive moods. After their heavy discussion this morning, Jonathan had kissed her cheek and wandered off to think things through.

That had been two hours ago, so Catherine had decided to follow. Not that she was invading his privacy, of course. That would be rude. However, there was no law that said she, too, couldn't enjoy the solace of a pristine wilderness. If she happened to run into Jonathan, well, life was full of little coincidences.

On the south side, the snow had nearly disappeared, and she lost her footing on a slick blanket of pine needles. Reaching up, she grabbed a low-slung branch to steady herself. At the top of the rise, she looked down into a small ravine. It didn't look familiar.

Maybe she was lost. That would be swell, she thought irritably. The idea of wandering through the forest waiting for another well-timed rescue was humiliating, and she pushed the unpleasant thought aside.

Then she heard a soft lapping sound. Squinting through the trees, she saw the reflection of sunlight on water. The creek. Thank goodness.

Relieved, she climbed over a large rock and started down the north side of the slope. It was colder here, with patches of snow still clinging stubbornly to the shady areas. Catherine was so engrossed with scanning the creek for Jonathan that she didn't pay attention to where she was stepping. Her foot hit a patch of ice and the next thing she knew, she was skidding down the hill on her bottom.

She made a sharp sound of surprise, then shrieked as her leg hooked a tree, spinning her around to continue her descent backward. She slammed into something hard and heard a masculine grunt of pain.

Dazed and panting, Catherine looked up at the swaying pine boughs and realized that she was stretched out on something warm. Gazing down the length of her prone body, she saw four legs. What an odd hallucination, she thought fuzzily and noted that two of the feet wore hunting boots suspiciously similar to Jonathan's.

Then she felt a strange vibration against her back and heard a low groan. The booted feet moved. Catherine blinked, then rolled to her side, propping herself up. "Jonathan! Are you all right?"

He winced. "I'd be a lot better if you'd get your elbow out of my stomach."

"Oh...sorry." Catherine scrambled to her knees and slipped her arm under Jonathan's shoulders.

He sat up rubbing the back of his head. "You sure know how to make an entrance."

Smiling weakly, she shrugged. "I should have been more careful."

"What are you doing here?"

"Just taking a little walk—" She flushed at his knowing stare. "Oh all right. I was looking for you."

"You found me," he muttered, massaging his sore stomach. "You shouldn't be wandering around alone, though. What would you have done if you'd gotten lost again?"

"I would have hugged a tree and waited for you to find me."

"What makes you think I would have looked?"

"Old habits die hard."

Smiling, Jonathan shook his head. "You're pretty sure of yourself, aren't you?"

"Not really. I just pretend to be confident. Actually, I'm scared to death."

He sobered and caressed her cheek with his thumb. "What are you scared of, honey? Me?"

"I'm scared *for* you, not *of* you."

"What does that mean?"

"You've been through so much, it's hardened you on the outside. But in here—" she touched his chest "—you're the same man, gentle and loving and soft. You can be wounded."

He regarded her for a moment, then stood and offered his hand. She took it and swung to her feet, brushing dried leaves from her pants. Jonathan gazed through the trees. "I like this part of the forest."

"I know. You always used to come here when you needed to be alone." Catherine pushed a rough pebble with the toe of her sneaker. "I never really understood that."

"What did you not understand?"

"Your need to be alone. I mean, you've always been pretty much by yourself and in a way, so have I. I hated the loneliness. When we were together, I felt so happy and so complete, that I couldn't understand why you needed to get away from me."

"I wasn't trying to get away from you. I was trying to get in touch with myself." He plucked a twig off a nearby branch and absently rolled it in his palm. "The universe is a big place, and each of us holds such a tiny part of it. Being surrounded by nature reminds me of that and puts things back in perspective. I begin to see myself differently."

"And how do you see yourself now?"

He pursed his lips and shredded the twig. "As a coward."

Stunned, Catherine stared for a moment, then emitted a dry laugh. "Stone, you're a lot of things—some of them a bit unpleasant—but you are not now nor have you ever been a coward."

"I was ready to run from you and from my own feelings because I was afraid of being hurt. If that's not cowardice, then I don't know what is."

The admission touched Catherine deeply. "Does that mean that you've decided to stand your ground and face whatever comes?"

"I'm going to try." Dropping the pulpy remains of the twig, Jonathan met Catherine's questioning gaze. "I've spent so many years looking for you that I lost sight of why. The search became more important than the reason."

"And what was the reason?" She held her breath, awaiting his answer.

"The reason was that I couldn't accept that what we had was gone. I wouldn't admit it then but suddenly you were here and I had to face you. Then I had to face myself." He took her hand and kissed it. "You were right, Cat. We don't know what the future holds but if you're willing to take things one day at a time, so am I."

Tears blurred her vision, and she wiped away the moisture. "That's all I want."

"Then you have it." He took a deep breath and released her hand. Before he looked away, Catherine saw his red eyes and knew that he, too, had been deeply affected. "Are you ready to go back?"

She sniffed. "Back to the cabin or back to the city?"

"Both," he said seriously. "We can't hide out here forever and we'll never be able to go forward while we're living in the past."

He was right. Catherine knew that, but was deeply saddened by the thought of leaving. "All right," she said softly. "When would you like to leave?"

He jammed his hands in his jacket pocket and stared at the patch of blue sky peeking through the thick treetops. "I suppose if we left now, we could be back in L.A. by dinnertime."

Catherine's heart sank. "I suppose so."

"On the other hand, we'd probably be more rested tomorrow morning."

She latched onto his cue. "Absolutely. In fact, I'm really a bit too tired right now to take on such a long trip. Tomorrow morning would be much better."

Jonathan was still gazing upward, but she saw the corner of his mouth twitch. "Tomorrow, then."

"Yes," she whispered breathlessly. "Tomorrow."

That gave them tonight. Intuitively, Catherine knew that those remaining hours would be special. Very special.

The hike back to the cabin worked up a healthy appetite. Since this would be their last evening at the cabin, they decided to drive into Lake Arrowhead Village for the makings of a special dinner.

Pink with excitement, Catherine climbed into the cab of Jonathan's truck. She loved the village with its quaint elfin motif framed by the sparkling blue lake.

Amused by her enthusiasm, Jonathan slid into the driver's seat and flipped the ignition. The engine roared to life. Suddenly, Catherine felt uneasy. Something was missing. The truck cab seemed oddly empty.

She stared at the vacant seat between them. In Jonathan's old pickup, that had been Mackie's place. The silly dog had absolutely loved riding in the truck. Catherine remembered how the wiry little animal would run in circles around the pickup, whining hopefully, then jumping up with his paws on the door handle.

Smiling, Catherine recalled the day Jonathan's key ring had disappeared. After tearing the cabin apart, they'd noticed Mackie waiting patiently beside the truck with Jonathan's keys dangling from his whiskered mouth.

Naturally, such chutzpa should be rewarded, so they'd all hopped into the truck and driven aimlessly around the mountain. As always, Mackie had perched politely in the middle, tongue lolling happily while his bright little eyes took in the sights.

Catherine touched the seat, brushing her fingertips over the upholstery and fighting an unexpected surge of emotion. Jonathan's hand covered hers and when she looked up, she saw compassion in his eyes. He understood.

Jonathan squeezed her hand, and she managed a thin smile. "I'm fine," she said. "Let's go."

Nodding, Jonathan put the car into gear and steered toward the narrow rutted road. Catherine studied the scenery. She recognized a fallen log rotting beside the path and an unusually shaped pine that resembled a huge bonsai.

Before she was expecting it, the road melted into a paved highway. "That didn't take long," she said.

"The cabin is only a half mile back," Jonathan replied. "The access road is so poor that it can be walked faster than it can be driven, so it seems farther than it really is."

Up ahead, Catherine saw a large service station on the right. Jonathan slowed, then turned in and pulled up to a gas pump.

"This will just take a minute," he said, then popped the hood and exited the cab.

While Jonathan tended to the mundane necessities of gas and oil, Catherine glanced around the new facility. There used to be a tiny garage with a couple of ancient pumps in this location. All that had been replaced by a huge full-serve station, 24-hour grocery and a spiffy service bay complete with a fleet of shiny new tow trucks.

Then she noticed a row of pay telephones. She should call the hotel.

No, she wasn't going to do it. Any messages she might have could wait for her return. Uncle Brad would have learned about her change in plans two days ago and had probably called several times leaving messages that ranged from fairly furious to downright hysterical. Another day's delay wouldn't matter.

On the other hand . . .

With a sigh, Catherine climbed out and ran to the nearest telephone. She just wanted to be certain that there were no real emergencies. One of her uncle's tantrums was hardly an emergency but she couldn't suppress a niggling fear that when she hadn't been on that plane, he might have had a heart attack or something equally awful.

Dropping coins into the slot, she dialed. The telephone rang.

"Regency Plaza" came the crisp response.

Catherine covered one ear to muffle traffic noise. "This is Catherine LeClerc. Do I have any messages?"

"One moment, please." After a pause, the desk clerk returned and read the list. There had been one call from Mrs. Waldenhoff, two from Maurice and only one from Uncle Brad.

But that one had been a shock. "Could...you repeat that last message?"

"Certainly, Miss LeClerc. Mr. Madison will be arriving at LAX tonight at ten and will come directly to the hotel."

"I...see. Ah, when Mr. Madison arrives please tell him that I will meet him in the suite sometime tomorrow. Thank you." Numbly, Catherine hung up the phone. This was bad news. Jonathan would be driving her directly to the hotel and he'd probably insist on seeing her to the room. No way did Catherine want Jonathan Stone and Bradford Madison in the same room. Actually, she didn't even want them in the same city. Jonathan obviously hated her uncle.

Until things had been resolved, Catherine simply had to keep the two of them apart. She decided to keep the news of Bradford's arrival to herself.

As Catherine walked back toward the truck, she noticed a large lot containing row after row of cars and a sign proclaiming it a Park-And-Ride facility. She saw a bright yellow minibus with the words Valley Shuttle emblazoned on the side. That was also a new addition. The mountain was changing and that saddened her.

She climbed into the truck just as Jonathan opened the driver's door. He winked at Catherine, reached under the seat for his wallet then extracted a plastic card and handed it to a greasy attendant. "How are things going, Ralph?" Jonathan asked politely.

Ralph's Adam's apple bounced. "Better'n fair. Need more snow, though. Flatlanders don't come spend their money if'n there ain't no snow."

After filling out the charge slip, Ralph handed the small clipboard to Jonathan and peered into the cab. "'Afternoon, ma'am. Havin' a nice day?"

Catherine smiled. "Yes, thank you. I haven't been up here in quite a while and things have certainly changed."

"Yep, that they have." Ralph took the signed slip and ripped out the carbons. "So many folks moving up here, can't hardly get down the hill during rush hour. My partner and me put in that little bus a few years back. Best move we coulda' made."

Jonathan put his copy of the slip in his wallet. "I take it that the shuttle business is booming."

"Yep." Ralph pursed his thin lips, then spit on the oily pavement. "Paid for a whole new station. Next year, we're gonna' get us two more of them buses and buy the whole damn mountain." Cackling at his own joke, Ralph tipped his hat at Catherine, gave her a toothy grin, then sauntered off to the next customer.

"Quite a colorful character," Catherine commented as Jonathan steered back onto the highway. "What happened to the little gray-haired man who used to own the station?"

"He sold out years ago."

"That's too bad. I liked him."

"It got too crowded around here for him, as I recall." Jonathan slid a glance at Catherine. "Civilization is moving up the hill. There's even a realtor from San Bernardino who's been after me to sell out."

"Sell the cabin?" Catherine went cold at the very thought.

"They'd just bulldoze the cabin. They're after the forty acres that goes with it for a time-share condo development."

"You're not going to let them do that, are you?"

"They're offering serious money," Jonathan replied thoughtfully.

"But the cabin...*our cabin*? Oh, Jonathan, you wouldn't—" She saw the mischievous glint in his eyes as he tried to suppress a grin and realized he'd been teasing. "Very funny."

"So was the look on your face."

"I'd forgotten about your macabre sense of humor."

"And I'd forgotten how much fun it is watching you puff like an indignant blowfish."

"I don't puff."

"You puff," Jonathan said matter-of-factly. "Your cheeks pooch out and your face gets red and your eyes kind of bulge— Ouch!" He rubbed his pinched thigh and quickly added, "But on you it looks good."

She smiled sweetly. "Thank you."

They drove in silence for several minutes. Catherine felt relaxed and happier than she'd been in many years. Then niggling doubts crept into her mind. She wondered why her uncle had been so upset that he'd jumped on the first available flight to Los Angeles. That didn't make sense, but then a lot of things were still a mystery to Catherine. For example, she still couldn't understand why Jonathan had waited so long to contact her. He'd mentioned something about a search, but a man with his resources certainly should have been able to locate her.

If he'd really wanted to, that is.

Jonathan noted her mood change. "A penny for your thoughts."

She managed a smile. "That might be a bit cheap."

"Name your price." His response was casual but his eyes were sharp. "What's on your mind?"

"I was just wondering..." She chewed her lip briefly, then took a deep breath and blurted her question. "Why couldn't you find me? I know France isn't exactly around the corner, but I wasn't in hiding."

"Weren't you?" Jonathan's knuckles whitened as he tightened his grasp on the steering wheel. "What do you remember about those first few months in Europe?"

"Bits and pieces, mostly, but I've already told you that." Catherine felt a bit queasy as she tried again to pull those days into focus. "I wasn't completely recovered, I guess. Things are still hazy, as though I'd been tranquilized or something."

"Then you can't know for certain what happened during that time."

She reluctantly acknowledged that. "But I know we had a forwarding address."

"Yes. It was a post office box in Chicago."

"Chicago?" That was a shock to Catherine's system. "But we were never in Chicago... at least, I don't believe we were."

"You weren't." Jonathan sighed. "For the first year, I admit that I didn't do anything except try to get my head together. When I did try to find you, I ran into one stone wall after another. You may not have been hiding, but Madison did a pretty good job of covering your tracks."

"What are you talking about?"

"It turns out that your uncle had a friend in Chicago. The guy picked up the forwarded mail, repacked it and sent it on to France."

"How do you know that?"

"Eventually I went to Chicago and confronted him. By that time, the post office box had been closed and I had no way of tracking any farther unless Madison's cohort admitted where he'd sent the mail. He wouldn't. The trail died."

Catherine considered this. "But what about my passport? That's public record and every destination would be accounted for."

"True enough," Jonathan said grimly. "But there was never a passport issued for Cathy Greer, so I had no reason to suspect you'd left the country."

"Oh Lord. I never thought about it, but—" Catherine swallowed, feeling as though she'd swallowed a brick.

"What is it?"

She moaned and rubbed her forehead. "My passport was in the name of Catherine Elaine Madison."

The truck lurched, and Jonathan quickly dragged his eyes back to the road. He said nothing, but his jaw twitched madly.

"I know what you're thinking, but it's not true." Catherine stared into her lap and fidgeted. "Uncle Brad was my guardian so it was easier to use his last name on school records and medical files, that kind of thing. Since the guardianship papers were in the name of Madison, he used them instead of my birth certificate. It just saved a lot of time and questions."

"It was also illegal as hell."

"Technically, I suppose." Catherine cleared her throat. "But as you can see, it wasn't any kind of deliberate deception."

"Of course not." Jonathan bit off each word, then turned into the village parking lot.

Catherine gasped and rolled down the window. "It hasn't changed a bit."

"Not much. There's a video arcade where the pizza parlor used to be, but other than that it's not much different."

As soon as the truck was parked, Catherine leaped out and looked around. Memories flooded her. "Do you think that the candy shop still sells Gummy Bears? Remember that marvelous fudge? Oh look! There's the bakery where we bought that beautiful cake for..." The word trailed away and Catherine frowned. For what?

She vividly remembered every nuance of that wonderful day. They'd been planning a big celebration dinner, but for the life of her, Catherine couldn't recall what they'd been celebrating.

Jonathan spoke tensely. "What is it, Catherine?"

"I don't know exactly." A pit of fear opened deep inside, frightening her. It was the same icy feeling that had been assaulting her for weeks, an emotional warning that subconscious secrets were boiling to the surface.

No more, she begged silently. Another shattering revelation would be more than she could endure.

Chapter Ten

It was dark when they returned to the cabin. Jonathan lit the oil lamp while Catherine unloaded groceries on the small kitchen counter. She was quiet and withdrawn. Something was obviously bothering her but his repeated queries had met with limp assurance or stony silence.

During the shopping trip, Catherine had been methodical and specific in selecting menu items. At first, Jonathan had believed her choices merely coincidence. Eventually, he came to the unnerving conclusion that whether she realized it or not, she was meticulously duplicating the meal they'd shared on one very special night. If she remembered that night, sooner or later she would remember what they'd been celebrating.

That was a terrifying realization.

Jonathan pushed back the chair and went to the window. He was angry with himself. After all, he had *wanted* her to recall that night; it held the key to his final elusive answer. Now he wasn't certain that he wanted to know. What's more, he had severe doubts about Catherine's ability to even handle the memory.

Only a fool set dynamite on a snow ridge and then tried to stop the avalanche.

Jonathan wasn't a fool. He'd had ample opportunity to stop the detonation of memories Catherine had endured, but he hadn't done so. Because he still needed to know. He hated himself, but he had to have that final answer. That's why he had allowed this to continue and, God help him, that's why he would see it through.

A soft clunking sound distracted him. Turning, he saw Catherine placing two candlesticks on the table, just as she'd done so long ago. Then she turned on the portable radio, adjusting the station until she found the mellow background music she wanted. Her expression was strange, determined yet unsure. He wondered if she realized how precisely she was recreating the past.

She chewed her lower lip in concentration, then began to set the table. "The dishes are different," she murmured.

A lump formed in his chest. "The old ones were broken."

"Of course. The explosion." Her voice was mechanical, devoid of emotion. "These will do."

He made no response, and Catherine robotically completed her task. If she pulled out the teak bowl and wanted him to—

"Would you please make the salad?" she asked suddenly.

Swallowing, Jonathan stared at the wooden bowl she offered, then managed to nod. There was no doubt now as to where this evening would lead.

For the next half hour they quietly busied themselves with preparations, each lost in thought. Finally Catherine placed the roast chicken on the table and called over her shoulder. "The ginger ale should be chilled by now. Could you open it, please?"

Without awaiting his answer, Catherine stared at the table. Everything seemed about right, she thought, except the bowl of new potatoes should be by Jonathan's plate. She made the adjustment without considering why such a minute detail had even concerned her.

Actually, she felt a bit strange and wondered if she was coming down with some kind of virus. Her head buzzed a little, and she felt numb, not quite here. That alone was odd, because this dinner was so very important to her. She wasn't sure why, but everything had to be just perfect.

Standing back, she took a final look at the table and was satisfied.

Jonathan walked up beside her holding a bottle and two small tumblers. "I don't know why we couldn't have gotten a decent champagne."

"I thought you preferred soft drinks," Catherine replied, frowning. Although she couldn't remember the specifics of their last celebration dinner, she vividly recalled that they'd toasted the future with ginger ale. Of course, she'd only been seventeen at the time, not old enough to drink.

Catherine had been too young for a lot of things in those days, things like falling in love and getting married. At least, that's what the law had said. But her heart had said otherwise, and Cathy Greer had always followed her heart; Catherine LeClerc had not.

That realization offered Catherine's first real insight into why the preceding years could have been so superficially successful, yet so emotionally unsatisfying. She'd tried to please others—her uncle, her teachers, her audience—and yet had always suppressed her own unhappiness. Catherine's secret grief had always been hidden; even from herself.

"Do you know what you're doing, Cat?" Jonathan's soft voice startled her.

"I'm setting the table."

"But do you realize *how*?" With a sweep of his hand, Jonathan encompassed the scene. "The candlesticks, the menu, even the ginger ale is exactly as it was eleven years ago."

"Is it?" Catherine knew that it was; she simply didn't know why. She sighed. "Yes, I guess it is."

He set the glasses on the table and poured the bubbly drink. "Do you remember that evening?"

"Parts of it. It happened before that...last weekend, didn't it?"

"Yes, it was a couple of weeks earlier. What else do you recall?"

Catherine rearranged the filled glasses to just the proper spot. "I remember that we were both happy and excited about something. It was a big celebration about—" she concentrated briefly "—about our wedding? Why are you looking at me like that?"

"Like what?"

"You know, like I've suddenly grown antlers or something."

"Sorry." Jonathan pulled out the chair for Catherine. "Just hungry I guess."

"Oh." She sat down, then quietly waited until Jonathan had seated himself. "Was that it? Was that the night you asked me to marry you?"

Jonathan appeared to be totally engrossed in carving the main course. "We discussed marriage that evening. Hold up your plate."

Catherine complied and Jonathan served a healthy portion of roast chicken. Since he obviously was more interested in dinner than historical events, Catherine shrugged off a disquieting sense of doom.

After a few minutes, their conversation grew light and soon both were laughing as they reminisced about their happy times together. They recalled the rainstorm that had caught them unaware during a walk in the woods. Drenched and freezing, they'd struggled through the blinding downpour searching for Mackie, who had disappeared with the first raindrop. When they'd finally given up and managed to crawl back to the cabin, the dog had been perfectly dry, sitting on the front porch and impatiently wagging his tail.

There had been unnerving times as well. Neither of them had thrived on the deception required by their relationship, and the constant secrecy had been a strain.

As she sliced the angel food cake, Catherine commented on the furtive bustle of those days. "It seemed that we were always rushing."

"That's because we were," Jonathan replied casually, accepting the dessert she offered. "There was always a deadline, either pushing to get away the minute your uncle stepped out of the house so we'd have more time together or—"

Catherine sat down and finished his sentence. "Or there was a mad frenzy to beat him back home. Sometimes I didn't quite make it, either. I remember driving up right after he got home and trying to explain the mud all over my tires."

"Is that the day you told him you'd been drag racing in the riverbed?"

"Umm. I was grounded for a week, but it was better than being sent to a convent." Catherine's eyes gleamed. "It was all so exciting and romantic."

Jonathan laid down his fork. "It was duplicitous and clandestine. I loathed it."

Catherine sobered. "I know. Eventually I did, too. Uncle Brad trusted me, and I lied to him. He was going through a crisis in his own life but instead of supporting him, I was sneaking out to be with you." Pushing away the unwanted cake, Catherine sighed. "I'm not proud of that."

"We both did things we didn't want to do," Jonathan said quietly. "There were alternatives but at the time, we didn't see them."

Catherine twisted her napkin. "You saw them. You wanted to be truthful and open about our feelings. I wouldn't let you."

"You were afraid. I understood."

She smiled. "You always understood me, even when I didn't understand myself. I loved that about you."

Jonathan's expression didn't change but his eyes reflected a hopelessness that Catherine couldn't understand. She would have been alarmed but the flash quickly disappeared, replaced by a dazzling smile that instantly turned her heart into butter.

The flickering candles and soothing music created a romantic mood. In the fireplace, red embers glowed with the same intense heat burning in Jonathan's eyes. Catherine's skin warmed, then grew hot, spellbound by the hypnotic Scorpio gaze.

Jonathan had always had an almost mystical power over her. That had never changed. With a look, a touch, a knowing smile, he took control of her deepest emotions. She felt exposed and vulnerable, yet oddly unafraid. Jonathan would never hurt her.

Instinctively, Catherine knew they were both captives, propelled by a love too strong to deny, too dangerous to ignore. She felt powerful and powerless, controlling and controlled.

Music drifted into Catherine's consciousness. She closed her eyes, gently swaying to the sweet melody, allowing the soft tones to caress her like a loving touch. She sighed contentedly, then realized that the delicate stroke across her cheek was quite warm and quite real.

She opened her eyes. Jonathan stood beside her, delicately tracing the contour of her cheek.

"May I have this dance?" He spoke in a throaty whisper, then lifted her into his arms before she could do more than nod.

Their fingers laced tightly, as though daring the world to pull them apart. Catherine laid her head on his shoulder, holding him close. As they moved together, she wished this moment could last for eternity. She was cocooned in his strong embrace, enveloped by his warmth. Woodsmoke and pine mingled with desire, an erotic blend of masculine scents that made Catherine's blood pressure soar.

His mouth rested lightly against her cheekbone. She felt his lips move as he turned his face into hers, then his mouth was moist against her skin. She moaned and moved her head back, allowing more extensive exploration.

Half-kissing, half-tasting, Jonathan slid his lips to her throat, then touched her throbbing pulse with his tongue. The gesture was so arousing that Catherine nearly pierced his shoulder with her fingernails. He didn't even flinch. Instead, he lifted his head and captured her mouth with searing intensity.

With a desperate whimper, Catherine tangled her fingers in his thick hair and pulled him closer. She opened her lips to him, then shuddered at his intimate response. Dizzy with the taste of him, she made a tiny sound of pleasure and realized that she couldn't feel the floor beneath her feet. After a moment's confusion, she realized that Jonathan had lifted her in his arms and was carrying her to the bed.

The room was swaying, and Jonathan was murmuring sweet words, and Catherine was lost in the erotic sensations flooding her. He had carried her like this before, cradling her sweetly in his arms as though she were infinitely fragile.

But was this then, she wondered hazily, or was this now? Time had stopped. There was no past and no future, only the present, only this glorious moment.

Burying her face in the curve of his shoulder, Catherine clung to him, shivering with delight as he whispered all the delicious details of how they were going to make love. Then he stumbled slightly, bouncing her.

"Be careful," she said dreamily. "Don't jostle the baby."

Jonathan froze.

Alarm bells went off in Catherine's brain, distant at first, then quickly growing louder and stronger. She felt an odd prickling sensation. Something was wrong but she was confused, dazed. The arms that held her were rigid, stiff with sudden tension.

Jonathan spoke in a strained voice. "What...did you say?"

"What did I say?" Catherine repeated numbly, then lifted her head from his taut shoulder and gazed blankly around. "I don't remember."

Lowering her feet to the floor, Jonathan straightened, then grasped her shoulders firmly, forcing her to meet his gaze. "Yes you do, Cat. Think."

She tried but her stomach knotted painfully, and her skull throbbed with the effort. "I don't want to talk any more, Jonny. Please. Let's go to bed."

"Not now." His voice broke, and he took a deep breath. "Think about the baby, Cat, think about our child."

"Our chi—" The word fell back into her throat, replaced by a low, moaning sound.

What was he saying? Why was he talking about babies and children and—

An image flashed through her mind. She remembered details of their first celebration dinner so clearly that she could have been watching a mental video. They had been toasting each other, laughing and clinking their glasses.

"Here's to our son," Jonny had said. "May he be first-string quarterback and the Superbowl's Most Valuable Player."

Cathy had feigned indignation. "No child of mine will grow up throwing a funny-shaped ball and being squashed by a stampede of uniformed neanderthals. Besides—" she rubbed her swelling tummy as confirmation "*—our daughter* will probably be valedictorian of her Harvard law class, then go on to become Attorney General of the United States."

Jonny flashed a delightfully crooked grin. "Don't you think that's a little ambitious?"

"For mere mortals, maybe." Cathy slid a sly look over the rim of her glass. "But not for one inheriting genetic superiority."

"Are you so sure that *he* will inherit my brains and your beauty?"

With a slitty-eyed stare, Cathy replied frostily, "You have that backward."

"I do? Hmm." Jonny managed to look contrite. "Then you could be right. In fact, *our daughter* just might skip the preliminaries and shoot straight to the presidency."

"That's better," Cathy replied, somewhat mollified.

Jonny's expression warmed, and he reached across the table to caress her hand. "I guess we don't need to worry about birth control any more, do we?"

Cathy smiled. "Apparently we didn't worry enough about that in the first place."

"I must have been careless," he said, sobering.

"It wasn't your fault. For all you know, I might have attacked those funny foil packets with a pin when your back was turned."

"Did you?"

"No." Cathy chewed her lower lip. "Are you sorry, Jonny? I mean, about the baby? I know we hadn't planned it this soon, but—"

"Shh." He placed a fingertip gently on her lips. "I'm the happiest man in the world. All my life, I've wanted a real family. Our baby is a miracle that we've created and there's nothing more important to me."

"So you still like me a little?" Cathy murmured.

Jonny lifted her hand to his lips, kissing the meadow grass ring on her finger. "You're everything to me, Cat. You're my love, my life and my future."

The memory slowly dissipated.

Trembling, Catherine swayed slightly and felt Jonathan's arms steady her. Oh God, she thought wildly. It was true. She'd been pregnant.

"Catherine, please." Jonathan's voice urged her softly but she felt his desperation. "Tell me about our child."

Frantically she pushed away, stumbling backward. "Let me think," she mumbled. "I have to think."

But Jonathan was too close to the answer he'd sought for a decade. His voice was ragged. "Was our baby born in Europe? God, Catherine, can't you even tell me if I have a son or a daughter? I have a right to know—" With a raw gasp, he fell silent.

Cool air brushed Catherine's back, and she knew he'd turned away from her. She covered her face, warming her icy skin with her palms. Knowing that she had been pregnant, Jonathan had assumed that somewhere they had a baby. No wonder he had searched all these years. It hadn't been some deep romantic bonding of souls; he had been looking for his child—their child.

The child he believed that she had taken from him.

And that's what they had argued about on that final fateful afternoon. Jonathan had insisted that they tell her uncle about the baby. Catherine had been terrified, knowing that Brad would be livid. At that time, Bradford Madison had been capable of almost anything. He was unpredictable and unstable from years of alcohol abuse and the emotional trauma of a disintegrating marriage. Catherine had tried everything to make Jonathan understand what could happen, what her uncle could do to destroy them.

In desperation, she had threatened to leave Jonathan, and they had quarreled fiercely. Then she had run out of the cabin and into the arms of fate.

But their baby... what had happened to their baby?

Catherine couldn't remember. Lord help her, she *couldn't remember*. An anguished cry bubbled from her throat, and she buried her face in her hands.

From what seemed a great distance, Catherine heard Jonathan's voice, strained by emotion. "Forgive me, Catherine. I shouldn't have pushed so hard, but we're so close now...please try."

Lowering her hands, she looked over her shoulder and saw agony in his eyes. He was afraid, she realized, every bit as frightened as she by what they might both discover. Panic made her irrational. "I-it was a mistake, a false alarm."

Slowly, he shook his head. "We went to the doctor together. He confirmed the pregnancy."

"It was too early to know for sure. Doctors aren't perfect, they don't know everything." Catherine raked her fingers through her hair and wildly scanned the room like a cornered animal. "I would know if I'd borne a child. Dear God, don't you think that I'd know that?"

"Catherine—"

"I can't talk about this." She grabbed her jacket and started for the door.

He stopped her, pulled the garment from her grasp and tossed it away. "This time, you're not going to run away. We're going to deal with this together."

"Not now—"

"Yes, now." He bit off the words angrily. "Face it, Catherine, face it now or you'll spend the rest of your life running, and I'll spend the rest of mine chasing you."

In his determined expression, Catherine saw the truth of his words. She *had* been running. Even as a child, she had dealt with problems by seeking escape. The ostrich approach had become so deeply ingrained that even her mind had followed suit, blocking out unpleasant memories, tucking them neatly away and hiding the hurt.

Jonathan was right. It was time to stop running, no matter what the cost. But what he was saying, what she was remembering boggled her mind. Her shoulders slumped and her head fell forward as though her neck could no longer support the weight. She murmured softly, thoughts escaping without conscious effort. "It must have been devastating for you to find me and not find our child."

The pressure on her arms instantly disappeared as Jonathan released his grip. Catherine couldn't look at him, couldn't face the torment she knew would be etched in his eyes. She heard him walk across the room, then pause and speak softly. "When you told me that you had no children, it almost killed me. All these years, I believed that you were somewhere raising our baby. Every August, I silently celebrated, knowing our baby was another year older and each time I saw a little boy or a little girl of the right age, I wondered if we had a daughter with soft green eyes like her mother. Sometimes I fantasized about a son, a strong boy with dark hair who would someday look like me."

Catherine wiped away invading tears and swallowed the sob surging up from deep inside her. Seeing Jonathan's torment cut her to the bone. Her amnesia had been a blessing, a protective shield of ignorance.

But Jonathan *had* remembered. All these years, he'd endured in the vain hope that Catherine could relieve his suffering only to have his pain increased tenfold.

Looking up, she saw him staring out the window, rigid and expressionless. "But when you saw the magazine article about me, you must have discovered that I had no children."

Jonathan raked his hair, then squeezed the back of his neck, loosening the stiff muscles. He spoke in a flat monotone. "I didn't believe it. You'd never been married, and your public relations people would have concealed any illegit—any children you might have had." A hint of bitterness seeped into his voice. "I told myself that you'd probably sent our child to a boarding school so you could further your career."

"You knew I wouldn't have done that."

"Did I?" He turned, his eyes hot and accusing. "You had surprised me before, Catherine. I wasn't going to underestimate you this time."

With some effort, she lifted her chin and met his hard stare. "Under the circumstances, I can see why you felt the way you did. But over the past weeks, you must have realized that hadn't happened."

"Yes." His eyes clouded with sadness. "The truth became painfully clear."

"What... truth?" she asked cautiously.

"You were injured and traumatized by your experience. Madison took advantage of that."

"Uncle Brad? What on earth could he possibly have to do with any of this?"

"I think that's rather obvious. You said yourself that you don't remember much about those first few months in Europe. Maybe he kept you sedated until the baby was born."

Catherine simply stared, unable to speak. What was Jonathan implying?

"Madison was your guardian. He had control over your legal affairs. Don't you understand?" Jonathan asked harshly, annoyed by her expression of disbelief. "He probably kept you doped up so you wouldn't know what he'd done."

"What could he have done? I don't understand why you're so angry with him. You act as though he—" Catherine's eyes widened in horrified comprehension. "You think he stole our baby, don't you?" The smoldering fury in Jonathan's eyes answered her question and she clutched her churning stomach. "No... you're wrong."

"Am I?" Jonathan growled. "Then tell me what happened, Catherine. Did *you* give our child up for adoption?"

"No!" She whirled on him. "How dare you even ask such a question?"

"Because I'm desperate," he snapped angrily. "Because somewhere in the world is a ten-year-old child who doesn't even know I exist. Somebody knows what happened to our baby and if it isn't you, there's only one other person it could be."

Catherine couldn't deny that. Weak and trembling, she stumbled to the table and sat down. Could Jonathan's theory be right? No. She couldn't believe it. Bradford Madison had faults, but he never would have done such a vile thing. There had to be another answer, an explanation locked deep in her mind.

"We have to know, Catherine," Jonathan said softly.

She took a deep breath. "Yes, we have to know."

"Then let's start at the beginning." He sat at the table and took her hand. "Tell me what you remember about being in the hospital."

"I've already told you everything."

"Tell me again."

Forcing her mind back, she recalled the white walls and antiseptic smell. As each image flowed into her mind, she dutifully related what she saw, what she heard. For half an hour, Jonathan urged and questioned; Catherine concentrated until her head throbbed, then responded the best she could.

The only new memory she had was of overhearing her uncle talking with a doctor. They'd been discussing Catherine—when she could travel and what kind of care she would require over the next few months. But their footsteps had grown faint and the voices had faded away.

Catherine could remember the silent, empty room. She had been heavily sedated, and Bradford had been extremely careful not to discuss anything of consequence in Catherine's presence. Apparently, he had allowed no one else to do so either.

Although obviously disappointed, Jonathan simply nodded and urged her on. "What happened when you arrived in France? Do you recall getting off the plane?"

"No, but I remember seeing the house my uncle rented in Versailles for the first time. It was a stone cottage with wild roses tangling over a picket fence. I thought it was lovely."

Closing her eyes, Catherine remembered the French countryside, green and lush, sprawling over gentle hills as far as the eye could see. The image was clouded, as though she was viewing a film shot through filmy gauze fabric.

Concentrating, she related her memories to Jonathan. There had been a garden behind the cottage. Catherine recalled sitting on a stone bench as a woman dressed in white gave her some kind of medication.

"What time of year was it?" Jonathan asked urgently.

"I don't know. It was cool, though. The nurse was wearing a sweater, and I wore a heavy coat. The sky was gray."

Pursing her lips, Catherine tried to focus the memory. It had still been winter then, she was sure of it. But there were other memories, warmer days when the garden had bloomed with young leaves and colorful flowers. She'd been picking daisies when Uncle Brad had brought a stranger onto the veranda. The man had been introduced as Catherine's tutor.

Jonathan's voice interrupted her thoughts. "Was that man your piano instructor?"

"No, he was from the American Embassy. I needed three additional credits for my high school diploma and I recall studying for an equivalency examination."

"When did you take the test?"

"In July. Uncle Brad drove me into Paris and after the exam, we had lunch in a quaint little bistro. The tables were all outdoors and were shaded by blue umbrellas."

Jonathan made a raspy sound, then spoke slowly. "Are you sure it was July?"

"Yes. The examination date is posted on my educational records. I have certified copies."

"What—" Jonathan cleared his throat and took a deep breath. "What were you wearing?"

"Wearing?" Catherine sounded hollow, even to her own ears. She felt as though she were in an echo chamber. "I don't know. A dress, I suppose."

She knew exactly what he was asking and why. By July, her eight-month pregnancy would have been obvious to all.

"Think, Catherine. You're sitting at the bistro having lunch. Picture the blue umbrellas and the patrons at the next table. Feel the breeze on your face. Close your eyes. Remember."

She complied, concentrating until she could actually hear her uncle's deep laughter and taste the creamy wine sauce that had been spooned over her meal. It had been a very warm day. She remembered dabbing her damp face and bare arms with the linen napkin.

Bare arms. Catherine suddenly remembered the dress.

It had been full-skirted and sleeveless, a blue cotton fabric printed with tiny white flowers. Lace had been appliqued across the fitted bodice and the matching sash belt.

As she went even deeper into her mind, she saw the scene with crystal clarity. Everything about that moment was strikingly vivid, street sounds and swaying shadows across the sidewalk, the hustle of the busy cafe . . . everything.

And her heart twisted in her chest.

She met Jonathan's anxious gaze, extending her hand in a gesture of grief and sorrow. The tiny flame of hope in his eyes flickered, then faded to blackness. Neither spoke, yet both knew. At that moment in time, in a quaint bistro somewhere in Paris, Catherine had not been pregnant.

The cabin was black as a tomb. Catherine shivered against the chill, sitting up in bed and pulling the blanket around her. From the sofa, she heard Jonathan's soft breathing and realized that he'd finally fallen into a fitful sleep. She was thankful that he'd found at least a few minutes of peace.

If she lived a thousand years, Catherine would never forget the hopelessness she'd seen in his eyes last night. Still, he'd stubbornly refused to accept the obvious and had insisted that the child could have been born prematurely. Catherine hadn't disputed him. Her own grief was too deep, too raw. She'd pleaded a headache and gone to bed alone, staring wakefully into the darkness while Jonathan had paced long into the night.

She'd told herself he was wrong, then silently wondered if he was right until her mind swirled with conflict and confusion.

There were two things of which Catherine was certain: Bradford Madison had answers, and Jonathan would go to any length to get those answers.

If Jonathan discovered that her uncle was in Los Angeles, the result would be too horrible to contemplate. Catherine hadn't forgotten the ugly altercation with Maurice. There was a seething rage buried deep in Jonathan that could explode with devastating consequences. Catherine couldn't allow that to happen. She had to confront Uncle Brad alone.

Quietly, she dressed and packed her suitcase. Through the window, she saw a gray pall and realized that it would soon be dawn. Hopefully, Jonathan would be exhausted enough to sleep for several hours. That would give her ample opportunity to walk to Ralph's service station and catch the earliest shuttle down the mountain.

Stealthily she tiptoed into the kitchen, easing a pad and pencil from a drawer. There was barely enough light to see the paper, but she managed to scrawl a brief note. She set the note on the table, then swallowed an overwhelming urge to wad up the paper and burn it. She didn't want to leave Jonathan, even for a day. But she had to. He'd be angry, but once he realized why she'd had to do this, he would understand.

A sound startled her.

On the sofa, Jonathan moaned, rolling his head painfully. He'd fallen asleep sitting up. Catherine went to the bed and pulled off a blanket, then gently covered him. His shoulders jerked, and she suppressed an urge to smooth his mussed hair.

She loved him so much. No matter what the future brought, she always would.

Picking up her suitcase, Catherine crept out the front door and down the porch steps. The air was cold, the sky as gray and heavy as her heart. Beyond the farthest peak, the white glow of sunrise barely illuminated distant storm clouds. The sun wouldn't shine today.

And as Catherine slowly walked down the icy rutted road, she wondered if the sun would ever shine again.

Chapter Eleven

Jonathan awakened with his head dangling over the sofa. Squinting into the gray pall, he massaged his knotted muscles and pushed himself into a sitting position. His neck responded with a sharp spasm, and he groaned. Beneath the jagged scar, his stiff shoulder protested the effort with searing pain. The weakened ligaments felt as though they would snap like dried-out rubber bands.

His bones ached. His head throbbed. It was hell to get old. Blinking, Jonathan glanced down at the blanket tangled around his body and smiled. Catherine had covered him. That was sweet.

Looking toward the tiny kitchen, he saw that the coffeepot still sat on the counter, empty and cold. Catherine wasn't awake yet. Good. She needed the rest. Last night, he'd heard her crying, a soft muffled sound as though she'd tried to conceal her sobs with a pillow. When he'd gone to offer comfort, she'd pretended to be asleep but he'd known that she wasn't. Hell, her entire body was stiff as she had tried to suppress the involuntary trembling. But he had respected her silent request and had left her alone. Eventually, the sobs had stilled, and the night had grown quiet.

Leaning forward, Jonathan propped his elbows on his knees and rubbed his stinging eyes. He could understand her grief and confusion. They both had suffered over the years, but they had suffered alone; now they would help each other. Together, they would get through this.

In spite of the nightmare they'd already survived, there was a ray of hope for the future. For Jonathan, the impossible dream had already become a reality. Catherine still loved him. Hope surged like a warming light. From now on, they would go forward, not back. They would share a future as well as a past.

And they would find their child.

In spite of everything he'd learned, Jonathan couldn't bring himself to give up. Bradford Madison was the key, he was sure of it. Somewhere, their child was waiting. He had to believe that, although he understood why the realization would be difficult for Catherine to accept. It would take time. After all, it had taken Jonathan eleven years to come to terms with their history; Catherine had only eleven days.

Eventually, she'd be a believer; she'd recognize the truth. Once they'd found their child, they would be the family destiny had intended.

Tossing off the twisted blanket, he stretched his arms and rotated his shoulders until the muscles relaxed slightly. He rolled his head, then stood, wincing while his bones cracked and popped. After six hours twisted like a frozen pretzel, he was lucky he could even move.

With a cup of coffee under his belt, he might even be able to think.

As stealthily as his creaking body would allow, Jonathan crept into the kitchen and put the pot on to boil. He glanced at the bedroom curtain and pictured how Catherine must look at this very moment. She'd be curled on her side with blankets pulled nearly over her head, and her face buried in the soft pillow. The urge to join her was almost overwhelming.

If he tiptoed in, easing back the bedcovers to kiss her soft neck, she'd moan and turn into his arms. He'd stroke her sleek body, caressing her until she gasped softly and made the little love sounds that drove him to the brink of madness. She'd beg him to love her and he'd—

He'd do nothing, damn it. What in hell was wrong with him, anyway? Just the thought of Catherine's sweetness made his entire body snap to attention, but the last thing she needed right now was a confrontation with his raging hormones. What she *did* need was consideration, understanding and support; and Jonathan was determined to provide that.

From the corner of his eye, he noticed a sheet of paper laying on the table. He stared at the white sheet and knew instantly that something was terribly wrong. The hairs on his neck stood up. He took two giant strides and snatched up the note.

Jonathan,
I must do this alone. Forgive me.

All my love, Cat

For a moment, his numb brain couldn't comprehend the meaning of the cryptic message. Dazed, he stared at the scrawl, reading it again and again, until his mind cleared and his heart went cold.

His hand, still grasping the paper, fell to his side, and he raised his head, staring at the bedroom curtain. Slowly, he walked across the wooden floor, each footstep echoing through the empty room like a pounding dirge drum. When he reached the curtain, he stopped and flexed his hand once before ripping the fabric aside.

She was gone.

He'd known that she would be, yet some spark of foolish hope had compelled him to look. Through narrowed eyes, he saw the evidence of her hasty departure. The bed was rumpled and unmade. The armoire door was still ajar. On the floor beside the bed lay a single brown mitten—used, discarded and forgotten. How appropriate.

The scene was self-explanatory, and a sane man would have accepted that. A man in love, however, was not sane. At that moment, a deadly fear dropped over him, the fear that Catherine was out there somewhere, hurt or freezing.

Grabbing his keys, he ran out the front door toward his truck. He yanked open the driver's door, then paused. Which way had she gone? Surely, she wouldn't have tried to cut through the forest. That would be suicide.

He paced the clearing, searching for a telltale footprint. There were dozens, his and hers, remnants of the past few days. He walked to the rutted road, looking for some clue that she'd passed this way.

He found it. Like a seasoned tracker, Jonathan examined every dent in the road's icy crust. There was a small footprint, then another. He saw a deep gouge at the side of the path, like something heavy had been dragged there. Something like a suitcase.

His jaw twitched in determination and with a final look down the road, he returned to his truck. If she'd made it, fine. If not, he couldn't leave her to fate.

Only his heart wasn't as logical and unyielding as his mind. Inside, he was in terrible pain. Catherine had left him. Again.

Why couldn't he accept that? Why was he speeding along this frozen path, airborne at every bump and fishtailing through every ice patch? Because he was driven by some irrational hope that she'd be just around the next curve, sitting on her suitcase and patiently waiting for him to appear.

But she wasn't. The highway loomed ahead, empty gray pavement, slickened by the dampness of an empty gray day.

His stomach burned as though he'd swallowed a vat of acid, but he drove on, scanning the roadside for a familiar figure. When he pulled into the station, even Jonathan's ever-vigilant, ever-hopeful heart had turned black and cold.

Ralph appeared, wiping his hands on a greasy rag and sporting a crooked grin. "Fill 'er up?" he asked cheerfully.

Jonathan shook his head. "Do you remember the woman who was with me yesterday?"

"Yep. Funny eyes, pointy nose . . . cute, that one."

"Have you seen her this morning?"

Ralph made an unpleasant sound then spit on the cold pavement. "'Bout an hour ago. Took the early shuttle."

Jonathan closed his eyes and took a deep breath. "Did she seem . . . all right?"

Pursing his thin lips, Ralph scratched his stubbly chin and considered the question. "Guess so. Gave her some coffee to warm her up, but she didn't talk much." The man's eyes narrowed. "Say, she didn't steal nothing did she? 'Cause if'n she did, I'll call down the hill and have 'em hold her at the station."

For a brief moment, Jonathan considered his answer. She *was* a thief, the worst kind. She'd stolen his trust; she'd stolen his heart.

But she hadn't stolen his self-respect. He wouldn't chase her. His pride was slightly frayed, but it was still intact.

Shaking off Ralph's inquiry, Jonathan jammed the truck into gear and peeled onto the highway heading back toward the cabin. His jaw clamped so tightly that his teeth ached, and he felt like a lump of molten lead had been dropped in his chest.

Jonathan was hurt and angry. After everything they had shared this weekend, Catherine had still turned away from him. Maybe she didn't trust him enough; maybe she was still ashamed of him, as he'd believed her to be so many years ago. Money didn't make the man. In Catherine's eyes, maybe Jonathan would always be a tough street kid spitting in society's face.

Regardless of her motives, she was gone and that was a bitter blow. Still, he was suspicious and wondered if she had remembered something more about their child, something that she was trying to conceal.

Either way, she'd obviously run back to her world of glitz and glamour. If she thought he would slink back into the shadows, she was sorely mistaken. He would find his own answers, and if Catherine Greer Madison LeClerc got in his way, she'd discover just how formidable an enemy Jonathan Stone could be.

* * *

The elevator slid open. Shakily, Catherine stepped out and leaned against the wall. An hour in the shuttle and two more hours on a smelly bus had been exhausting, but her ordeal was just beginning and she knew it.

According to the desk clerk, Uncle Brad had arrived last night and was driving the harried concierge to distraction with repeated inquiries as to Catherine's whereabouts. Apparently the message she'd left for her uncle had done little to quell his mounting hysteria.

She wanted to turn around and run back to the cabin, back to the safety of Jonathan's warm arms. But she couldn't, not yet, not until she'd found all the missing pieces to the past. Once the puzzle was solved, they could begin a new life together.

Strengthened by that thought, Catherine picked up her suitcase and marched resolutely to her room.

When she opened the door, Bradford was screaming into the telephone. "Listen, you insipid buffoon, I haven't the slightest interest in a recital of your ludicrous regulations. My niece is missing *now* and I insist that your department initiate an immediate search— Pardon me?" He paused, then exploded with outrage. "Forty-eight hours? That is totally unacceptable, sir. I demand to speak to your superior—"

"That's enough," Catherine said tiredly, dropping her suitcase and closing the suite door. "You seem to have a penchant for calling the police any time I disappear without leaving a notarized itinerary."

Whirling, Bradford saw Catherine, and his jaw sagged. Finally he found his voice, mumbled unintelligibly into the telephone and cradled the receiver. He cleared his throat. "You have some explaining to do, young lady."

She hitched one brow. "I'm not in the mood for a lecture, so drop the authoritarian attitude."

Bradford's pale eyes widened in surprise, and he absently smoothed his thinning gray hair. "I've been extremely concerned about you."

"I'm sorry you were worried. I left a message for you at the desk."

With a contemptuous snort, Bradford grasped his hands behind his back and lifted his sharp chin, exuding the commanding presence that was such an asset to his profession. While conducting, his long arms dominated the stage, riveting the attention of both orchestra and audience. Baton in hand, Madison became the focal point of his music, arms sweeping with bold strokes and an almost frenzied intensity. During a performance, his eyes would shine with joy and pride and confidence in his craft. At such times he seemed younger than his fifty-eight years.

Yet offstage, he seemed a rangy man, loose-boned and physically awkward. The transformation went even further, as professional confidence faded to the arrogance of frightened insecurity.

Catherine understood this. Others did not; consequently, Bradford was frequently shunned by those whose friendship he craved. In his loneliness, he turned to Catherine, the one person who tolerated his frailties and truly cared about him.

Sometimes she felt smothered by her uncle's need for comfort and reassurance. This was one of those times.

Catherine avoided her uncle's accusatory gaze and rubbed her eyelids. At least she wouldn't have a transcontinental flight to endure before she got some answers. For that she was grateful. Still, she was so tired, so emotionally drained that she wasn't at all certain that she'd be able to survive what was ahead.

Perhaps she could take a brief nap first—

But Bradford had other ideas. "I've come a very long way, Catherine. Surely, I'm entitled to an explanation."

Anger swelled inside her. She opened her eyes and defiantly lifted her chin. "No one asked you to drop everything and fly out here in a hysterical moment. I'm twenty-eight years old and have a right to conduct my own life as I see fit."

"And I have a right to be concerned when my own niece disappears without a word," he responded harshly.

"I sent word with Maurice, or didn't you bother to talk to him?"

Bradford emitted a sound of disgust. "Maurice was most uncooperative. All he said was that you had decided to take an unscheduled vacation. Frankly, my dear, I believe Mr. Bouchard has exhausted his usefulness as your manager."

"Oh you do, do you?" Catherine rose from the sofa, eyes flashing. "That is *my* decision to make. It's also my decision to go where I wish and be with whomever I choose without your pompous interference."

"Pompous?" Bradford sputtered, and his eyes bulged in shock. "What has come over you, Cathy? You haven't behaved in such a disrespectful manner since..." His words dissipated and his eyes narrowed suspiciously.

With a humorless smile, she finished his thought. "Since I was a teenager."

"Yes," he acknowledged cautiously. "You were quite rebellious then."

"And deceitful?" Catherine asked sweetly. "Poor Uncle Brad, you didn't know what to do with me, did you? All those raging adolescent hormones bursting out and suddenly, you'd lost control."

Although Bradford's expression remained impassive, his skin paled. Turning away, he walked stiffly to the window. After a few moments, he spoke quietly. "You've spoken with Stone, haven't you?"

The direct question took Catherine by surprise. "Yes."

His shoulders shook slightly, and his voice trembled. "I knew it. He is an evil man, Catherine. He's dangerous. Whatever he told you is a lie."

"You seem very certain of that."

He faced her, terror etched in his tight expression. "He's desperate. He would say anything, do anything to get what he wants."

"What is it he wants?" Catherine asked slowly, then held her breath and awaited the answer.

Bradford squared his shoulders and looked right at her. "Vengeance. He wants to destroy us."

Catherine's first instinct was to instantly deny the accusation and tell her uncle everything that she'd remembered. Something told her to wait, to see what information would be offered. At this point, she was still bewildered. These men were sworn enemies. She loved them both yet one of them could be deliberately deceiving her. All she trusted at this point were her own memories, but her recollections were flawed and incomplete.

She opted for discretion. "Why would he want revenge?"

Bradford regarded her thoughtfully, as though considering his answer carefully. "You knew him once, kitten, a long time ago."

Catherine was relieved at the honest answer. Still, she was cautious and settled for a neutral response. "Oh?"

Clearing his throat, Bradford stared into space, seeming lost in thought. "There was a misunderstanding that led to some... unpleasantness and misfortune."

"Misfortune for whom?" Catherine inquired innocently.

"For all of us. It was a very tragic time in our lives—and in his."

"Then why have we never discussed this before?"

"There seemed no point," Bradford said bleakly. "The accident took your memory and at the time, I believed that a blessing."

"It was eleven years ago." Catherine felt a surge of desperation and fought the inner panic. "After I recovered, you still never told me what had happened. You deliberately deceived me."

"No... I never lied to you, kitten." Bradford's voice broke. "You were very ill for so long—my God, sometimes you went for days without saying a word. I was terrified that you'd never be the same again. Slowly, you began to speak and to smile. You were happy again. The doctors didn't know how you would react if the memories returned, and I couldn't bear the thought of seeing you in such pain again. Years went by, and your life went on. You became a woman, forging into the world to carve a career for yourself. I was so proud of you and eventually, that time seemed insignificant."

"Insignificant?" The impact of the word made her tremble. "A man almost died because of me, and you call it insignificant?"

Bradford went white. "You were not responsible."

"No, *you* were responsible." The turmoil within spilled out in a fury. "How could you do it? How could you take advantage of my illness and rush me out of the country, leaving an innocent man to rot in jail? Do you know what that did to him? Do you even care?"

Anguish flashed through Bradford's eyes and he extended his hand in a pleading gesture. "Is that what he told you?"

"No! That's what I remember."

Bradford's expression changed from shock to disbelief. "You remember... everything?"

A sharp retort died on her tongue. She didn't remember everything and was lashing out at her uncle to conceal the pain of the one unanswered question that still haunted her. The anger left Catherine as quickly as air from a deflated balloon. She'd wanted to vent the rage and frustration, but realized that her fury had been misplaced.

Shakily, she turned away and sat heavily on the sofa. She felt drained. "I remember most of it, but there are still some things missing."

Bradford wrung his hands. "What things are missing?"

She slid him a tired look. "If I knew that, they wouldn't be missing."

It had been the perfect opportunity to ask about her child, but Catherine wasn't ready. She was still confused, still unsure if her uncle would respond truthfully. And deep down, she was afraid of what she might learn.

After a moment, Bradford sat beside her. "Perhaps I should have handled things differently, but I can't change what happened. My mistakes have caused you pain and for that I'm deeply sorry, but I have no remorse toward Jonathan Stone. Whatever the price he paid, it wasn't high enough for what he did to you."

Stunned, Catherine could only stare.

Calmly, Bradford related the events of that winter from his own perspective. "We were having a difficult time then, Cathy, and I realized that it was my fault. After Lois left me and I lost my job, I realized that drowning myself in vodka was the cause of my problems instead of the solution. So I was determined to get my life back on course, except I went from one addiction to another. I was so wrapped up in AA meetings and job interviews, that I completely ignored you."

His candor shocked Catherine. Her uncle had always believed that exposing emotions was a distasteful breach of etiquette. To him, sensitivity equaled weakness, and few had dared accuse Bradford Madison of either. Now, he was quietly discussing his innermost feelings as though it was the most natural thing in the world. Catherine was too choked to speak.

Bradford leaned back, staring blankly into space and spoke quietly. "You were the only stable person in my life, Cathy. I loved you deeply, but I took you for granted. When I came home that day and found you gone, I realized that I might have lost you forever. At that moment, I prayed harder than I'd ever prayed for anything in my life. I promised that if you were returned safely, I'd never leave you alone again."

Catherine swallowed hard. "That's why you've been so controlling all these years?"

He smiled sadly. "I prefer to consider my behavior as protective. You almost died, Cathy."

"But that wasn't Jonathan's fault."

"Of course it was his fault." Anger flashed in Bradford's pale eyes. "None of it would have happened if he hadn't taken you away."

"I wanted to be with him. Didn't you realize that?"

He looked away. "No. I honestly believed you had been taken against your will. When you began to struggle and call out his name, I was confused. Suddenly, everything was in chaos and I thought of nothing except the fact that you were hurt. Later, in the hospital—" Quickly, he clamped his lips together as though he'd inadvertently revealed something.

Catherine zeroed in. "What happened in the hospital? Tell me!"

"You . . . were delirious."

"That's not what you were going to say." Catherine took her uncle's hand and squeezed it imploringly. "Please. I have to know."

He closed his eyes and sighed. "You called out for him."

"For Jonathan?"

"Yes," he whispered. "At first, I believed that you were afraid of him, so I told you that he'd been killed. It was my understanding that he wasn't going to survive, and I wanted you to feel safe, but—" he swallowed hard "—But your eyes widened in horror and you screamed. It was the most agonized sound I'd ever heard in my life. Then . . . I knew."

For a moment, Catherine couldn't breathe. She didn't remember that moment, but instinctively knew that her uncle had told her the truth. Still, something didn't quite add up. "You knew he'd been unjustly accused, yet you did nothing to stop it. Why?"

"Assault charges had already been filed by the state. There was nothing I could do."

"But when you found out that Jonathan was alive, why didn't you tell me?"

Bradford hesitated, then answered slowly and cautiously. "By then it was clear that you were suffering from traumatic amnesia. You were unaware that Jonathan Stone even existed, and the doctors felt another upset could adversely affect your recovery."

Catherine regarded him thoughtfully. "It wasn't the doctors who made that decision. It was you."

He met her gaze. "Yes and I stand by that choice. The shock could have been detrimental to your health. There was nothing to be gained by telling you or putting you through another ordeal."

She was flabbergasted. "Nothing except freeing an innocent man from jail."

"You couldn't have done anything about that."

"I could have told them the truth."

"You didn't know the truth."

"If you had told me, I would have..." The impact of her words seeped through. Her uncle was right. She simply would have been parroting what she'd been told, and no court in the land would have believed her a credible witness.

"There, there." Bradford slid his arm around Catherine's shoulders, comforting her. "You didn't pick up that rifle. He brought it on himself."

"He didn't know those men were policemen. He was trying to protect me." Catherine pulled away, stunned by her uncle's lack of concern. "You know how much he suffered. How can you be so cold?"

Bradford's expression hardened. "He took advantage of your loneliness and your vulnerability. You were a child."

"I was seventeen, and Jonathan was twenty. We were both young, but we were hardly children." Catherine tilted her head. "But it had nothing to do with age, did it? If I fell in love and got married, then you'd be alone and you couldn't deal with that."

"That's not fair, Catherine."

"No, it's not fair, but it's the truth. You rushed me from my hospital bed to an airplane before I even had a chance to remember anything."

"I told you, I didn't want the police questioning you. If there had been any kind of trial, you would have been subjected to publicity, your reputation would have been destroyed."

"My reputation—or yours?" Catherine didn't recognize her own voice. Words rushed out without conscious thought, and she seemed to be a disembodied observer, watching herself from a distant universe. "Those early days in France are vague, like I'm looking through some kind of fog, but I remember enough to know that something was horribly wrong. There was a woman in white. She came every day, didn't she? She gave me pills, lots and lots of pills."

Bradford regarded her and in his eyes, Catherine saw a flash of fear. Tension hardened his voice. "You were ill. Medication was necessary."

"Was it?" Catherine's exhausted mind seemed caught in a time warp, hovering in an odd dimension between the past and the present. She saw images of the woman, her crisp uniform partially concealed beneath the heavy wool sweater she'd always worn. There had been an antiseptic scent about her as she'd moved soundlessly through the room on thick, rubber-soled shoes.

She'd spoken in a hushed voice, with the condescending manner one uses on recalcitrant children. Her smile had been superficial; her eyes had been shrewd. Catherine had feared her, feared the tiny paper cup filled with colorful tablets and the numbing blackness that soon would follow.

As the blurred memory unfolded in her mind, Catherine saw herself knocking the pills away and struggling to get out of the bed. But her legs had been leaden and she'd fallen. The woman had cursed her, then called out. Bradford had appeared and Catherine remembered his soothing voice, his strong hands lifting her.

She'd fought him. Her tongue was thick, her words slurred but Catherine remembered trying to push her uncle away. Then the woman's rough hands were on Catherine's mouth, prying her teeth apart, choking her as the pills were thrust down her throat. Gagging, Catherine had sobbed. She remembered Bradford's angry voice berating the nurse, then the sounds had grown faint.

And the final voice she remembered had been her own, screaming.

Now, dry-eyed and numbed by the memories, Catherine faced her uncle and repeated her question. "Was it necessary to force drugs down my throat, or was it simply convenient?"

"What?" His face twisted in disbelief. "Good Lord, kitten, what are you saying?"

A cold pit yawned open in the very core of her. "You didn't want me to get well, to know what you'd done."

Bradford grasped her shoulders, turning her to face his anguished expression. "You were delusional, almost catatonic. I did everything I could to help you get through it. My God, Cathy, don't you understand how much I love you?"

For a moment, his anguished plea reached her. Then she remembered his hands holding her down as the nurse forced her lips apart.

Shaking him off, she backed away, the breath catching in her throat. Panting and trembling, she said, "Is that why you kept me doped up for weeks and weeks? Were you trying to make certain my brain cells were totally fried?" The high-pitched voice emanating from her body seemed to belong to a stranger. Catherine suddenly had no control over her words or the agonizing rush of emotion clouding her judgment. "It didn't work. All the pills, all the brainwashing didn't work. *I remember* what you did. *I remember my baby.*"

Bradford went rigid.

With a horrified gasp, Catherine pressed her hands to her mouth. Her heart rushed into her throat as she waited and prayed for him to deny her accusation. Her uncle's eyes were empty, and he seemed a broken man, but his only response was smothering silence.

Deep inside, Catherine wept silent tears and wondered if Jonathan had been right.

"Howard, I need your help." Swiveling his chair, Jonathan stared out over the L.A. skyline and tightened his grip on the receiver. "I hate to ask for favors, but it's important."

Howard Dylan's response was instantaneous. "Name it."

Jonathan took a deep breath. "I need some investigative work done—fast."

"I thought you worked with some guy out of Santa Monica."

"He was an incompetent fool. I hoped you'd be able to refer me to someone with a less orthodox style."

After a thoughtful moment, Howard clarified the request with usual bluntness. "You want someone who values results over the means, eh?"

Wincing, Jonathan answered succinctly. "Yes."

"I think I've got a man who can help you. Ethics isn't his strongest attribute, but he gets the job done."

"How can I get in touch with him?"

"Might be best if I contact him myself. He doesn't much cotton to strangers," Howard replied cautiously. "What kind of information are you looking for?"

Hesitating, Jonathan rubbed his head. He regretted this move already, but knew that the black fury boiling deep inside would never cool until the truth had been exposed. He'd hoped to work with Catherine, not against her. But then over the years, he had hoped for a lot of things. Hope was for fools.

Subconsciously he squared his shoulders. "I need some old hospital records."

Howard emitted a low whistle. "That's privileged information."

"Are you saying it can't be done?"

"There's nothing that can't be done—for a price." Howard was silent for a moment, then said, "Give me the details. I'll see to it."

Instead of relief, Jonathan felt sick. Words lodged in his throat, but anger forced them out. "It's about Catherine. I've discovered that right after the accident, she spent a couple of weeks in a local hospital under the name Catherine Madison. Put a check on the names of Greer and LeClerc, just in case. There was a passport issued in the name of Catherine Elaine Madison, and I want travel details for the following year."

Howard chuckled. "You don't want much do you? Anything else?"

Jonathan rubbed his head. "I may need you to grease some skids at the French embassy."

"Foreign ambassadors are a bit out of my field," Howard admitted. "Just what are you up to? What'n the devil do you expect to find in France?"

"Birth records," Jonathan replied brusquely.

A moan filtered over the line, then a muffled curse. After a pause, Howard grunted once, then cleared his throat. "This isn't any of my business, son, but are you sure you know what you're doing?"

"How soon can I get the information?" Jonathan asked flatly.

Howard sighed. "Let me see how many strings I've got to pull, then I'll get back to you."

"You're a good friend, Howard."

"If I was such a good friend, I'd be sitting in your lap right now trying to pound some sense into your thick head. Nothing good is going to come out of this and that's a fact, but I'll do it because you asked me to. I just hope the whole thing doesn't blow up in your face."

"I'll risk it," Jonathan snapped, annoyed with himself. Howard was absolutely right and deep down, Jonathan knew it. But his quest had become a dangerous obsession. He couldn't quit, couldn't control the gnawing need to know.

After hanging up the telephone, Jonathan stared out over the horizon. He wondered where Catherine was at this very moment. Was she still in Los Angeles or had she taken the first available flight to Europe? Was she thinking about the days they'd just spent together?

He told himself that it didn't matter. All he'd ever wanted was to find the missing pieces of his past and now his search was nearly over. He'd never expected or wanted to rekindle an old flame. Even in his wildest dreams, Jonathan had never imagined that he and Cat could respond to each other with such unbridled passion. Holding her in his arms, Jonathan could almost believe that the empty years never existed, as though he and Cat had never really been apart.

But that was a fool's fable. They'd simply been carried away by sweet memories; no more, no less.

Jonathan's mind had accepted that. His heart hadn't.

Chapter Twelve

Bradford Madison stared at Catherine with hollow eyes, then turned away, shoulders rounded by the weight of his misery.

"It's true," Catherine whispered. "How could you?"

"I took care of you," Bradford mumbled. "I did everything I could for you."

Catherine shook her head, the images rushing through her brain. "You held me down while that horrible woman forced pills down my throat."

"You needed the medication. It was the only way—"

"To keep me unconscious?"

Bradford stiffened and met her accusatory gaze. "Yes. And to keep away the nightmares."

Involuntarily, Catherine's hand went to her throat. When her uncle reached out in a pleading gesture, she stepped backward.

His hand fell limply to his side. "For the first two weeks, you were very ill and very weak. You needed time to rest and recuperate from your ordeal and you couldn't be left alone. I hired a woman, a registered nurse, but when I saw how she treated you, I fired her and took care of you myself. Then you began to recover."

Closing her eyes, Catherine pictured the small gray room. She remembered her uncle, seated on the edge of the soft feather bed as he'd held her hand and helped her sip hot broth.

It was true. She could remember—couldn't she?

Or was her mind simply creating the image of what she was being told? The implications of that thought made her shudder. If she was that gullible, that mentally confused, how many other images had merely been figments of her own imagination? Had the memories of Jonathan and what they'd shared been some kind of delusion? Had she simply manufactured memories to support what he'd told her?

Was she losing her mind?

No. She couldn't accept that. Jonathan had been so careful to reveal nothing that she hadn't remembered on her own. The cabin had been real. Their lovemaking had been real. Her memories had been real. Their baby had been real.

Tentatively, Catherine raised her eyes, meeting her uncle's empty stare. "But my baby? Where is my child?"

His shoulders shuddered, and he spoke slowly. "You never bore a child."

The room undulated, and Catherine steadied herself. "I . . . don't believe you."

"What you believe or don't believe doesn't change the truth," he said sadly.

"I *remember*."

"No you don't, but you want to. You're creating things in your mind, things that never existed."

Confusion circled Catherine like a bird of prey. Her mind buzzed with disjointed images. She remembered Jonathan's laughter when she'd told him she was pregnant. He'd swooped her up, spinning her around the cabin until she'd begged for mercy. Then they'd celebrated, toasting each other with ginger ale, sharing the dream of a bright future.

Had that never happened? Had the baby that they'd wanted so desperately never even existed?

Catherine couldn't cope with the thought. With a soft moan, she stumbled toward her room. Bradford called out. When she ignored him, he quickly crossed the room and took her arm.

She shook him off. "Don't touch me."

"Cathy, listen to me."

"No. You're lying, and I don't want to hear any more."

Grasping her shoulders, he forced her to look at him. "I know how difficult this must be for you, but you have to see it through. It's the only way you can put the past behind you once and for all."

She lifted her chin and stared up defiantly. "I want my baby."

Bradford's mouth contorted as though he were in terrible pain. His hands fell helplessly to his side. "You must believe me, Cathy. When you were ill, you had hallucinations. What you think you remember, it never happened."

"*Yes it did.* Jonny and I were going to have a baby. We got this little book of names and made a list of our favorites." Tears spilled down her cheeks as she looked at her left hand. Her ring finger suddenly seemed bare without the tiny circle of woven grass. "We were going to be married," she whispered.

Bradford's pale eyes went cold but he said nothing.

Turning away, Catherine wiped her face. "That's what we were quarreling about when I ran out of the cabin. Jonny wanted to tell you about the baby, but I was afraid of what you might do. I wanted to elope but he was so old-fashioned..." The words trailed away, and she smiled. When she spoke again, her voice softened. "He actually planned to ask you for my hand in marriage. Can you imagine that? He wanted your blessing. That's sweet, isn't it?"

Bradford's lips fell apart, and his eyes registered surprise. He stared briefly, then his expression tightened.

"You believe me, don't you?" Catherine asked anxiously.

Regarding her thoughtfully, Bradford's forehead creased and he pursed his lips. Finally, he sighed. "Yes. I believe that you both were convinced that... certain things occurred."

Catherine felt the blood drain from her face. "What are you saying?"

"I don't want to hurt you, kitten, you must know that. I've made grievous errors in the past. I admit it. I've done things I've not been proud of and perhaps I've not always behaved in an honorable manner, but I've always done what I thought best for you." Bradford looked right at her. "Do you remember the day we toured Bourdeaux?"

Startled by the unexpected question, Catherine frowned. "No...wait a minute." Closing her eyes, she recalled the French countryside. They'd been laughing and driving down a twisting road lined by miles and miles of grape arbors. The gnarled branches were tinged by the first green blush of spring growth, and they'd pulled into a small clearing for a picnic. "Yes, I remember. It was your birthday, and we drove to the country to celebrate."

"Yes." Bradford took a deep breath. "Do you recall everything that happened that day?"

"Why? What has that to do with—"

"Please, Cathy. Think."

"All right." She didn't understand why her uncle was so vehement, but shrugged and brought the image of that time back into focus. "We spread out a cloth and lunched beneath a big apple tree. I teased you about being old and you pretended to be offended. Then I challenged you to a tree-climbing contest and I won." She looked up expectantly.

Bradford nodded sadly, as though her words had offered some kind of revelation. When she continued to stare blankly, he prodded her gently. "My birthday is in April."

"I know that, but I still don't see what that has to do—" Suddenly, the truth hit Catherine like a speeding truck. She could see herself clearly, scrambling up the trunk with athletic grace, then balancing on a thick branch, taunting her panting uncle. After he'd acknowledged defeat, she'd shown off by using a fat limb as a trapeze before dropping into a laughing heap onto the soft earth.

Now Catherine realized why Bradford had wanted her to remember that day. She'd been nimble and strong and obviously recovered from her injuries. And she hadn't been pregnant.

Air rushed from her lungs. In April of that year, she should have been five months pregnant. Shakily, she turned away, remembering that July outing in Paris and how she'd clung to the possibility of a premature birth. Now even that hope had been dashed.

She went to the window, looking out over the gleaming city. It was a rare day, the air as clear as sparkling glass. In the distance, snow-covered peaks loomed invitingly, surrounding the L.A. basin like stoic white soldiers. The mountains were strong and solid, a foundation of permanence in a tumultuous world.

Everything else was transient. Even life was but a fleeting moment in earth's calender, where eons tick as mere moments in time. In the presence of such a grand scale, the existence of an individual human being would seem insignificant, and an entire lifetime no more than a heartbeat in the universe.

But ethereal philosophy couldn't ease Catherine's pain. Each life was crucial, each tiny soul a miracle of love. Yet deep inside, she knew the truth. There had been no child.

The realization broke her heart.

Storm clouds gathered over the Pacific and in the distance, silent lightning licked at the black horizon. Jonathan leaned on the deck railing and stared out at the dark sea. A cold wind whipped the ocean into choppy peaks. Huge waves surged upward, curling like angry fists, then unleashed a punishing force on the helpless shore.

Inside himself Jonathan felt the same mounting tension, nerves sparking like distant lightning, fear boiling like the turbulent sea.

He waited, knowing that the storm within would soon break. At any moment the doorbell would ring and a clandestine exchange would occur. The payoff had been arranged by a raspy voice on the telephone, making Jonathan feel like a bit player in a clichéd spy film. The entire charade left a bad taste in his mouth but desperation played hell with moral fiber.

As he thought back over the past few days, he realized just what an emotional roller coaster he'd been riding. His hopes had been alternately raised and dashed, surging up like the swelling surf only to be splintered like so much driftwood.

Had it only been yesterday morning that he'd awakened in the cabin to find Catherine gone? It seemed a lifetime ago. Now he was waiting for information that would tell him . . . what? What did he hope to accomplish? Did he honestly believe that he'd discover anything that would lead to a fictional happy ending? All the evidence he'd uncovered so far pointed to the fallacy of that hope and had led to one inescapable conclusion: history could not be relived or rewritten.

Doubt gnawed at him but he'd come too far to give up. No matter how brutal the truth, Jonathan would see this through to the bitter end.

Determined, he turned and walked into his house, closing the French doors behind him. He glanced at his watch, then nervously picked up his briefcase and recounted the agreed-upon cash.

The front bell jangled, and he stiffened. He stared at the door, unable to move. The bell rang again, followed by an impatient knock. Finally, he managed to answer.

A short toady man stood on the porch. "Stone?" he rasped, clutching a large manilla envelope.

Jonathan nodded.

The man's amphibian eyes moved rapidly. "Got the money?"

"That depends," Jonathan responded coolly. "What information do you have?"

Bulging eyes regarded Jonathan shrewdly, then handed him the envelope. "See for yourself."

Jonathan held the package for a moment, then opened the clasp and scanned the contents. There were a half-dozen photocopies of medical forms and hospital records. The name "C. E. Madison" leaped out from every page. The breath caught in his throat, and he stared spellbound at the copies.

The investigator coughed significantly. At the sound, Jonathan shoved the papers back into the envelope and went to get the money.

After counting the bills, the man grinned. "It's a pleasure doin' business with you," he said, then disappeared into the night.

Jonathan closed the door and stared at the envelope laying by his briefcase. He tried to shake off the deep sense of foreboding, but the metallic taste of fear flooded his mouth. He felt nauseous.

After eleven years of uncertainty, the answer was within his grasp, yet he had an overwhelming urge to throw the entire package into the fireplace and watch the unread pages curl into black ash.

Coward.

Forcing himself, he lifted the envelope with stiff fingers and removed the papers. One by one, he scanned them, trying to decipher the myriad handwritten scrawls. Much of it was hopeless, abbreviated medical terms that might as well have been Theban hieroglyphics. There were bits and pieces he could interpret and he tried to make sense of them. In the emergency room, Catherine had apparently been treated for a severe concussion and deep scalp lacerations. She'd suffered contusions and abrasions, and X-rays had revealed two cracked ribs.

Jonathan frowned. The attending physician had indicated that she could be released, pending follow-up with her personal doctor. But Catherine had recalled being in the hospital for at least two weeks. Why?

He flipped through the papers, then saw something that caught his attention. Something had happened immediately after the emergency room examination. There was some kind of surgical release form signed by Bradford Madison, but the technical description of the procedure meant nothing to Jonathan. It was apparent, though, that Catherine had been more seriously injured than first believed.

Baffled, he flipped back to the detailed patient records and searched for some kind of clue. He'd just about decided that he'd have to have the entire package interpreted by a medical professional when an all-too familiar word screamed out at him.

He felt like he'd been kicked in the gut. His stomach twisted, and he murmured in disbelief. No. There was a mistake. It couldn't be true.

But it was true and Jonathan was devastated by the revelation.

He couldn't breathe, couldn't move. Even when a distant jangling seeped into his consciousness, he felt frozen in time.

Never in his wildest worst-case scenario, could Jonathan have conceived this horrible reality. God, how could he have been so blind?

He dropped his head into his hands. The doorbell rang again, followed by a tentative knocking. The sound seemed so far away, so surrealistic that he simply couldn't focus on it. His own pain was too deep and too real.

When he heard her voice, he looked up, wondering if he'd imagined it. She called out his name and again knocked softly.

It was no dream. Catherine was on the other side of that door.

Rubbing her arms against the evening chill, Catherine nervously wondered if Jonathan had gone for a walk on the beach. His car was in the driveway, and his secretary said he'd left the office hours ago. Light emanated from several rooms in the house and it certainly appeared as though someone should be home.

Again she tapped on the door, then waited anxiously. She wanted to see him, to hear his comforting voice and feel the safe warmth of his arms. It had only been yesterday morning that she'd covered his sleeping body and walked into the cold mountain dawn; it seemed eons ago. After the soul-wrenching confrontation with her uncle, Catherine had lain awake for the second night in a row trying desperately to cope with what she had learned. She'd been devastated by the truth.

The worst part would be telling Jonathan. He'd lived with hope for so long, Catherine was sick about brutally dashing those hopes; but she had no choice. After all the years of torment, he was entitled to the truth.

And that truth was deeply disappointing.

The thought that their child might be out there somewhere, lost in a world of strangers had tormented Catherine to the point of madness. But she had also felt a spark of joy that their love had created a tiny life, a small person that was a part of them both. A flame of hope had been ignited, burning brightly beside the agony of loss; but that flame had been cruelly extinguished. Their child had never existed. That was a bitter blow.

She shivered, then turned toward the walkway leading to the beach. After she'd taken a couple of steps, the front door flew open, startling her. She jumped, clutching her throat as her heart pounded wildly. A familiar shape was silhouetted in the doorway.

She lit up. "Hello," she whispered, and her heart ached at the sight of him. His only response was the slight tilt of his head, and Catherine was taken aback by his cool reception. "May... I come in?"

"Why?" he asked bluntly.

Her shoulders automatically stiffened. She licked her lips and spoke slowly. "I understand that you're upset at the way I left yesterday, but I'd hoped you'd be courteous enough to hear me out."

Pausing, he regarded her for a moment, then his teeth flashed unpleasantly. "I certainly wouldn't want to be considered discourteous," he said sarcastically, stepping aside and sweeping his arm in an exaggerated gesture. "Please do come in, Miss LeClerc."

Catherine hesitated briefly, then lifted her chin and brushed by him into the warmly lit living room. The chrome and leather furnishings were distinctly masculine and except for a few papers scattered on the coffee table, the room was surprisingly neat. A fireplace blazed in the corner and wide glass doors led out to the deck. Beyond, the Pacific Ocean licked the cold sand with a foamy tongue, before withdrawing into the silent blackness.

Clasping her cold hands together, she bit her quivering lip, keeping her back to him until the front door clicked shut and she had regained her composure.

From the corner of her eye she saw Jonathan walk to a small wet bar by the adjoining dining area. He lifted a bottle, then paused. "Would you like something, Miss LeClerc?" He inquired with exaggerated politeness. "Cognac, bourbon... ginger ale?"

The reference wasn't lost on Catherine. She refused his offer, then took a deep breath and faced him. "I didn't mean to hurt you."

"You never do," he said coolly, pouring a measure of amber liquid into a sparkling glass. After a hefty swallow, he winced slightly and fixed her with a hard stare. "Is that all you wanted to say?"

"No." Catherine was confused by Jonathan's coldness. He looked terrible, as though he hadn't slept for a week and had been wearing the same clothes for as long. The Scorpio eyes seemed sunken, hollow and strangely impotent. Confusion turned to concern for him. "Are you all right?"

He made a dry sound. "I'm swell, just swell."

She took a step toward him, stopping when he gave her a frigid stare. "Jonathan, I'm sorry I left the cabin so abruptly but I had my reasons."

"Ah." He took another gulp of liquor, then pressed his lips together and nodded knowingly. "Well as long as you had your reasons that makes everything okay, doesn't it?"

"I had no idea you'd be this upset. I left you a note—"

"Of course you did," he said harshly. "That's the part that's supposed to soothe your conscience, isn't it? I mean, it's not as though you simply disappeared without a word. You'd *never* do that, would you Cat?" Jonathan's eyes narrowed, and his face contorted with raw fury. He seemed a man teetering on the verge of losing control.

Stunned, Catherine stepped back. She wasn't as much frightened as confused by his irrational anger.

Suddenly, his rage melted into the deepest agony Catherine had ever seen. With a choked sound, he turned away, shoulders vibrating as he fought the demons within. Then he straightened, shuddered once, and when he looked at her again his eyes were as blank and cold as the mountain. "Just say what you have to, Catherine, then leave me in peace."

"Leave—?" Catherine swallowed hard and looked away. When Jonathan realized why she had left, he'd understand. Everything would be all right then. She found her voice. "I don't want to leave. I want to be with you."

"Well we can't always have what we want, can we?"

There was a double meaning to his cynical response, but Catherine didn't understand it. He was obviously agitated, but she still assumed that he was angry that she'd left the cabin without telling him. She hastened to explain. "Do you remember the telephone call I made at the service station?"

Jonathan blinked, then furrowed his brow. "What about it?"

"I called the hotel for messages and discovered that my uncle was flying in that evening." Catherine paused, searching his tight expression for a sigh of comprehension. She saw none, so she continued her explanation. "Uncle Brad is the only one who knows what really happened eleven years ago. I wanted answers from him."

"Didn't it occur to you that I might have one or two questions myself?"

"I didn't believe your interrogation methods would be particularly effective," Catherine snapped. Jonathan's sharp tone and accusatory manner was beginning to irritate her immensely. "Besides, I wanted to talk to him alone."

He stared for a moment, his jaw twitching madly. Then he emitted a dry, humorless laugh. "Some things never change."

"What do you mean by that?"

"You're still ashamed of me."

It took a moment for her to find her voice. "That's not true."

"No? Then why did you run yourself ragged trying to hide me from your uncle all those years ago?" The Scorpio eyes blazed, and he didn't wait for her answer. "I was a tough street kid, someone you found dangerous and exciting but much too common for your high-brow friends. Maybe for you our relationship was a rebellious thrill but things didn't work out, did they? Because you couldn't control me and you couldn't hide me. I became your embarrassment."

"I was never ashamed of you. Never." Aghast, Catherine shook her head trying to exorcise the horrible words. "I didn't realize that you felt that way."

He shrugged casually. "It doesn't matter any more."

"I'm so sorry," she whispered, stepping toward him and reaching out.

He froze her with a look. "I don't need your pity."

Slowly, she withdrew her hand. Whatever was going on inside of Jonathan extended much deeper than the insecurities of youth. Something else had happened, something terrible. The air was thick with tension and a raw torment that Catherine could feel, but couldn't even begin to comprehend.

Baring his teeth in a cold smile, Jonathan spoke with deceptive softness. "All right, now we've established that you wanted to talk to him alone and since this is the first I've heard from you since yesterday morning, I'll assume that you've had ample opportunity to do that."

"I'd planned to call you sooner, but—"

"Time just flies when you're having fun, doesn't it?"

Catherine took a sharp breath. "I realize you're annoyed, but sarcasm isn't going to help."

"Forgive me, *mademoiselle*," he said mockingly. "Please enlighten me as to the cause of your delay."

"I... overslept." She felt her cheeks heat and hurriedly completed the explanation. "I didn't get to sleep until nearly dawn and by the time I woke up, it was dark again."

"You and Uncle Brad must have had quite a reunion."

"We had a lot to talk about."

"I don't doubt it." Jonathan set the empty glass on the bar. "So tell me, Catherine, exactly what did your illustrious uncle have to say?"

She licked her lips and turned away. "He... helped me to remember certain... things."

"Oh? How interesting. Do go on." Jonathan's light tone was not particularly pleasant.

Catherine took a ragged breath, then in a thin halting voice, she told of how her uncle had reacted to protect her and about those first horrible weeks in Europe. Jonathan listened in stony silence.

Finally, she could put off the inevitable no longer. Facing him, she fought a rush of tears and laced her trembling fingers together. "I asked him about our baby."

Jonathan's mouth twitched revealing. He said nothing.

"I—" Her voice broke, and she tucked her clamped hands beneath her chin, struggling for composure. "I was never pregnant. It was... a mistake."

When he made no response, Catherine forced herself to look up. His expression shocked her. She'd expected him to be hurt and disappointed, but she could never have anticipated such black hatred.

Her mind whirled, and her voice was tinged with desperation. "I never meant to deceive you. I honestly believed that we were going to have a baby, but I was so young and impressionable. Maybe I wanted your child so very much that I just fooled myself into believing . . ." The words dissipated.

Jonathan leaned casually against the bar. There was nothing casual about the smoldering fury in his eyes or his taut, grim expression. "The clinic was fooled, too? How did you manage to fake the pregnancy test? Did you pay off an orderly?"

Stung by the insinuation, Catherine stiffened. "No test is one hundred percent accurate. Obviously, there was an error."

"Obviously." He gave the word a contemptuous inflection. "And the morning sickness was all—" he tapped his skull "—up here, a psychosomatic reaction to being so young and impressionable."

Her mouth went dry. "I suppose it was."

"That certainly explains everything," he said savagely. "I feel so much better now, knowing the *truth*."

"Why are you looking at me as though I'm some kind of an insect that just crawled out of your cereal box?" Anger and indignation surged like a hot geyser. "I understand your disappointment and sadness, but that doesn't give you the right to attack me this way. You're not the only one with feelings. How dare you treat my pain as insignificant?"

He whirled on her. "And how dare you insult my intelligence with that ludicrous piece of fiction? What kind of an idiot do you think I am?"

"A thickheaded one," Catherine snapped. "You wouldn't recognize the truth if it jumped up and bit your skinny nose off."

Jonathan spoke through clamped teeth. "Drop the act, lady. I've seen this performance before." He made an unpleasant sound and raked his fingers through his hair. "The lies are over. At least have the decency to admit that."

Catherine willed herself to be calm. An argument between them would only exacerbate the pain they were both feeling. They needed each other for comfort and support. Hurling accusations helped no one. Finally, she spoke in a clear, composed voice. "I know you don't want to accept this but I'm not lying to you, Jonathan. I wish we'd had a baby, God knows how much I wish that, but I can't change the facts. I was never pregnant."

His eyes impaled her. "Is that what your uncle told you?"

Catherine paused, remembering Bradford's exact words. *You never bore a child, Catherine.* "Yes, but it doesn't matter what he said. I remember everything now."

"How convenient for you."

"That's not fair."

"The world isn't fair, Catherine, and I've become an expert on life's little injustices."

"Yes, you've had a tough time, and I'm truly sorry for that," she replied sharply. "You were very noble and very righteous and the world had 'done you wrong,' but that was a long time ago. Self-pity is not a particularly attractive emotion and quite frankly, it doesn't suit you."

"Thank you for pointing that out," he said dryly.

"You're welcome." Catherine's anger dissipated and she tiredly massaged her eyelids. Nothing made sense to her anymore, not Jonathan's inexplicable rage, not the deepening sense of impending doom shrouding her heart. "I don't understand what has happened between us. Two days ago, we were so close, recapturing the feelings that had lain dormant for so many years. Now I look at you and see a spiteful stranger."

"We've always been strangers, Catherine. We just didn't realize it."

"I don't believe that. What we've shared is too special to be so easily dismissed, and you know it." Catherine maintained a composed veneer but inside, she felt frantic. Where was the man who had held her so lovingly, whispering soft words of comfort and passion? Surely, this hard-eyed stranger couldn't be the same man.

This must be a dream, a horrible nightmare from which she simply must awaken. It couldn't be happening. She would go mad if this was truly happening. Her voice faltered and she extended her palm in a pleading gesture. "We loved each other."

"Did we? Or did we simply use each other? Don't look so shocked, Catherine. Biology is a fact of nature and when peeled down to the most basic instincts, humans are no different than any other animal." He faced her grimly. "I take that back. Animals don't prey on their own kind."

Catherine's voice failed. Shakily, she turned away staring blankly out over the dark ocean. Whether Jonathan had acted for revenge or merely amusement, one fact had become crystal clear: everything that had passed between them this weekend had been nothing more than a cruel charade. He'd pretended to care, pretended to love her, when all he'd wanted was—What? To hurt her? To humiliate her in some kind of misguided feat of vengeance?

When she spoke again, her voice was as empty as her heart. "If I meant so little to you, why didn't you leave me alone? Why did you seek me out and dupe me into playing this sick little game with you?"

"It was no game to me," he replied in a voice that could etch cold steel. "I wanted my child."

She shivered. "I'm sorry to have disappointed you."

"Yes," he hissed angrily. "I can see how very sorry you are."

With every ounce of pride she could muster, Catherine ignored her screaming heart and faced Jonathan squarely. "I don't know why you've suddenly decided that everything that passed between us has been a lie, but I can't accept that. I know what I know. I loved you. You were my life."

His eyes darkened as he clenched his fists, then with a sudden movement and a guttural sound, he backhanded the neat row of glasses with a single furious swipe. "Damn what you do to me!" His fist slammed onto the marble counter and the entire room seemed to vibrate.

The outburst stunned Catherine motionless. Before she could move, Jonathan crossed the room and framed her face between his palms. His eyes reflected his pain, and his breath came in panting gasps.

"Even now I don't want to believe what I know. Do you realize what kind of man that makes me?" he rasped, then crushed his mouth against hers in a desperate kiss. Catherine clung to his wrists as her legs turned to rubber.

With a groan that seemed torn from his very soul, Jonathan ripped his mouth away. His hands bounced apart as though spring loaded, pausing midair as he looked at her with an expression of total shock. Then he closed his eyes, grabbed the back of his neck with both hands and turned from her.

A shudder raced through his body, and he squeezed his neck as though holding his head in place. Reaching out, Catherine touched his shoulder, wanting only to offer comfort but his arms stiffened, his palms pushing air.

"Don't—"

Hurt, Catherine pulled her hand away. "I don't understand what I've done to make you so angry."

"No, you probably don't, and that's the saddest part of all."

"Then tell me! I'm not a seer, I can't read your mind. Talk to me!" She felt frantic, bewildered to the point of absolute terror.

"Words are too easy, Catherine. That's why they don't count for much." Rolling his head, his hands fell limply to his side and he walked slowly toward the coffee table. "When you appeared tonight, curiosity got the better of me. I wondered what kind of story you and dear Uncle Brad had cooked up this time. I even toyed with the idea that you might have turned over a new leaf and decided to confess the truth. Silly me."

As Catherine watched in confusion, Jonathan fingered the papers strewn across the table's gleaming glass surface. His expression was as bleak as a gray winter day, and he spoke in a dull monotone. "The worst part is that even when I saw the truth in black and white, I still couldn't believe it. Part of me was locked in this foolish, futile hope that this, too, was a mistake."

"What was a mistake? Jonathan, what are you talking about?"

He ignored her question. "If you'd told me the truth, I would have been hurt and angry, but I would have tried to understand. Maybe I could have even learned to live with it. But this—" his hand shot out and snatched up the papers, then shook the wadded sheets in her startled face "—this can't be forgiven. It's over, Catherine . . . the pretense, the lies, the grand deception . . . all over."

Furiously he flung the crumpled sheets, and they fluttered to the floor. With two angry strides, Jonathan slammed his hands on the bar and his body sagged between stiff arms. He sucked in a ragged breath. "Get out, Catherine. Please, get out while I still have the strength to let you go."

Catherine hesitated, then numbly knelt and picked up a piece of paper. She looked at it and frowned. "What is this?" she asked, glancing over at Jonathan. His back quivered but he didn't answer.

Lifting another sheet, Catherine saw that they were forms of some kind, then the name of a hospital leaped out at her. Scanning the illegible scrawls, she felt like an unwilling participant in some kind of bizarre hallucination. After a few moments, she'd just about given up understanding anything except the most basic notations, when she saw something that made the blood drain from her face.

She gasped, staring at the writing until the lines blurred. A tiny whimper rushed from her lips, then she heard a series of agonized moans and realized that the sound had come from her.

This couldn't be true. This couldn't be happening. Oh God, please...

"No," she whispered. "*No!*" she screamed.

Buried in a line of nondescript double-talk, was a single legible phrase: Pregnancy terminated.

The room spun into blackness.

Chapter Thirteen

Green people surrounded her. A light shone in her eyes, so white and blinding that for a moment, Catherine thought heaven itself had opened to her. There were hushed voices and the smell of antiseptic. She fought. She struggled. She cried out. No one listened, no one cared...

With a sharp gasp, Catherine sat up and stared numbly into the darkness. The hotel window glowed red, reflecting the neon brightness of the city at night. For a moment, she hoped that the confrontation with Jonathan and the vile sheets of paper had been part of her nightmare.

Then her head cleared and she realized that the evening had been all too real. Vaguely, she remembered that Jonathan had pried the paper from her convulsive grip. She'd sat on the floor, dazed, staring into space as though her brain had been switched off. There had been a voice in the distance, Jonathan's voice, then the click of a telephone receiver being cradled.

She barely remembered the cab ride back to the hotel and her uncle's alarmed inquiries. Like a zombie, she'd walked slowly to her room and closed the door. After a while, Bradford had stopped knocking and begging to be let in. After a longer while, exhaustion had sucked Catherine into a fitful sleep.

Now she was awake, focusing on memories triggered by the dream. Suddenly, she recalled the hospital as clearly as if it had happened yesterday. Details were sharply ingrained in her mind; the kind blue eyes of the paramedic, the frightening tubes attached to her arm and the harrowing ambulance ride. Uncle Brad had been with her, holding her hand and murmuring softly. She had cried, sobbed with uncontrollable spasms that turned her desperate questions into blubbering gasps. Only when she'd reached the hospital had Cathy regained her voice.

Two men in white jackets had been leaning over her, shining a tiny flashlight in her face. Cathy had pushed the instrument away and grabbed a white lapel. "J-Jonny," she had stammered, repeating his name over and over.

A stabbing pain pierced her belly and she moaned, folding her legs and turning on her side.

"Hold still, miss, you're going to be all right." A competent hand cradled Cathy's head. Something wet stung her scalp and the sharp smell of antiseptic was nauseating. The thin beam of light refocused, and a sharp voice snapped orders. "Call radiology. We need a full skull series, stat."

"No X-rays," Cathy protested weakly as her abdomen knotted with knifelike spasms. "Baby... my baby."

The examining hands stilled. Cathy moaned again, doubling up on the table. Something was wrong. Oh God, something was wrong.

"Please," she croaked. "Please don't let anything happen to my baby."

A round-faced woman leaned over. Her voice was firm but she looked worried. "How far along are you, Miss Madison?"

Cathy tried to speak, but her lips stuck to her teeth. Another pain hit with jackhammer force and she screamed. From what seemed a great distance, she heard a voice. "She's hemorrhaging, doctor."

"Type and cross-match," someone shouted. "Prep O.R. five. *Now*, people! Move!"

Chaos broke out, a madhouse of shouted commands and rushing bodies. Hands lifted her and then the ceiling tiles were flying as she was wheeled into a long hall.

Uncle Brad's drawn face loomed over her and Cathy grabbed his wrist. "D-don't let them hurt my baby," she pleaded, then cried out in pain. "Jonny, where's Jonny?"

"He's gone, kitten," Bradford had whispered. "He'll never bother you again."

Before she could scream out, a mask covered her face and she fell unconscious.

Later, much later, Cathy awoke in a quiet hospital room. Venetian blinds blocked the window and slanted strips of dim light fell over the room like gray prison bars. She was alone.

Moaning, she felt her throbbing head. When she moved one leg a searing pain took her breath away. She felt eviscerated, sliced and sectioned like so much butchered meat. Licking her cracked lips, she gently moved one hand down to her belly and touched the thick gauze pad taped below her navel. Panic formed around the pain, swelling like a black ball.

Outside the room, two men were talking softly. She recognized her uncle's voice and tried to call out. Her throat was paralyzed.

Her uncle spoke in a hushed whisper. "Will she be all right, doctor?"

"The surgery went well, and her vital signs are strong. The uterine damage was repaired without complication." The unfamiliar male voice changed from brisk to sympathetic. "The pregnancy was terminated but she's young and strong. She can have other children."

"Yes, of course. Thank you for all that you've done—" Bradford's voice cracked. "What about the man . . . this Stone person?"

"He was transferred to another facility." There was a pause. "I don't believe he made it. I'm sorry."

Bradford made an unsympathetic response but Cathy didn't hear it. Her mind was swimming, drowning in the horror of what she'd just learned.

Jonny was dead. Their baby was gone.

A low moaning sound filled the room, glowing louder and more primal until her anguished screams drew a crowd of anxious hospital personnel. With the prick of a needle, the tortured howls ceased. Freed from her unbearable torment, Cathy sank into amnesiac blackness.

Now Catherine sat alone in her dark hotel room and absently touched the tiny pelvic scar unnoticeable except in the brightest light. She remembered it all, the horror and the desperation, the agonizing loss of her child and the man she loved. Her grieving mind, unable to cope with the dual tragedy, had simply shut down.

She'd fought to remember, fought to reclaim that part of her mind. Suddenly, Catherine longed to reach inside her head and again pull that switch to sweet oblivion.

Ignorance *had* been bliss; she simply hadn't realized that until now.

The suitcase lay open on the bed and Catherine tossed a handful of lingerie into its yawning mouth. Empty drawers hung out of the dresser and except for a few wire hangers, the closet stood vacant. After a final glance around the room, Catherine closed the suitcase and snapped the clasps.

"Cathy?" Bradford knocked impatiently, as he had done every few minutes for the past two hours. "Please, kitten, let me in. We have to talk."

Under ordinary circumstances, she couldn't have denied his pitiful plea, but the circumstances were far from ordinary and Catherine's heart had turned to granite. At the moment, she didn't want to talk to anyone, least of all her uncle.

The rapping grew louder. "I shall acquire a key from the front desk," he warned, using a firm parental tone for effect. "I know you're in there. I can hear you."

Ignoring him, Catherine pushed the drawers closed and piled her luggage on the bed. Satisfied that nothing had been forgotten, she took a deep breath and opened the door.

Bradford almost fell into the room. "Thank heavens," he mumbled, then froze and stared at the pile of suitcases. A broad grin split his face. "I'll call the airport and reserve two seats for the next flight."

"I'm not going to Paris," Catherine replied crisply, then picked up the telephone. "This is Catherine LeClerc. I'll be checking out within the hour. Would you please prepare my bill and send someone for my luggage? Thank you." She cradled the receiver.

"But I thought..." Bradford's jaw drooped, and his eyes blinked rapidly. "All right, we don't have to go back home right away."

"You can leave any time you want. I'm not going."

"Oh," he muttered, obviously confused. "How long will you be?"

"I'm not going back to Europe—not now, not ever."

Bradford looked stricken. "You...don't want to go home?"

Catherine whirled on him. "Paris has *never* been my home, don't you understand that? *This* is my home, this is where I was born and raised."

For a moment, Bradford seemed too stunned for words, then his eyes narrowed. "It's Stone, isn't it? He's convinced you to stay."

With a dry laugh, Catherine shoved a strand of hair from her eyes. "Nothing could be further from the truth. Jonathan Stone would be the happiest man on earth if he never set eyes on me again." A small sob caught in her throat, and she was annoyed by the weakness. Turning, she busied herself arranging and rearranging her luggage.

"Then what has happened? Why have you turned away from me?"

Her hands went still. Slowly, she straightened and looked back over her shoulder. Her voice was low and deadly. "You lied to me."

His shock was genuine. "What are you talking about?"

She faced him. "I was ten weeks pregnant when the accident happened."

He paled three shades. "Yes, you were."

"Oh, thank you so much for your honesty. A bit late, of course, but appreciated nonetheless." Angrily, Catherine went to the window and opened the curtains with a vicious yank.

"I didn't lie to you, Catherine. I said that you'd never had a child and that was the truth."

"The truth?" With a furious gasp, she whirled around. "The truth is that *my baby is dead*. But then, you already know that, don't you? You were there. You told them to do it."

"My God, Catherine, what are you saying?"

"I saw your signature, I saw it!" She wiped the wetness from her face. "You gave them permission to kill my baby, then you lied to me. All these years you've been lying to me. You can't deny it anymore because I know what happened...*I know what you did!*"

Bradford went ashen, then seemed to age ten years in as many seconds. Eyes sunken, his translucent skin stretched across the deep hollows under his cheekbones. He shook his head, a minute movement that could have merely been a shudder, then his shoulders slumped and he eased himself into a nearby chair.

For a moment, he sat silently and stared at the floor. Then he looked up, eyes clear yet infinitely sad. "How did you find out?"

"Does it matter?"

"Yes."

"Jonathan showed me copies of the hospital records."

Bradford smiled sadly. "I underestimated his resourcefulness."

The statement was ironic. "Jonathan said that it was dangerous to underestimate one's adversaries." Her eyes were dry, and she remembered his thunderous expression. "He hates me, you know. He believes that I did it, that I deliberately aborted our child."

"How could he possibly believe such a thing? If he had the records—"

"The records are very clear and very ugly. At first I didn't believe them, because I know that I wanted our baby, more than anything in the entire world. A bump on the head couldn't have changed that. A nuclear explosion couldn't have changed that. That child meant everything to Jonny and me." Feeling strangely detached, Catherine wrapped her arms around herself and sat on the bed, rocking gently. "Then later, I remembered everything that happened at the hospital. I begged them not to hurt my baby. But they did. And you let them."

"I did no such thing!"

"You signed the form."

"I consented to the surgery that saved your life. The baby...your child was already gone." Desperation sharpened his tone. "I don't know what you saw in those records, but I do know that the explosion caused a miscarriage. There was nothing the doctors could do except try to repair the damage. You almost bled to death."

As her uncle's words seeped into her mind, Catherine raised her head and stared right at him, recalling those horrible hours in the hospital.

She's hemorrhaging, doctor.

...O.R. five...stat!

Now, people! Move!

She covered her ears to blunt the voices in her mind, ward off the unwanted memories. But the pain, she could still feel the horrible pain, like her insides were being squeezed in a barbed wire noose.

Now, people! Move!

"I'm sorry. I—I know it wasn't your fault," she whispered as tears slid down her face. "Maybe I just need someone to blame because I can't face my own responsibility. If I hadn't been so frightened to tell you the truth, none of this would have happened."

In an instant, Bradford was beside her. Holding her as though she were still a child, he smoothed her soft hair and rocked her. "You weren't responsible."

"Jonathan doesn't believe that. He'll never forgive me."

Bradford emitted a sound of disgust. "The man is a rogue and a cad. If anyone is to blame for all that you have suffered, it is Jonathan Stone."

Catherine shook her head sadly. "You accuse Jonathan, he accuses me, and I accuse you. It's a never-ending cycle of blame that perpetuates anger and bitterness but solves nothing. I can't bring back my baby. I can't recapture those lost years."

"No, but you can look to the future and go on with your life." Bradford squeezed her shoulders and lovingly kissed her forehead. "Forget him, Catherine. He isn't worthy of your tears."

Sitting up, Catherine wiped her eyes. "It's not that easy. I wish it was. I wish I could just snap my fingers and magically erase Jonathan Stone from my mind, but I can't."

"You can if you try."

"Have you been able to forget Lois?" Bradford's eyes softened nostalgically and grew moist. Catherine touched his hand, knowing her uncle was still desperately in love with his ex-wife. "You told me once that each of us has only one chance for real love and when destroyed, it's gone forever. Lois was your chance. Jonathan was mine."

Discreetly dabbing his eyes, Bradford took a shuddering breath. Finally, he spoke so softly she could hardly hear. "My impulse is to deny that you, or anyone else in this world, could experience the loss I have lived with all these years. It is arrogance but I am an arrogant man. Still, your comparison may be valid. I... must consider this."

Choked with emotion, Catherine could only nod.

Sniffing and gruffly clearing his throat, Bradford stood and walked rigidly across the room. He folded his arms, paused, then spun to face her. "There is something I ask you to consider as well," he said. "Even if you stay, he won't come back to you."

"I realize that." Catherine swallowed. "I've hurt him too much."

"Then why would you give up your career, everything you've worked so hard to achieve?"

"Because what I've achieved is not what I want."

"I beg your pardon?" His double take might have been comical except for his distraught expression.

Catherine tried to mitigate her uncle's distress. "I enjoy my music, truly I do, but I never wanted to make a life of it. I hate the rigors of touring, I dislike the restriction of constant practice and quite frankly, as a concert pianist I'm not all that wonderful."

"That's absurd!" He appeared to be in shock, as though Catherine had muttered the vilest heresy. "You are a marvelous musician of enormous talent. You've dreamed of concerts at Carnegie Hall and of performing at the White House some day. Maurice says—"

"Pardon me, but Maurice's job is building confidence in his clients and he is superb at doing just that. The day he was born, he probably praised the doctor's sterling delivery technique." Seeing her uncle's crestfallen expression, Catherine softened her tone. "I know how much my career means to you and how much you've sacrificed, but Carnegie Hall is your dream, not mine."

Bradford stared in disbelief. "I thought you were happy."

"I was happy to please you and to make you proud." Sighing, Catherine raked her fingers through her hair. "I've changed and I've grown. Being a good little girl just isn't enough any more. I want to do something with my life that will make *me* proud."

"What will you do?" he asked in bewilderment.

"I'm not sure, but music is such a reclusive business. I'd like to be around people." Catherine thought of the cheerful Ms. Broughton at the Children's Care Center as she added wistfully, "Perhaps I could even teach."

Bradford was aghast at this revelation but before he could speak there was a loud knock.

"That's the bellboy." Catherine stood and began gathering suitcases as Bradford reluctantly opened the door.

In a few moments, the young man finished loading and wheeled the luggage cart away. Catherine took her purse and felt a hot lump form in her throat. A furtive glance confirmed that her uncle's eyes were as red as her own.

Awkwardly, Bradford brushed imaginary lint from his lapel and feigned unconcern. His choked voice gave him away. "Where will you be staying?"

"I've rented a small motel room," she replied with as much dignity as she could muster. "I can stay there a week for what one night here costs. When I find someplace permanent, I'll call you."

He managed a jerky nod. "We'll... keep in touch?"

"Ohh." With a soft cry, Catherine threw her arms around her uncle's neck. "I love you. I'll call as often as I can and I'll fly back for visits... Please, try to understand. I have to do this."

Patting her back, Bradford whispered, "I do understand, kitten. So would Lois."

Then he stepped away, concealing emotion by coughing noisily. But as Catherine left the room, his cough became a sob.

Jonathan stepped from the elevator and walked briskly toward his office. A stylish woman fell into step beside him carrying a steno pad and speaking rapidly. "Three calls from New York, two are urgent, and the bank executives are waiting in the north conference room. You have a luncheon appointment with the city comptroller to discuss municipal bonds." She simultaneously took a breath and flipped the page. "The Securities and Exchange Commission hearing has been scheduled for tomorrow afternoon, so I canceled your morning appointment in San Francisco as well as the dinner meeting in San Diego."

"Uncancel them," he snapped, pushing through the carved mahogany doors to his private office.

The woman followed, frowning. "That's impossible, even for you. Your schedule is too tight as it is and if you'll forgive the impertinence, you already look like hell."

"Thank you for the astute observation," he replied dryly. "Reschedule the meetings."

"But—"

Jonathan froze the hapless woman with a look. She licked her lips, nodded and backed out of his office. Before closing the door, she poked her head through the opening. "Ah, could you at least shave before the meeting? And there are clean shirts in the cabinet." The head disappeared, and the door slammed shut.

Tiredly, Jonathan eased himself into the plush executive chair and stared at the polished surface of his desk. This had been his universe, a world of luxury and power befitting a man at the top of his profession. These accomplishments had been earned by long hours and hard work.

There had been a time Jonathan would have given anything for what he'd achieved. Now it was all within his grasp and he'd cheerfully trade the elite surroundings to relive one weekend in a simple forest cabin. The notion was romantic but impractical. Wistful dreams couldn't change the past any more than compulsive exhaustion could quench his throbbing loneliness.

But it might silence the memories for a while.

The intercom buzzed at the same moment his office door flew open with a resounding bang.

Startled, Jonathan looked up as a man burst into the room and strode toward him with grim determination. The secretary appeared instantly, wringing her hands and stammering an apology for the intrusion.

The man stopped abruptly, hands clasped behind his back as though fighting for control. His expression was one of undisguised animosity.

Jonathan met his black gaze without blinking, then rose slowly and leaned across the desk. "Who the hell are you?"

Pale blue eyes regarded Jonathan with contempt. The man spat out his name. "Bradford Madison."

Jonathan instantly straightened as his stomach dropped like a rock. "Has something happened to Catherine?"

"Do you care?" Before Jonathan could grab his throat, Bradford spoke again. "Physically, she's fine."

Regaining his composure, Jonathan took a deep breath and met the man's hard stare. "Is this a social call?"

"It's not my habit to socialize with vipers," Bradford replied curtly.

Jonathan hitched one eyebrow. Seeing his nemesis march right into enemy territory was a surprise and he decided that Madison was either fearless or stupid. That intrigued him.

The secretary took a step forward. "Shall I call security?"

Shaking his head, Jonathan dismissed the frustrated woman, then scrutinized his adversary. So this fiftyish, gray-haired person was the man who had destroyed Jonathan's life, the man against whom he had planned vengeance in a thousand inventive ways.

Reality was disappointing. Bradford Madison didn't look so formidable. Gravity had done considerable damage, and the passing years had eroded his face into a road map of deep wrinkles. He looked old and as worn-out as Jonathan felt. Still, Bradford's eyes were belligerent and angry; the man was obviously prepared for war.

Jonathan found that mildly amusing. Smiling, he sat lazily on the edge of his desk. "Did you bring your own scabbard or would you prefer pistols at dawn?"

"You're a bastard, Stone."

Every muscle in Jonathan's body tensed. He leaned forward, balancing on the ball of one foot, ready to spring. "A wise man knows when he's treading dangerously. Take care with your next step."

Ignoring the warning, Madison glanced around the plush office with obvious disapproval. "You've come up in the world, boy. How many lives were shattered, how many young girls were defiled to satisfy your obsessive greed?"

Instantly Jonathan was on his feet, fists clenched. "Get out, old man, while you can move under your own power."

Madison stood his ground, meeting Jonathan's blazing stare with glacial coldness. "Eleven years ago Catherine was a beautiful, happy young woman with talent and ambition. You nearly destroyed her once and you've tried to do so again, simply to prove that you could."

Shaking with fury, Jonathan's voice was low and deadly. "You've got nerve, Madison, I'll give you that. You and your precious niece set me up then jetted off to bask on the Riviera while I languished in a prison hospital with everyone and his dog waiting for me to die. But I fooled them, didn't I? And do you know why? Do you know what kept me taking the next breath and the next and the next?"

With each question Jonathan moved toward Madison until he was close enough to spit in his eye. He spoke with venomous fury, his words lashing out with the brutality of a fist. "Ignorance kept me alive, the naive belief that I had to survive for Catherine and the baby. I thought *my family* needed me. That's a laugh, isn't it?"

Disbelief flickered across Bradford's face, mingled with shock and confusion.

Stepping back, Jonathan raked shaky fingers through his hair and regarded Bradford through narrowed eyes. "You don't think that's funny? Maybe you'll like this better. In fact, I know you will. This is a real scream."

As though unable to control the rush of pain and anger, Jonathan's face contorted and words pulsed out like machine-gun bullets. "For years I actually searched for her and—this is where it gets hilarious—when I finally found her, I allowed myself to be convinced that *she* had been the victim. Isn't that a riot? What's the matter, Madison? You're not laughing."

Bradford's eyes filled with sadness, and he shook his head. "You're an idiot, Stone. But worse than that, you're a fool."

Stiffening, Jonathan swallowed a surge of blind rage. "You must have a death wish. I've silenced better men than you with less provocation."

"Grandiose self-pity aside, you are not the only one who has suffered," Bradford snapped angrily. "Catherine has endured more than you could ever imagine, nearly losing her mind and her life because you couldn't control your lust. Even as she lay convulsed in agony, her life's blood seeping away, she cried out your name."

The image of Catherine's pain froze Jonathan to the core. He stumbled back a step and sagged against the desk. She had called his name?

Bradford shook his fist at Jonathan, and his voice dripped with cold fury. "I comforted Catherine when she woke up screaming in the night and I held her hand while she wept for the child she would never hold. *I* was the one who was always there to love her." His face turned red, and his mouth twisted grotesquely. "*I* picked up the pieces, Stone, *I* nursed her back to health. I'm not going to stand idly by and watch you wreak havoc on her emotions again."

Numbly, Jonathan wiped icy perspiration from his upper lip. He was sickened by Bradford's words, but he was also perplexed. The older man seemed sincere enough as he described Catherine's grief, but the facts were contradictory.

"Catherine wept for our child?" he mumbled, unaware that he had spoken aloud. "But she let them destroy it—"

"Are you insane? What do you think drove her to the edge of madness in the first place?" Bradford's hands shot out and grabbed hold of Jonathan's shirt, hauling him upright. "She begged the doctors to save her child, but they couldn't. The explosion caused a miscarriage that nearly killed her."

Clamping a steely grip on Bradford's wrists, Jonathan effortlessly broke Madison's hold and pushed him away. "I saw the reports," Jonathan hissed. "I know what she did... what you helped her to do."

"For an intelligent man you are amazingly obtuse." Disgusted, Bradford rolled his head and massaged his neck. After a silent moment, he spoke. "Perhaps I can explain this to you in a language you'll understand. You are a businessman and as such I would imagine you procure technical experts for everything from tax laws to computer programs, do you not?"

Scowling, Jonathan nodded.

"Then will you kindly explain to me why a man of your obvious corporate acumen hasn't got the sense to seek a professional opinion for the interpretation of medical records?" With a contemptuous sound, Bradford turned away.

Jonathan took a deep breath. His mind was churning, his stomach was in turmoil and he wondered if Madison was right. He remembered Catherine's horrified expression when confronted with the records. At the time, he'd believed her to be chagrined at having her secret exposed. Now, he wondered.

"She didn't deny it," Jonathan protested weakly.

With his back to Jonathan, Bradford raised his arms in a gesture of frustration. "Good Lord, man, she was in shock! She still didn't remember—" whirling, he faced Jonathan with an accusatory expression "—or do you believe that the amnesia was just part of some elaborate ruse constructed for the sole purpose of deceiving you?"

Rubbing his eyelids, Jonathan simply shook his head. He didn't know what to believe. He'd conditioned himself to be decisive, always in control, yet at the moment he felt in over his head. He was confused, unable to focus his mind.

And God, he was tired. Jonathan felt drained, as though someone had pulled a secret plug, and his strength was leaking away. He felt the buried rage slipping out of him and weakly fought to hold on. Anger had driven him too long to be so easily surrendered.

Meeting Bradford's eyes, Jonathan spoke through clenched teeth. "Why did you take her away from me?"

Bradford lowered his gaze. "I was afraid, for Catherine and for myself."

"That doesn't make any sense."

"I... was losing her. Even before she met you, things between us had changed. It was my fault, I know, and I always planned to make it up to her. But then she met you and I realized that time had run out. It would have been too late, except that..." The words dissipated.

Jonathan got the gist. "So when Catherine lost her memory, it was an opportunity to regain what you'd lost and go back to the way things had been."

"Yes," Bradford whispered. "I believed it was best."

"Best for whom?" Jonathan asked bitterly.

"Best for everyone." Bradford lifted his chin defiantly. "When I thought she'd been abducted, I was terrified. Afterward, when I realized my error, I was furious and sick at heart. Her innocence had been sacrificed and her trust betrayed."

"I never betrayed her." Even as Jonathan spoke the words, he felt a niggling doubt. She *had* trusted him, and he had taken her innocence. Finally, he said simply, "Catherine and the baby were my life."

"In my place, what would you have believed? If it had been your daughter, would you have simply sat back and thought 'isn't love grand?' I didn't know that the relationship was serious until it was too late."

"You didn't want to know," Jonathan replied grimly. "You didn't want to share Catherine, or jeopardize the rigid control you had over her life."

To Jonathan's surprise, Bradford's expression grew thoughtful. His lips pursed and after a moment, he spoke softly. "That is unfortunately true, although in my own defense, I didn't realize it then. By the time that idiotic detective came snooping around, Catherine had already started a new life. I wouldn't allow that to be jeopardized."

Jonathan froze. "My investigator found her?"

"Of course he did," Bradford snapped. "Good Lord, I was working under my own name in front of God and everybody. After the first year, the greedy fool you hired had little trouble in locating me."

"So you paid off my investigator."

"Yes and you allowed it. I guessed that your motives were based more on noble pretense than determination and apparently I was right. We were never bothered again."

Jonathan turned away, realizing that Madison was right. Deep down Jonathan had known something was amiss. The detective had had a convincing line, always reporting that new information had been uncovered while carefully obscuring the details. Jonathan had blithely bought into the deception because the guy had consistently offered a glimmer of hope. Now the word "sucker" came to mind, and Jonathan silently cursed his own gullibility.

Bradford spoke again, more softly now. "I admit to making grave errors in judgment over the years. For those, I shall most assuredly accept the consequences. If you must hate someone for the injustice of your life, hate me. Don't turn on a woman whose only crime is having the misfortune to have fallen in love."

The final drop of anger drained out, and Jonathan felt limp. For most of his life, rage had been his driving force. Whenever he'd wanted to give up, fury had propelled him forward and propped him up so he wouldn't fall. Without the smoldering blackness, he felt empty and hollow.

And without the protective sheath of fury, the pain was waiting.

Deep in the very pit of his heart, Jonathan realized that Bradford had spoken the shattering truth. Catherine's only crime was having loved both him and their child so deeply that she couldn't live with the memory of loss.

He remembered his bitter accusations and her tortured eyes. That memory would haunt him to the grave.

"Why did you come here?" Jonathan asked bleakly.

"I'm not sure." Clasping his hands, Bradford stared out the window. "Catherine is a strong woman, but with the return of her memory, she is dealing with all the grief that she couldn't face years ago. Perhaps I didn't want her to go through that alone."

"She's . . . not returning with you?"

"No." Bradford's voice was sad and distant. "Catherine has declared her independence by discarding a career built over a decade."

"Where is she?"

"I don't know." Bradford's eyes narrowed. "You have the resources to locate her, unless you'd prefer licking your own wounds and casting blame. But before you make that choice, be very certain you've considered the consequences."

"What consequences?"

Bradford shrugged sadly. "You're a proud man. So am I, but pride is a jealous mistress. Pride drives away all who would love you until finally you look around and realize that you are alone. Pride must have you all to herself."

"Why are you telling me this?"

"Because I have followed the road you're traveling and it's a trip I wouldn't wish on my worst enemy." Then he looked at his watch and said, "I have a plane to catch."

Stunned, Jonathan watched as Bradford Madison squared his shoulders and strode to the door. With his hand on the knob, the older man paused and glanced over his shoulder. "I still don't like you, Stone."

With that, Bradford spun on his heel and walked out of the office.

Chapter Fourteen

The tiny room was sparsely furnished but provided what Catherine needed most: solace. For days she had isolated herself and begun the long process of healing. Her soul ached. She mourned all that had been lost; her child, her love, her innocence. Grief devoured her like a merciless predator.

Over the years that grief had been suppressed along with the hidden memories. Now she faced what had been concealed for so long. As would an addict, Catherine suffered the throes of anguished withdrawal. Without the numbing amnesia that had been her narcotic, she was consumed with pain.

And guilt.

Catherine blamed herself. Jonathan had begged her to be honest with her uncle, but she had been afraid. Cowardice had kept her silent all those years ago. The lies and deceit that followed had led directly to the tragedy that had destroyed them all.

If only—

She cut off the thought. It was useless to dwell on what couldn't be changed. Her intellect accepted that but she couldn't erase the memories and was overwhelmed by a poignant yearning to hold her baby in her arms, if only to say goodbye.

Shuddering, Catherine sat at the wobbly table and buried her face in her hands. She stopped fighting the pain, allowing it to flow along with the stream of hot tears.

She wept for Jonathan and the torment he'd endured. She wept for the child they'd loved and lost. And she wept for her uncle because no matter how misguided his actions, he'd always truly loved her. Now he was alone.

But something else was happening to Catherine. She was changing, evolving in a way that was oddly comforting. After the accident, Catherine had withdrawn, becoming malleable and uncertain, willing to let others make judgments on the direction of her life. That was changing.

Deep inside, Catherine's strength and resolve was being rebuilt. She felt strong and capable of joining the world as a productive member of society. She was almost whole again.

Standing, Catherine wiped her damp face and went to the small motel room window, then whipped open the drapes. Sunlight streamed in, bathing the interior with golden rays. It was a beautiful day. Outside, people scurried about, some smiling and some frowning, all busily accomplishing the task of living.

She was nearly strong enough to join that hustling throng. Jonathan was out there somewhere. She remembered her uncle's ominous prediction that Jonathan would never return. While silently acknowledging that possibility, she wasn't going down without a fight. Every day she would find a thousand small ways to remind Jonathan of her existence.

And that was a promise he could take to the bank with his corporate stock options.

Returning from another grueling business trip, Jonathan found himself in the parking lot without realizing that he'd left the plane. His preoccupation was no surprise. Over the past week, thoughts of Catherine had constantly teetered on the brink of his mind. He'd tried to bury those thoughts through overwork and fatigue but now the final drop of his resistance drained away. He released the memories and reveled in the image of Catherine's loveliness. As the vision faded, he felt a stab of panic and the ache of crushing loss.

Madison had been right. Pride *was* a jealous mistress.

If Catherine was gone forever, Jonathan had no one to blame but himself. In spite of his protestations to the contrary, he realized that Bradford had been right. Jonathan could have located Catherine years ago if he'd put enough effort into the search. But blind anger had dulled his mind, and a stubborn ego had kept him away from Catherine when she'd needed him most. Now history was repeating itself and he was allowing it to happen.

Tired, he unlocked the car door and slid onto the soft velour seat. The interior was cold as a tomb, and he instantly turned the ignition and switched on the heater. A storm was brewing off the coast. Rain would bring snow to the mountains, and Jonathan's mind wandered to a vision of Catherine laughing and wet, fervently scooping balls of icy white snow for a sneak attack. If he lived to be a hundred, he'd never forget how she'd looked that morning, cheeks flushed pink, and eyes sparkling with mischief.

Nor would he forget those same eyes a few days later, dulled by shock and filled with torment as he'd hurled those vicious accusations. How could she ever forgive him for that when he could never forgive himself?

Shaking off the painful recollections, Jonathan glanced at his watch. It was late afternoon and ordinarily he wouldn't have thought twice about driving straight to the office for another five or six hours work. But not today.

Today, he needed to be around smiling faces and happy giggles. Today, he needed to be with the kids.

Picking up the car phone, he dialed and waited impatiently for his secretary's brusque greeting. Their conversation was brief, and she efficiently assured Jonathan that nothing required his immediate attention.

After a pause she added, "There was a delivery for you this afternoon."

"Can someone else handle it?"

A soft laugh filtered through the line. "I don't believe it's related to business."

He frowned. "What is it?"

"It's a plant of some kind," she replied. "I've never seen anything quite like it. It's a bush with dark shiny leaves and the most delicate white blossoms."

Jonathan sucked in a sharp breath. "Is . . . there a card?"

"No. Just an affectionate token from one of your many secret admirers, I suppose." She didn't try to hide her amusement. "Shall I put it in your office? Mr. Stone? Hello...are you there?"

"Hmm? Oh. Sorry." He swallowed hard. "Ah, what was the question?"

She emitted a long-suffering sigh. "Shall I put the plant in your office or would you prefer it delivered to your home?"

"That's fine," Jonathan replied absently, then stared out the window and cradled the receiver.

Suddenly, the world seemed a more pleasant place. Sunlight edged the clouds with blinding brilliance and as though the scent had filtered through the phone line, the air suddenly seemed thick with sweet mountain laurel.

There was no doubt about who had sent the flowers or what the gift had meant. Catherine had forgiven him. Now if only he could forgive himself.

Catherine leaned in the doorway of the Children's Center and watched the laughing youngsters. Beside her stood Margaret Broughton, smiling and radiant.

"I'm so grateful that you've volunteered to work with us," Margaret said.

The praise humbled Catherine. "I'm the one who is grateful. These children are so special, being around them tends to put the rest of the world in perspective. I hope I can do something worthwhile."

Margaret laughed. "Your help is more than worthwhile. It's a godsend. Most people are too wound up in their own problems and their own lives to make time for kids like these."

"Three afternoons a week and a few hours on Saturday isn't much."

"Don't forget that you've volunteered to perform at our benefit concert." Margaret regarded Catherine curiously. "I must admit that I was surprised. When I spoke to Mr. Bouchard a couple of weeks ago, he indicated that there was a conflict in your schedule—something about a tour in Eastern Europe."

"There was a change in plans." Catherine smiled too brightly. "In fact, the benefit may turn out to be my farewell performance. I plan to stay in Los Angeles."

Margaret straightened. "You're giving up music? That seems a terrible waste."

"I'm just changing gears a bit." Leaning forward, Catherine's voice took on a tone that was both confidential and enthusiastic. "The local musician's union sent me on an audition this morning. One of the larger recording studios is looking for versatile backup musicians, and I think I've got a good chance."

"Really?" The woman seemed skeptical. "Well, I'm sure you've given this a great deal of thought. I hope everything works out as you've planned."

Before Catherine could respond, a thin blond child bounced into the room and demanded attention. Margaret listened intently to the boy's lisping complaint, then stood and took his hand. Before leaving the room, the woman glanced over her shoulder. "I know you have to catch the last bus before the storm breaks, but the children do so love your singalongs. Could you play a couple of short pieces?"

Catherine smiled. "I thought you'd never ask."

The first wet drops plopped on Jonathan's face as he struggled to carry several bags up the winding walk. A clap of distant thunder warned that the sky would soon open and release a raging torrent, and he made a mental note to check the skylights when he returned home. It rained so seldom in Los Angeles that during the last storm, he'd awakened to find a small river churning down his hallway.

Balancing the parcels, he managed to poke the doorbell. From inside the warmly lit building, he heard the sweet sounds of singing children and happy laughter. He needed that. Over the years, he'd given money to the children's home, but little time. That was an oversight he would remedy. Time was infinitely more precious, and these beautiful children deserved that.

Later tonight, after he'd summoned his courage, he'd go to Catherine. Maybe he could find the words—

The door opened.

"Why, Mr. Stone. What an unexpected pleasure." Margaret Broughton stood aside as Jonathan stepped into the warmth.

"I hope I haven't come at a bad time," he said as Margaret rescued the bag slipping from his arm.

"Not at all." She peered inside the bag and beamed with pleasure. "This is wonderful. Thank you so much."

"It's nothing, really." Jonathan shuffled uncomfortably. "I thought the kids might need some warm clothes."

"Yes, they certainly do. This was very kind of you."

Smiling stiffly, Jonathan heard a familiar sound and the hairs on his nape stood at attention. Childish voices belted out "Home on the Range" accompanied by a piano played with the style and tempo that was unmistakably—

Ignoring Mrs. Broughton's startled gasp, Jonathan whirled and strode toward the huge parlor. There, surrounded by a gaggle of giggling youngsters, was Catherine, her back to the doorway as her fingers danced across the keys. His heart surged as though seeing her for the first time, and he knew that this particular visit to the Children's Center had been scheduled by fate.

Suddenly, the music faltered. Jonathan saw her arms stiffen, and the great Catherine LeClerc hit a flat note that made him wince. Hesitantly, she glanced over her shoulder. Their eyes met. Sparks shot between them like jagged lightning.

Catherine paled, trembled, then licked her lips. She seemed unable to look away, as though unwilling to break the fragile link between them. Finally, a dark-haired tot stepped forward and tugged Catherine's sleeve in silent entreaty. Blinking, she nodded at the child and turned back to the piano.

Catherine's arms felt like lead. She tried desperately to force her stiff fingers to move, but they seemed frozen in place. My God, what was Jonathan doing here at this time of the afternoon? What would he think to find her here?

It was one thing to let him know with subtle hints that she was still around; it was quite another for him to believe that she'd use the children to force herself into his life.

Perspiration beaded her forehead. She was embarrassed and flustered, but somehow managed to complete the piece. As the final note hung in the air like flattened tin, Catherine shuddered and emitted a sigh of relief. Now, all she had to do was manage a graceful exit.

Margaret Broughton had other ideas. The woman dragged Jonathan across the room with a cheery, "Look who's here."

Jonathan's expression was impassive but his potent gaze had lost none of its power over her. Catherine was immobilized by the brilliant intensity of those Scorpio eyes. He didn't speak.

Catherine forced a thin smile.

Seeming confused by the sudden tension, Margaret wrung her hands and spoke with exaggerated brightness. "Mr. Stone brought some things for the children."

Testing her voice, Catherine managed a weak reply. "That was very thoughtful."

Jonathan's eyes smoldered silently, and the final drop of moisture evaporated from Catherine's mouth. The stretched smile made her cheeks ache, and her heart thudded against her ribs as though seeking escape.

Margaret frowned briefly, then turned to Jonathan. "Catherine has volunteered to help out at the center."

"Has she now?" Jonathan drawled. The corner of his mouth twitched. "How very gracious of her."

Catherine flushed to the roots of her hair. Obviously, he thought this was all part of some kind of elaborate plan to throw herself at his feet. She *did* have such a plan, of course, but it had never included using the children as pawns. Catherine had volunteered to work at the center because she felt a deep need to be there, not because of any ulterior motives revolving around Jonathan Stone.

Still, the amused twinkle in his eyes was humiliating, and all Catherine wanted at the moment was for the earth to swallow her whole.

With her last ounce of dignity, she lifted her chin. "It was nice to see you again, Jonathan," she said formally, then turned to Margaret. "I'll be back on Thursday."

"Of course." Margaret's brow puckered, and her shrewd eyes narrowed. "I'll see you to the door."

Jonathan blocked Catherine's way. "I'd be happy to drive you home."

"The bus stop is right around the corner, but thank you for the offer." She stepped around him.

He followed. "It's raining."

"I like rain."

"So do I. I'll walk you to the bus stop."

Jonathan politely opened the front door, waiting for Catherine to exit before following her outside. Rain fell in fat lazy drops, and she carefully picked her way down the slick walkway, painfully aware that Jonathan was right behind her.

When they reached the gate, Catherine took a deep breath then turned to face him. "You don't have to do this."

"I know."

She swallowed. "Jonathan, I didn't know you'd be here. I would never purposely intrude upon your time with the children."

"I know that, too." He jammed his hands in his pocket and rocked back on his heels. Rain dripped from his hair and ran down his face. "We have to talk, Cat."

Air backed up in her lungs, and her chest felt so tight she feared she might explode. All she could manage was a jerky nod.

"There's no sense getting pneumonia," he said quietly, then took her arm and guided her to his car as though afraid she might change her mind and bolt away.

Once inside, his nearness overwhelmed her. The air was filled with his maleness, and the sexy scent of him made her weak. In spite of the weather, she opened the window slightly and gulped cold wet air. Even turned away from him, she could feel his eyes caressing her, warming her to the core. She felt giddy, yet frightened.

Jonathan cleared his throat, as though wanting to speak. But then he sighed, and the engine roared to life. Stiffly Catherine stared out the window watching the rain. They drove for several silent minutes.

Finally, Jonathan spoke. "Why did you send the mountain laurel?"

"I don't know. Perhaps I just didn't want you to forget me."

"That could never happen," he murmured, then paused. "There was no return address."

She shrugged. "I didn't want to be pushy. It would be easy enough to find me."

"Hmm. Let's see, for the first four days you were at the TraveLodge on Oak Place, then you moved to a furnished apartment six blocks east of the Children's Center."

In spite of herself, she smiled. "I see you've done your homework."

"You left a trail wide enough for a blind scout to follow."

"Those forwarding addresses were necessary for business reasons," she replied primly.

He laughed. "Of course they were."

She gave in gracefully. "I figured you'd spent enough money on private investigators."

"I appreciate your thoughtfulness."

Fidgeting with the hem of her sweater, she chewed her lip nervously. Jonathan had known where she was all along, yet had never contacted her. There was a reason for that, a reason that Catherine didn't want to consider.

He hadn't wanted to see her again and if not for the coincidental meeting tonight, he would probably have gotten his wish.

She slid a glance at his strong profile and saw that his expression had grown serious. He stared out the window, his mouth tight. She felt a surge of panic. What was he going to say? Was he going to be kind and gentle as he sent her away forever?

The attraction between them was even more intense than before, but pure magnetism wasn't enough to build a future. Too much had passed between them, too much heartache and too much hell. Jonathan's sacrifices had been too great, and her own mistakes too enormous to be so quickly forgiven.

Catherine had been a fool to believe otherwise. Her heart felt like lead, and she struggled for composure. Later, she could fall apart. Now, she was determined to accept Jonathan's dismissal with quiet dignity.

She realized that the car was no longer moving and noted a salty tang in the air. Through the rain, Catherine saw the boiling surf pounding on a storm-whipped beach. The black sky cried over the boiling turbulence and provided an appropriate mood for what was to come.

After a moment's silence, Jonathan spoke hesitantly. "I'm sorry, Catherine. When I got the hospital report, I let anger overwhelm my common sense. I didn't want to admit that the indomitable Jonathan Stone was vulnerable, that some things were beyond my control. I needed someone to blame for my disappointment. You were handy."

"I know," she whispered. "I was hurt—desperately hurt—so I turned around and blamed my uncle, even though I knew in my heart that he wasn't at fault either."

"No he wasn't," Jonathan said slowly. "Like us, he was victimized by a situation that spiraled out of control."

"Pardon me?" Catherine stared. After all the years of blind fury, was Jonathan actually defending Bradford Madison? "How did you come to that conclusion?"

Jonathan rubbed his neck and smiled sheepishly. "The esteemed Mr. Madison dropped by my office on his way to the airport. Our discussion was quite informative and, uh, rather lively."

"I can imagine," Catherine mumbled. Jonathan and Uncle Brad in the same room? And both had survived the experience? This was all too much to absorb. "What did you talk about?"

"Pride, for one thing. And loneliness. I saw things from his perspective and realized what he must have felt all those years ago. In his eyes, you were still a child. He envisioned you playing with dolls. Instead, you were playing house and he couldn't deal with that. He hadn't let go, hadn't seen the woman in you emerging. To him, I was some kind of vile cad taking advantage of a young girl for purely carnal purposes."

Jonathan shook his head, then shifted behind the steering wheel and faced Catherine. "Madison asked me how I would have felt if you'd been my daughter. When I thought about that, I began to understand what he'd been through."

Catherine was touched to tears. "It takes an intelligent man to analyze himself so objectively."

"Being intelligent is one thing, being smart is quite another. I didn't achieve success in business by ignoring past mistakes, yet with you I seem doomed to repeat history."

"What do you mean?"

"I don't want to forget the past. We've both paid too dearly for the lessons we learned then."

Catherine's throat closed as though squeezed by a giant hand. Jonathan was talking about payments and lessons and all kinds of clever analogies, but the bottom line was that he was simply trying to let her down easily. Jonathan couldn't forget the past and he couldn't forgive it. He was going to send her away.

Mustering all of her strength, Catherine lifted her chin. "So, shall we sound the retreat?"

"Retreating out of fear is a coward's game and I'd never considered myself a coward . . . until now, Cat. Until you."

She couldn't stand it. "Jonathan, please. You don't have to—"

"Please let me finish before I lose my nerve." He took a deep breath and spoke in a voice that would have seemed brusque if not for a slight tremor. "In my business, I take risks every day. If I win, I win big. If I lose, it's only money. But risking your heart . . . well, that's something else entirely. The stakes are too high, the loss too deep. That's what scares me, Cat. That's what has me walking in circles and talking to myself. Love is dangerous."

"Yes, yes it is, and that's why I understand that yo—" The word was cut in half as her mouth snapped shut. She blinked in disbelief. Love? During their entire weekend together, Jonathan had never mentioned love, and Catherine wasn't certain she'd heard correctly. "W-what did you say?"

Raking his hair, Jonathan took a shuddering breath and stared out at the rain. "I love you, Cat. I don't know if you can ever forgive what I've put you through, but I do know this—I've loved you since the day I pulled you out of a snowbank and I'll go to my grave with your image engraved in my heart."

"Oh." It was more of a breath than a word. Jonathan still loved her. She couldn't speak.

Anxiety roughened his tone. "There's no excuse for the things I said to you. I guess I wanted to believe the worst because I was afraid of my own feelings, afraid of being hurt again. I wouldn't blame you if you never wanted to see me again—"

"No!" Whirling, she laid a fingertip on his lips to silence him. "I should be begging forgiveness of you. You were shot and violated and unjustly accused, all because I was too much a coward to face my uncle with the truth. If I'd had the strength to be honest, our b-baby might not have been lost." In spite of her determination to be strong, tears seeped from her eyes.

"Shh, honey. It's all right." Jonathan brushed the moisture away with his thumb, then gently traced the contour of her face. "Neither of us is perfect but that doesn't matter. I've never loved anyone else, Cat. I don't believe that I ever could. We're stuck with each other, you and me. Destiny just keeps throwing us together."

She managed a wet smile. "Then I guess we might as well grin and bear it."

His lips hovered inches from her mouth. "Might as well," he murmured, then kissed her deeply, savoring her sweetness as though tasting her for the very first time.

Reluctantly releasing her, Jonathan nervously reached into his pocket for a tiny velvet box. "I, ah, gave you a ring once, woven out of meadow grass. I promised that someday I'd buy you diamonds." He opened the box.

Catherine gasped. "It's . . . beautiful."

Tugging at his collar, Jonathan started to speak, coughed nervously, then tried again. "I told you a long time ago that I couldn't even imagine my life if you weren't a part of it. I still can't. Please marry me, Cat. I want you to be my wife."

Catherine bit her lip to keep from crying out. Tears of happiness blurred Jonathan's face and the shimmering diamond that symbolized his love. When she finally spoke, her voice quivered with emotion. "I promised you once that I would never marry anyone else. I've kept that promise. I want to be your wife, Jonny. I want that more than anything else in the world."

With a ragged groan, Jonathan pulled her into his arms. Catherine melted into his loving embrace. She was home.

Through all the years and the tears, the pain and the joy, they had always loved each other. Nothing had diminished that love; nothing ever could.